Off the Mark

OFF THE MARK

LINDA SANCHE

Signature EDITIONS

Cover design by Doowah Design.
Cover image by Robert Major.
Photo of Linda Sanche by Jillian Faulkner Photography Ltd.

This book was printed on Ancient Forest Friendly paper.
Printed and bound in Canada by Hignell Book Printing Inc.

Library and Archives Canada Cataloguing in Publication

Title: Off the mark / Linda Sanche.
Names: Sanche, Linda, author.
Identifiers: Canadiana 20260248096 | ISBN 9781773241739 (softcover)
Subjects: LCGFT: Detective and mystery fiction. | LCGFT: Novels.
Classification: LCC PS8637.A538762 O33 2026 | DDC C813/.6—dc23

We acknowledge the support of the Canada Council for the Arts the Manitoba Arts Council, and the Manitoba Government for our publishing program.

Canada Council for the Arts Conseil des arts du Canada
MANITOBA ARTS COUNCIL CONSEIL DES ARTS DU MANITOBA
Manitoba

Signature Editions
P.O. Box 206, RPO Corydon, Winnipeg, Manitoba, R3M 3S7
www.signature-editions.com

1

Kate practised her yoga breath, inhaling the cedar scent of the sauna. She tried to clear her mind and tune out the '90s rock ballad blaring through the gym's loudspeakers. No use. Her thoughts pinballed from that awful song to Henry to her latest case. She exhaled, tightened the towel around her torso, and squelched out of the sauna.

After she showered, she turned on the wall-mounted hairdryer and banged her head on the vent. She cursed, bemoaning her too-tall frame. When her long hair was reasonably dry, she changed and packed her bag, cursing again at the sound of muffled ringing. She dug through her backpack to retrieve her cellphone.

"You took your time," said Alma.

"Hello to you too, Mom."

"Good luck at brunch." Alma paused—Kate knew what was coming next. "Maybe he'll take you back."

"Don't want to talk about this. Gotta go." She tossed the phone back in her bag. Bloody hell. Thanks to her mother, she was back to thinking about Henry. Kate weaved her way through the rows of treadmills and weight machines to the lobby.

"Have a good day!" chirped the perky woman at the front desk.

Kate muttered, "Thanks," as she zipped up her parka and pulled on her knitted toque. Maybe Mom was right; he'd take her back. She'd find out soon enough.

An hour later, Kate sat in her SUV and stared at the modern two-storey she'd moved out of last summer. Taking a deep breath, she shut off the engine and grabbed the bright bouquet of gerberas she'd picked up from the grocery store. She walked up the cleared pathway, snow piled high on either side and hesitated at the door. Knock or walk in? She chose the latter. In the front hall, she took off her parka and unzipped her boots. "Hello? Henry? Samantha?"

"We're back here," Henry shouted from the kitchen.

Kate hesitated again. Her stomach queasy, like she was on a first date. Or job interview. She scrutinized her appearance in the hall mirror and undid another button on her blouse. What was she trying to do? Show enough cleavage to make him forget what she'd done? She gave her reflection the middle finger and made her way down the hall. "These are for you," she said.

Henry beamed at the sight of her holding the bouquet. "Thanks. Very colourful."

God, he was sexy when he smiled. She gave him the flowers, and her pulse quickened as his hand brushed hers. Did he do that on purpose, or wishful thinking on her part?

He eyed the cupboards. "Where do we keep the vases?"

She held her breath for a moment. He said *we*. Get a grip, thought Kate, I'm acting like a teenager, clinging to any signs of affection. She pointed to the large cupboard below the granite-topped island. "Under there."

She pulled up a stool as Henry rifled through the cupboard. "Found it!" He held the glass vase above his head in triumph, exposing his abs. He was looking fit. Must be back playing beer hockey with his buddies. He set the vase on the island and hummed as he cut the stems and arranged the flowers.

Over time, the spark between them had dimmed. Bored by her routine-filled life, she'd strayed. A brief, impulsive affair. An age-old story. But Kate could pinpoint the moment her attraction for Henry had reignited—when he'd tossed her clothes onto the bedroom floor and yelled at her to pack up and leave. His heavy breath, damp brow, and crazed eyes—a rare demonstration of anger—had made her hot. How sick was that? In that moment, she'd realized what a colossal mistake she'd made. Now, six months later, she clung to the hope that he'd let her move home, if only for the sake of Samantha. She'd take that. Maybe her mother was right—that he'd invited her over for brunch because he wanted her back.

"Hiya, Mom."

Kate gasped and grabbed the counter to keep from falling off her seat. "Sweetheart!" she said as she spun around to face her daughter.

"Sorry. Didn't mean to scare you…that much," said Samantha with a smirk.

Kate did a double take at the sight Samantha's lopsided hair—long and wavy on one side, the other shaved close to the scalp. "You never told me you were getting your hair cut."

Her brow furrowed. "I did. Last weekend. At your place."

Kate struggled to recall that conversation but came up short.

"What do you think?" Samantha spun around, giving Kate a 360-degree view of the new style.

Kate scrambled to come up with an appropriate answer. "It's very Cyndi Lauper-ish."

"Who's Cyndi Lauper?"

Kate glanced across the island at Henry. He rolled his eyes. "A famous singer from the '80s," she said.

"Was she any good?"

Kate shrugged. "Very unique."

Samantha pulled on an apron and announced, "I'm cooking. Pancakes and eggs."

Henry gestured for Kate to follow him into the living room. "Let's give the chef some space to work."

Kate settled on the sectional and Henry dragged over the ottoman. His proximity unnerved her; she hadn't been in the same room with him in months. Their Siamese cat strolled over and rubbed against her leg. She reached down to pet him, but he hissed and scurried away. "I see Simon's as unpredictable as ever."

Henry's probing gaze unsettled her. "I think the cat misses you."

Did he miss her, too?

Henry shifted in his seat. "How's work?" he asked. His knee brushed up against hers. Had he done that on purpose? She crossed her legs, intentionally bumping his leg.

"Sorry," he said, scooting back the ottoman.

She flushed. He hadn't done it on purpose. *I'm a desperate idiot.* "Work's busy," she said. "We're trying to track down the Bicycle Bandit." The local tabloid had given the jewellery store robber that moniker after the police department released a photo of him dressed in bike courier gear.

"How do you like the new unit?"

Kate relaxed back in the sofa; grateful he didn't bring up the reason she'd transferred out of homicide. "It's a nice change, but I'm the only analyst attached to this case, so the pressure's on." Using GIS software, Kate had mapped out the robbery locations and identified the Bicycle Bandit's pattern. Based on her data analysis, she had predicted where and when the next hit would likely take place. Her new boss had focused police resources in that area. If she was right, and the robber stuck to his pattern, they might have him in custody by the end of the week.

He reached out and held her hands. "They're lucky to have you."

His touch made her body throb. She bit her lip. This was her chance. Ask him. Now. "I…," said Kate.

"I…," said Henry, at the same moment.

Kate smiled and squeezed his hands. "Sorry, I interrupted you. What did you want to say?"

"Don't be angry with me," said Henry. "I spoke with Conor yesterday. You two should talk."

Kate pulled away from his grasp. What the hell? Why was he bringing up her pain-in-the-ass brother? Was this the reason he'd invited her over? To act as a mediator? "Well, he can pick up the phone." She still hadn't forgiven Conor for what he'd done.

"Sorry I mentioned him," said Henry. "What was it you wanted to ask?"

She'd lost her nerve. Steering them back to neutral territory, she asked, "How's your work going?"

Henry's eyes lit up. "We've been given the go-ahead for more field research in Fort McMurray."

Not so neutral territory after all. She tried to respond enthusiastically. "That's good news."

She wanted to avoid mentioning the way they'd secured funding—she'd already lost that debate, and there was no point in bringing it up again. "When are you leaving?"

"Wednesday. I'll be gone for a week. Michael's staying longer." His long-time research partner did most of the fieldwork while Henry crunched the data in the lab, an arrangement that suited them both.

"Samantha can come stay with me at the apartment while you're up north," said Kate.

"Or you can stay here while I'm away," said Henry. "That way she can walk to class."

"Good idea." Kate wanted to ask if she could stay when he got back.

Samantha called out from the kitchen, "May I remind you I'm sixteen and perfectly capable of being on my own. Besides, Mom's always working anyways."

Ouch. That one hurt. Kate shifted in her seat so she could see her daughter. "I'd love to spend more time with you." Not that she'd see much of her next week, even if they were under the same roof. Thanks to the Bicycle Bandit, Kate had plenty of overtime hours ahead of her.

Samantha shrugged. "Sure, I guess it makes sense for you to stay here."

Kate clapped her hands in excitement. Samantha rolled her eyes and flipped the pancakes. It'll take time to rebuild her trust, thought Kate, but things were getting better. For months after the separation, Samantha wouldn't even speak with her. Now she was spending every other weekend at Kate's apartment. But it wasn't enough. Samantha was growing up quickly. *I need more time with her.* If only she could move back home. *Just ask him.*

Before she had a chance to broach the subject again, Henry leaned in and lowered his voice. "Listen. After my trip, we need to discuss a divorce agreement."

Divorce? Kate dug her thumbnail into her palm to stave off the tears. No damn way she was going to break down in front of him. She nodded, not trusting herself to speak. That's why he'd asked her over for brunch. No hope now that she'd be moving back home.

Henry tapped his index finger on his lips. What else did he want to say? She straightened her back and braced for impact. "When you're staying here, please make sure to keep the doors locked and the alarm on."

She puzzled over his request. Why state the obvious? Maybe it was his clumsy way of changing the subject? Before she had a chance to question him, Samantha announced brunch was ready.

Kate plastered a smile on her face and piled a stack of pancakes onto her plate. Smart move on Henry's part, bringing up divorce with their daughter in the room. He knew she wasn't going to make a scene in front of Samantha. Kate stabbed at her pancake with a fork and sliced off a large piece, her knife making a scraping sound on the plate, then crammed it in her mouth and chewed.

"Taste okay?" asked Samantha.

Kate nodded and smiled as she swallowed the too-big slice. "Delicious." Her cell rang and she checked the number: the Saxony, an old haunt of her brother's. Shit. Back on the merry-go-round. Could this day get any worse? She set down her cutlery and answered the call. "Is he drunk?"

"Yes, you'll need to come get him," said the bartender.

She hung up and announced, "Conor's at the Saxony." Samantha cursed and thumped down the bottle of syrup.

"Listen, Kate," said Henry, rubbing the back of his head, "Why don't I pick him up and bring him back to your mother's? That way you can spend the afternoon with Samantha."

She touched his arm. "Thank you."

Betraying Henry had been the biggest mistake of her life.

She'd been young when she'd first met him. Her university professor. She'd enrolled in his biology class because she needed a science credit for her criminology degree. Over a decade younger than him, Kate had been attracted to his calm, quiet nature. His stability. Later, those same traits had irritated her.

She followed him to the front door and watched as he buttoned up his wool overcoat.

"Don't worry. It'll be fine," he reassured her.

She imagined herself clinging to him, begging to give her a second chance. She wanted to say how sorry she was that she hurt him and that she still loved him. But she kept quiet, telling herself it wasn't the right time. Next week. After he got back from Fort McMurray. The thought of his trip up north reminded her about what he'd said earlier. "Why did you mention about the alarm and door locks?" she asked. "Is there something going on that I need to be concerned about?"

"It's complicated," he said, tugging on his brown leather gloves. "I'll explain when I get back from dropping off your brother."

She nodded. "Thanks again for this."

He touched her arm. "Of course. You know how much I care about him."

She wanted to ask: *how much do you care for me?*

Henry called out to Samantha, "See you in a few hours, kiddo."

In the kitchen, her daughter poked at her half-eaten pancake. "Samantha, don't worry about your uncle," said Kate. "He'll be fine."

Or maybe not. She'd lost count of how many times her brother had relapsed over the years.

Samantha dropped her fork and glared at her. "By the way, I also told you last weekend that I'm going by Sam now."

Shit. Kate couldn't remember her saying that either. Where had her head been? Probably puzzling over her latest case. But she wasn't about to admit that. "Sorry...Sam. I'll try to remember."

After brunch, Sam chattered away about friends and school. Kate revelled in her company. When they got weary of talking, they put on a movie. As the end credits rolled, Kate pulled out her cell to check the time. What was taking Henry so long? He'd been gone for over five hours. Must be a problem with her stupid brother. Biting her lip to stop from cursing, she paced the room. Sam leaned forward on the sofa, one foot bouncing. "Why's Dad so late? Something's wrong."

Kate gave her what she hoped was a reassuring smile and called Henry. Straight to voicemail. She hung up and called Conor's cell. No answer. She tried her mom's home line, but no one picked up.

"Maybe Dad's car broke down on the highway?" asked Sam.

"Maybe. Or—" Kate scrolled through her contacts on the phone.

"What?"

"Your dad and Michael are going up to Fort McMurray next week. Maybe they had some last-minute details to work out." She called his research partner's number. "Is Henry there with you?"

"No, he's not," said Michael. "Is everything okay?"

"Just worried. We can't find him."

Michael cleared his throat. "Have you tried Jennifer?"

Kate clenched her fist. "Who's Jennifer?"

"Well—"

Kate cut him off. "Never mind." She couldn't think about that right now. "Do you have her number?"

"Yes. I'll reach out to her, see if she knows anything."

Kate hung up the phone and squeezed her eyes shut.

"What is it?" asked Sam, her eyes wide with alarm.

Get it together, thought Kate. Stop catastrophizing. "Did you know your dad was seeing someone?"

Sam crossed her arms. "You're the one that cheated, Mom. What'd you expect? That he'd take you back?"

Ouch. Another jab hit the mark. Kate bumped her shin on the corner of the glass coffee table. “Bloody hell.” She slumped down beside her daughter and rubbed her throbbing leg.

“I can’t stand this,” said Sam. She stomped upstairs to her room and slammed the door.

Kate pressed her palm to her chest. She felt the same ache as that long-ago night when her cousin went missing. She took a deep breath to clear the dark thoughts. She was overreacting. This is nothing like what happened to her cousin. There had to be a reasonable explanation.

2

Erik glanced at the dashboard thermometer and cursed the weather. Minus twenty. And a snowstorm forecast to blow in before morning.

Christina gripped the steering wheel of the Ford Taurus. "Why is it so dark out?"

Erik leaned forward in his seat, straining to see beyond the range of the car lights. He felt claustrophobic, like he was enveloped in a black canvas. It took him a moment to figure it out. "No streetlights here."

Christina rolled her eyes. "We make a fine pair of detectives." Although they were technically within Edmonton's city limits, this area on the northwest edge was still undeveloped scrub land.

Up ahead, on the side of the two-lane roadway, the flashing blue and red of a police cruiser guided their way. Christina pulled in behind the cruiser. They donned their police-issued hats and gloves and sat in silence for a moment, readying themselves. Erik glanced over at his partner. "My aching bones don't want to move."

She laughed and the rim of the wool toque slipped over her eyes. She pushed it up with her gloved hand, and said, "Come on, old man."

He braced himself for the cold.

"Body's on the other side of that," said Christina, pointing to the snow-covered embankment. Erik shone a flashlight, illuminating their path as they scrambled over the hill and down to a taped-off area at the edge of a snowy field. Intermittent flashes from a camera lit up the dark surroundings.

A uniformed officer standing guard greeted the homicide detectives. "Hello, Sergeant Jorgensen. Constable Wong."

"You were first on the scene?" asked Christina.

"Yes, ma'am. Around twenty-one-hundred hours, we responded to a call about suspicious activity. A trucker saw two people get out of a black van and toss something from over there." The officer pointed towards the cluster of flashlights flickering on top of the embankment.

Erik leaned over the tape and shone his flashlight at the body. An arm protruded from under a white tarp. Stained coat cuff, possibly blood. Brown leather-gloved hand.

The detectives stepped back as forensic officers set up portable lights around the perimeter of the crime scene. "Look how the white tarp blends in with the snow-covered field," said Erik.

His partner agreed. "Whoever dumped the body didn't want him found until the spring thaw."

When the lights were set up, two officers carefully unrolled the tarp and another filmed the proceedings. Once forensics gave the all-clear, the detectives moved in for a closer look. Erik studied the victim's face. Male. Middle-aged. Prominent nose and lean, fit-looking build. He glimpsed a deep red line and bruising on the exposed part of the victim's neck. Ligature marks. Erik frowned. He'd met this man before; he was certain of it. He never forgot a face but couldn't quite place where he'd seen him. He squeezed his eyes shut. Then it came to him, and he could feel his chest tighten. Things were about to get complicated.

3

Kate's phone buzzed, a text from Michael. No luck. This Jennifer woman, whoever the hell she was, hadn't seen Henry.

She ran through possible scenarios. What if his car veered into a ditch and he was too injured to call for help? In this weather, he'd already be dead from hypothermia. Fidgeting with the ring on her finger, she tried to quell her fears. She checked in with the traffic unit, but there were no reports of a serious accident. She tried the local hospitals, but no one fitting Henry's description had been admitted. She called her mother and brother again. Still no answer. Where the hell were they? Frustrated, Kate sat back down and turned on the TV, trying to distract herself. But the sitting and doing nothing drove her crazy. She'd give it one more hour, then she'd drive around and look for him.

Just before midnight, her cell rang. But her hopes were dashed when she saw the call display. Erik. What did he want? She hadn't talked to him in months and wasn't about to do so now. She let it go to voicemail. Then the bell rang. She clutched the door handle and hesitated. The bell rang again. She opened the door. Erik and his work partner, Christina, stood on the landing, serious expressions on their faces. "We're here about Henry," said Erik. "I'm afraid it's bad news—"

"No!" Kate didn't want to hear what they had to say. She tried to shut the door, but Erik stopped it with his arm. She turned and pressed her forehead against the wall; its coolness eased her nausea.

"I'm sorry, Kate, but Henry's dead," said Erik. He put his arm around her shoulders and guided her to the living room. She collapsed onto the couch, put her head between her knees, and sobbed. How could he be gone? It didn't seem possible.

"Christina, would you mind getting her a glass of water?" asked Erik.

Kate heard the tap running. She sat up and looked at Erik through blurry eyes. "Where did the accident happen? And why are *you* here?"

Erik cleared his throat. "It wasn't an accident, Kate. Patrol officers went to investigate reports of suspicious activity northwest of Anthony Henday Drive. They found a body and called homicide, and I recognized Henry."

It took her a moment to process. *Murder?* Her stomach churned, and she rushed to the bathroom to throw up. Afterwards, she leaned against the wall, resting her cheek on the cool tiles. At least Sam was still sleeping. Kate had to get her act together before telling her daughter the news.

"You okay?" Erik held out a hand to help her up. He watched from the doorway as she rinsed out her mouth in the pedestal sink. She looked at him through the bevelled mirror. "How do you know it was murder?"

Erik shook his head. "Kate, you know I can't discuss specifics, but there's no doubt, it was murder…and given our history, I can't lead this investigation."

She swung around and glared at him. "You can't back out. It'll look suspicious." He broke her gaze and looked down at his hands. "And after all that's happened," she said, "you owe it to me, and Henry."

Erik sighed and rubbed his eyes. He looked exhausted. She regretted her harsh tone. "I'm sorry Erik, but you're the best detective on the force. I need you on his case. Please?" Erik sighed again and nodded.

They settled back in the living room. Christina handed her a glass of water and perched on the edge of the ottoman where Henry had sat only a few hours earlier. And now he was dead. How was that possible?

"If you're up to it," said Christina, "we'd like to ask you a few questions."

Kate briefly closed her eyes and took a couple of calming breaths. "Yes, go ahead."

"Why are you here?" asked Christina. "I thought you and Henry had separated?"

Kate explained about the brunch and the phone call from the bar. "Henry offered to bring Conor back to our mom's place."

The detectives shared a look. "Do you know if Henry picked up your brother?" asked Erik.

She knew what Erik was thinking, but there was no way her brother was involved. "Yes, and I'm sure Mom can tell you when he brought home Conor." Kate covered her face with her hands. She couldn't delay this anymore. "Listen, can we talk some more later? I have to wake up Sam, tell her about her dad."

"We'll get the rest of your statement in the morning," said Erik. He stood up from the sofa and rested his hand on her shoulder. "You need us to stay while you talk to her?"

She shook her head no and the detectives let themselves out. The air felt viscous as she trudged upstairs. Sam lay on top of her covers, mouth open, lightly snoring. She was still in her jeans and T-shirt, headphones on. Kate hesitated. She wished with all her heart she could protect her daughter, soften the blow. Kate gently bushed her cheek. Sam stirred and looked up at her. "Where's Dad?" she asked, rubbing her eyes.

Kate sat on the edge of the bed. "Your dad…he's…" She struggled to find the right words.

Sam shot out of bed, her eyes wide. "Is it an accident? Where is he?"

Kate stood up put her arm around her. "Your dad—he's gone."

"What do you mean?" Sam's faced crumpled with grief and she collapsed into Kate's arms. "He's dead?"

Kate held her close and tried to keep it together. "Yes. I'm sorry, sweetheart."

Sam pushed her away. "There must be a mistake."

"I wish it was, but the police stopped by…" Kate bit her lip. She couldn't bring herself to tell Sam the rest.

"No! It can't be." Sam flung her body onto the bed and sobbed into her pillow. Kate stretched out on the bed, placing a protective arm around her.

"When can we see him?" Sam asked, her voice muffled.

Kate kept quiet, not knowing what to say.

Sam shifted her body to face Kate. "What aren't you telling me?"

Kate gazed into Sam's swollen eyes. "The police say his death is suspicious."

Sam's brow furrowed. "I don't understand."

"Neither do I, sweetheart." She reached out and brushed away Sam's tears. "Try to get some rest."

"How can I sleep? Dad's dead."

Sam burrowed under the comforter and sobbed. After a few hours, and many bouts of tears, she fell into a fitful sleep. Kate slowly turned onto her back and stared up at the stippled ceiling. Her feet dangled over the edge of the mattress. The enormity of the situation hit her like a punch to the stomach and she struggled to catch her breath. Murder? This can't be happening. Again. That long-ago night was still so clear in her mind. She and Conor frozen in terror by the sight of their thirteen-year-old cousin, Bridget, face down in the muck of the marsh.

Kate sat up in bed. *Mom doesn't know yet.* She slipped out of the room to call. This time, Alma answered the phone.

"Oh sweet Jesus, how can this be? I'm on my way over."

"Can you tell Conor?" asked Kate.

"No use trying to wake him. He's passed out on the sofa."

Kate slumped on the floor in the dark hallway and wept. Henry didn't deserve this ending. She replayed her conversation with him at brunch, what he'd said about setting the alarm and locking the doors. What had he meant by that? Had he been worried about their safety? Or his?

She sat in vigil outside Sam's bedroom, waiting for her mother to arrive. After what seemed like an eternity, she heard Alma let herself in to the house. The hall light flicked on, and Kate shielded her eyes from the brightness.

"Sweetheart, I'm so sorry." Alma turned off the lights and joined her on the hallway floor, holding her close and murmuring words of comfort.

That night, after they'd found Bridget's body, Kate, stricken with grief, had collapsed onto the muddy ground. "Get up. Now." Alma's sharp tone had shaken Kate to the core. *She's afraid.* That's when it dawned on Kate: someone had done that to her cousin. But who? And why? As they scrambled back to the village, she'd clung to her mom's hand and kept her gaze fixed on her feet, too fearful to look into the darkness beyond the reach of the flashlight.

Now, sitting beside her mom in the dark hallway, the same questions gnawed at her. Who killed Henry, and why?

4

On the drive back to the crime scene, Erik gazed out of the passenger window. His reflection, ghostly and distorted, stared back at him. What the hell was he doing keeping secrets from his work partner?

Gusty winds buffeted the Ford Taurus as Christina turned onto the two-lane road and pulled over in the same spot where they'd parked earlier. Although still dark, Erik could see a hint of light on the horizon. As he stepped out, the wind seized the car door and flung it wide, the hinges groaning under the strain. He grabbed the door and slammed it shut.

The detectives clambered to the top of the embankment to survey the dumpsite. "Good thing that trucker called it in," said Erik.

"And patrol actually got their butts out of the car to check it out," said Christina.

Erik smiled. A few of their fellow officers had a reputation for laziness, just doing the bare minimum on their shift. He'd been around long enough to shrug it off, but it drove Christina crazy.

The medical examiner's team had removed the body, but forensics was still processing the scene. Erik headed down to take a closer look while Christina walked over to the large tent that'd been erected further along the embankment.

By the time Erik got down the hill, a forensic officer was bagging a grey glove with a red truck logo on the wrist. "Where did this come from?" asked Erik.

"Hello, sir. It fell out of the tarp when the body was removed."

Erik's heart raced. Henry had been found wearing brown leather gloves. This one could be the killer's. "Would you mind texting me the photos of the glove as soon as possible?"

Erik slogged back up the embankment; the cold burned his cheeks. The tent at the top faced the full brunt of the wind and shook like it was possessed. He unzipped the flap and peeked inside.

Christina glanced over and indicated it was safe for him to come in. Erik squeezed his tall rugby-player frame through the small opening.

"The body was likely tossed from here," she said, shining her flashlight to a spot at the far side of the tent. "Forensics found two sets of prints. One size eleven, the other size nine."

Good thing forensics had the foresight to set up a tent to protect the prints before the storm blew in. 'We're looking for two suspects," he said.

"Yup. And that fits with what the trucker saw."

The sound of the tent flap unzipping signalled the arrival of the lead forensics investigator. She wore rubber gloves, a standard white forensics jumpsuit, and a headlamp. After closing the flap behind her, she set down a large black toolkit and grinned at the detectives.

"Hello, Sergeant Agarwal," said Christina.

"Hello, Christina. No need to be so formal. Just call me Manpreet." She punched Erik in the shoulder. "Glad you're on the case. Haven't worked with you in a while."

Erik laughed. With Manpreet at the helm, he knew the scene would be processed thoroughly.

"You two arrived just in time. I'm about to cast the shoe prints. Have you seen this done in the snow before?"

"Can't say I have," said Erik.

Manpreet directed her assistant to shine his flashlight over the footprints. "Portable lights could melt them." She pulled an aerosol can out of her kit and handed the detectives dust masks. "Grey auto primer highlights the details of the tread." She pulled on her own mask, sprayed the prints, and then leaned in to inspect her handiwork as the photographer took another series of shots.

"Now for the fun part. Potassium sulphate mixed with dental stone speeds up the hardening process." She gently poured the solution into each of the prints as the photographer documented the process. "Now we wait for it to dry."

The detectives left Manpreet and her team to finish processing the scene. Back in their car, Erik cranked up the heat and held his hands over the dashboard vent, trying to warm up.

"Right, want to swing by Timmies?" Christina asked. They had hours of work ahead before they'd get any chance to rest. Coffee and sugar would help them push through the fatigue. Christina pulled out onto the highway. "We start with the family," she said.

Erik pulled on his seat belt. The strap felt tighter than usual, pressing into his chest. He should've taken off his parka. Clearing his throat, he said, "Conor's got some stuff in his background we need to look into."

Christina gave him a quick glance before turning her attention back to the road. "What kind of stuff?"

"He recently fell off the wagon—started drinking again."

"Do you know why?"

"Not sure. And there's more…" Erik squirmed in his seat and yanked at the belt again. He was reluctant to betray Kate's trust, but under the circumstances, he felt he had to at least share what he'd learned about her family when they lived in Northern Ireland.

5

Kate awoke to the sound of her phone vibrating on the coffee table. A moment of oblivion. Then the memory of what happened came flooding back. Henry's dead. She sprung up from the sectional and answered the call.

"It's Erik. Sorry to disturb you, but we need to talk to you and your family."

"Mom's here, but Conor's still sleeping off his hangover back at her place."

"I understand. We're on our way to you now. We'll be there in fifteen."

Kate hung up and chucked an accent pillow. She knew what was coming. Across the room, Alma stirred on the chaise. "What's going on, sweetheart?"

"The police need to talk to us. And Conor."

"But your brother doesn't know what's happened to Henry."

"Don't worry." Kate draped her blanket over the sectional. "I'll go with the detectives and give him the bad news." She picked the pillow up off the floor and banged her shin on the corner of the coffee table. Same spot as last time. "Fuck." She rubbed her throbbing leg. Alma stared her down. "Sorry for swearing," said Kate.

"Why do the police have to talk to us now? Can't it wait?"

"The sooner they identify what he was doing in the hours before he was killed, the more likely they'll find the murderer."

"If you say so. You're the police officer."

Kate held her tongue. No point trying to correct her. Again. Every time she tried to explain her job as a crime analyst, her mother's eyes would glaze over, and she'd mutter something about how the modern world was strange. Alma had never used a computer in her life, while Kate spent her workdays in front of a screen, creating analytical reports to help guide the detectives in the field.

"Make sure they aren't too hard on your brother. He's struggling right now."

Kate's old resentments bubbled to the surface. She choked back the urge to blurt out, *What about me?*

Alma wandered over to the kitchen. "I should make some coffee for the detectives."

Kate pulled up her pantleg and inspected her red and tender shin. A hint of a bruise was already forming. "Why didn't you answer the phone?" she asked.

Alma paused, coffee pot in hand. "What do you mean?"

"Yesterday. When Henry went missing. I tried to reach you and Conor, but no one picked up."

Alma broke down in tears.

Shit, she'd made her mother cry. "Sorry, I didn't mean to upset you. But the police will want to know what time Henry dropped off Conor."

Alma eyes widened and she whispered, "What if—"

"No need to go there, Mom." Kate frowned. "You're Conor's alibi."

Alma busied herself with the coffeemaker. Kate tried to catch her eyes.

"Right?"

She looked up at Kate. "Right," she said and turned back to prep the coffee. "My phone was out of power, that's why you couldn't reach me. And when Conor got home, he went straight to the couch and passed out."

"Did you see Henry?"

Alma pushed the start brew button. Why wouldn't she answer the question? Before she could press her mom, the bell rang. That was quick. "We'll talk more later," Kate said over her shoulder as she rushed to answer the door. "Come in. Mom's making coffee."

They gathered around the kitchen island, and Kate introduced Alma to the detectives.

"I'm sorry for your loss," said Erik, holding out his hand. Her mother stared him down and Erik slowly lowered his arm. He looked at Kate quizzically. She gave him a barely perceptible shake of her head.

Christina pulled out her pad and took notes as Kate and Alma recounted their whereabouts on Saturday. After they'd finished,

Christina stood up to leave. "I'm sorry to disturb you during your time of grief."

"Anything we can do to help," said Alma, shaking her hand and completely ignoring Erik.

Erik walked ahead to the front entrance and Kate followed. "She knows about us?" he whispered.

Kate cringed. "Yes. Conor told her."

"Great," he said, rolling his eyes. "We're heading out to see your brother and we'd like you to come with us."

"Of course. Conor doesn't know yet about Henry. I have to break the news to him."

Before she left with the detectives, Kate checked in on Sam. She was cocooned in her comforter, fast asleep. Kate stood in the doorframe and listened to the sound of her daughter's rhythmic breathing. A deep sense of inertia washed over Kate; all she wanted to do was curl up beside Sam and block out the world. She rolled her shoulders to shake her stupor, then slipped out of the bedroom.

From the back seat of the unmarked police cruiser Kate stared out at the bleak winter landscape. The monotone palette of the grey roadway and white fields blended in with the overcast sky. Skiffs of snow drifted across the highway as they headed south from the city toward the bedroom community of Leduc.

The last time she'd seen her brother was more than six months earlier, when she and Henry had gone to retrieve him from a bar. Conor was precariously perched on a stool and Henry put an arm around his brother-in-law's shoulders to steady him. Conor pointed a finger at Kate and shouted, "Ya tramp. Tell him whatcha doin'."

Well lubricated by beer, his Northern Irish accent had reappeared. Turns out he'd spotted her coming out of a motel room earlier that week. At first, she'd blamed Conor for the breakup of her marriage, refused to talk to him for months; but deep down she knew it was her fault. That night at the bar, after Conor's outburst, Henry had looked over at her with an expression that broke her heart. And now what she had to tell Conor was going to break his heart. He loved Henry like a brother.

When they pulled up in front of her mother's vinyl-sided duplex, Kate turned to Erik and pleaded, "Take it easy on him. You know what he's been through."

"I've got to do my job."

Kate bristled at his blunt tone. He rang the doorbell and turned to look her in the eyes. "You're here to support your brother. Leave the questions to us."

Conor pulled back the lace curtain and peered through the small window in the front door before opening it. "What's wrong?" he asked, his voice hoarse. "Where's Mom?" His eyes darted to the detectives and back to Kate.

"Let's sit down." Kate took his hand and led him into the kitchen. She wrinkled her nose at the stink of his stale breath and funky body odour. She sat down at the table and he followed suit. He glanced again at the detectives standing by the kitchen sink before turning his attention back to Kate. "What's happened? Is it Mom?"

"It's Henry." She paused, searching for the right words. "He was found dead early this morning."

Conor jolted back in his seat. "No, that can't be true? I saw him yesterday."

She studied his face: remnants of vomit at the corner of his mouth, sleep caked in the corners of his long-lashed eyes, his dirty and dishevelled auburn hair. Her beautiful broken brother. Kate reached for his hand, noting the filthy, ragged nails and sandpaper skin. She felt the jagged edge of a cut on his wrist, but before she had a chance to inspect it, he jerked it away, wrapped his arms around his body and started rocking back and forth, tears streaming down his face. Kate was at a loss for how to comfort him.

Erik rifled through the cupboards for a glass, filled it with water and set it in front of Conor. "I'm sorry, but we need to ask you a few questions."

Conor wiped his eyes and looked to Kate. "I don't understand. What happened?"

"His body..." She struggled to keep her composure. "They think it's murder."

His eyes widened at the implications. "I'm the last one to have seen him before—" He covered his mouth with his hand to stifle a sob.

"That's why the detectives need to ask you some questions."

He picked up the glass, hand shaking, and guzzled down the water.

Kate leaned forward. "Please. This could help catch the killer."

He cradled the empty glass in his hands. "What do you want to know?"

The detectives pulled up chairs across from the siblings. "Tell us what happened yesterday," said Erik.

"I was drinking. Ended up at the Saxony midday."

"Do you remember Henry picking you up from the bar?" said Kate. Erik glared at her; she shrugged her shoulders.

"Yes," said Conor, his voice breaking. He wiped away his tears. "I was relieved to see him. He is…was…such a calm guy, and always knew how to make me feel better, like it was all going to be okay in the end." Kate pinched the web of skin between her thumb and forefinger, an old trick of hers to avoid crying in public. "He told me it was time to go home, or something of that sort, and drove me back here."

"Did you two talk about anything on the ride home?" asked Erik.

Conor paused for a second. Why's he hesitating? thought Kate. Christina lifted her head from writing in her notebook. She'd obviously picked up on it as well.

"No, I think I must've passed out for most of the ride. The next thing I know, I'm lying on the couch here. I can't remember much else."

"I have a photograph I'd like you take a look at." Christina unlocked her cell and set it on the table in front of Conor. "Do you recognize this glove?"

Conor stared at the screen, unnaturally still.

"You need to answer the detective," said Erik.

"No?"

Kate caught the upward inflection in her brother's voice. His hand shook as he ran his fingers through his hair.

Christina pushed her phone closer to Kate. "Do you recognize it?"

Kate leaned in to get a better look at the screen and prayed the shock hadn't registered on her face. A crime scene photo of a grey glove with a red truck logo on the snowy ground. She shook her head because she didn't trust her voice.

Erik stood abruptly, the metal chair legs scraping on the tiled floor. "I think it would be best for you two to come to the station for formal interviews."

"What for?" asked Conor. "I've already told you everything I know."

"Are you sure about that?" asked Erik.

Kate rested her hand on Conor's arm to stop him from responding. "Yes, we'll voluntarily come in," she said. "We have nothing to hide. But we need a few hours so my brother can shower and eat. He can come back to my place to get ready."

Christina raised her eyebrows and turned to Erik. "That's fine with us," he said.

On the ride back to Edmonton, a semi passed in the fast lane and whipped up the snow that had begun to fall out of a menacing sky. A swirl of white enveloped the windows of the car. Christina muttered something about truck drivers and tightened her grip on the steering wheel. Erik grunted in response. No one else spoke. In the back seat, Kate glanced over at Conor. He was hugging his backpack to his chest and staring out the side window. He'd lied, and she'd been forced to play along. Just like the night their cousin died.

Christina brought the cruiser to a stop in front of the house. "We'll see you soon," said Erik.

Inside, all was quiet. "Mom and Sam must be sleeping," Kate whispered to Conor, "You can clean up in the bathroom at the end of the hall."

While he showered, Kate went into the master suite she once shared with Henry and slid open the closet door. His side of the walk-in was crammed with clothes; he never gave anything away. She sniffed one of Henry's favourite blue shirts and caught a faint scent of sandalwood and bergamot. On her side swung bare plastic hangers. Six months earlier, she'd packed up all her stuff when she'd moved to the rental apartment, and now she was back, but not at all like she'd hoped.

Next, Kate peeked in on Sam. She was sitting beside her grandmother on the bed, poring over a photo album. Sam looked up, her face blotchy red and swollen. "Look, Mom, our trip last year to the Okanagan." In the picture, Henry stood beside his daughter at the edge of a vineyard, his bird-watching binoculars hanging around his neck and a big grin on his face. Kate smiled at the memory of that day. She pointed to his feet. "Remember we teased him for wearing socks with his sandals?" That holiday was one of the last times they were together as a family before it all fell apart.

"Where's Conor?" asked Alma.

"Downstairs showering. The police want us to go to the station to give our statements."

"Why?"

"Standard procedure." She plonked down beside Sam and put her arm around her. "How are you holding up?"

Sam shrugged in response.

"I'm sorry I have to go again, sweetheart. Once we finish up at the police station, I promise we'll spend some time together, okay?"

Sam nodded and went back to looking through the album.

Kate found Conor in the living room, slumped down on the sofa, hair dripping wet, dressed in clean clothes. She crushed the back of a chair with her grip, steadying her breath. "What the hell's going on? That's your glove in the photo from the crime scene."

Conor covered his face with his hands. "I didn't have anything to do with it."

Kate eased her grip. "Then why did you lie about the glove?"

"I panicked."

"Why? Because of what happened before? You've got to tell the detectives the truth."

"Does Erik know about Bridget?" His voice was shaky. She nodded, wondering what was going on in that mind of his.

He hung his head. "They're going to think I'm guilty."

Now's the time to ask him, she thought. Could he have killed Henry? Maybe it'd been an accident?

"It's all happening again," said Alma.

Startled, Kate and Conor looked up to see their mother standing in the doorway.

Kate sprung up from the sofa to comfort her. "Don't worry, I'll handle it." She led her mom upstairs to Sam's room. "Watch over her for me. Please."

Alma touched Kate's cheek. "I will. You keep your brother safe."

Kate slowly walked back downstairs and rejoined Conor. "Don't worry, it'll be fine," she said, trying to reassure herself as much as her brother. Their cousin's murder was going to bubble to the surface again, and there was nothing they could do to stop it. Conor was still a suspect in Bridget's case. And now another murder in the family. She sighed and leaned her head on his shoulder.

"I'm so sorry, sis. I still can't believe Henry is gone." That was all it took for her to break down; she clung to him and sobbed. After she was all cried out, she closed her sore, puffy eyes and dozed off.

When she woke up, she found herself lying on the sofa. Alone. A knitted blanket draped over her body. She sat up and called out for her brother. No answer. She rapped on the partially closed bathroom door before pushing it open. Empty. Heart racing, she rushed upstairs. Sam was curled up next to her granny on the bed, both fast asleep. She ran to the front closet. Conor's parka and boots were gone.

She felt like she was thirteen again, circling her big brother's empty bedroom, wondering why he'd taken off before the police could interview him about Bridget. This time, Kate was going to find Conor before things got out of hand. She checked the clock. She'd only slept for half an hour. She called Erik and told him they were running late. "Conor's not coping very well with the news about Henry." Which was true.

"You've got until six," he said, "then we'll have to come get him ourselves." Kate figured they didn't have enough evidence to arrest him, but she didn't want to test it. Far better to go in voluntarily. She had four more hours to find him and bring him to the station.

Kate looked out of the window. Mom's Civic was gone from the driveway. She glanced down at the side table. Keys missing. That shithead had stolen her car. She left a message for Brenda Littlechild, family friend and Conor's business partner, asking her to call back. If he was going to run anywhere, it'd likely be to her place. Next, she tried his ex-boyfriend, Jeremy. He picked up on the first ring.

"I'm looking for Conor. Have you talked to him recently?"

A long pause before he answered. "He left a drunken message on my phone a couple of days ago, but I didn't call him back."

"What did he say?"

"He wasn't making much sense. Something about being scared and not knowing what to do."

Kate's heart skipped a beat. "Do you still have the message?"

"No, I deleted it. I couldn't bear to hear him like that. Sorry I couldn't be more—" Kate hung up on him. How fucking lame. Jeremy abandoned her brother when he needed him most. Then again, who was she to judge? Conor wasn't the easiest person to love when he was drinking.

She texted Brenda. Just left a phone message. Looking for Conor.

She texted right back. He's here.

Kate dreaded going back on the highway, but by the time she passed the city limits and headed south, the snow had stopped falling and the graders were out clearing the way.

She rubbed the dull ache in her stomach. Stress or hunger or both. Here she was, tracking down Conor when she should be back at home with Sam. What if…she didn't want to think about it, but what if he did it? She punched the steering wheel. There had to be another explanation.

By the time she pulled up in front of Brenda's house on the outskirts of Devon, a forty-minute drive southwest of the city, the sun was low on the horizon. The Civic was parked in the driveway. Good, he's still here. The light from the front porch flicked on as she climbed the steps and rang the doorbell. Brenda looked out through the living room window and waved to Kate. After a brief pause, Kate heard the click of the door unlocking.

Brenda pulled her into a bear hug. "I'm real sorry about Henry."

Kate clung to her for a moment, comforted by her familiar scent of engine oil and laundry detergent. She pulled back from the embrace and wiped away the tears stinging her eyes. "Sorry you had to find out from Conor. I was going to call and tell you, then he took off…"

There was no need for Kate to explain any further; they'd known each other a long time. Brenda was the first friend the siblings made when they moved to Canada and she was Conor's business partner in their courier company, Northern Shipping.

Kate found Conor at the kitchen table, sipping tea and smoking. She kept quiet about the cigarette. Better than drinking. "You stole Mom's car?" she asked.

Conor took a drag before answering her. "I borrowed it."

Brenda stood behind Conor and placed her hands firmly on his shoulders. "You're going to tell her what's going on, right?"

6

Conor stubbed out his cigarette in a saucer. "Someone's trying to blackmail me."

Kate slumped in a chair. Of course. Blackmail. This was her brother. Trouble always seemed to swirl around him. But what Kate could never quite grasp was how much was his fault, and how much was just bad luck. "What the hell?" she said.

He hung his head, unable to look her in the eye. "My drinking's getting out of hand."

That was the understatement of the year.

Brenda muttered to herself as she paced the cozy kitchen. Kate marvelled for the umpteenth time at how, and why, Brenda still had a business partnership with her messed-up brother.

"I've never drank at work—until a few weeks back. At an airport bar."

Kate banged her fist on the table. "Shit, Conor, you drove drunk? In your work truck? You could've killed someone."

Conor lit another cigarette. "Don't you think I know that? I only drove for about five minutes before I pulled over and called Brenda."

Brenda stopped pacing and tucked her thick shoulder-length hair behind her ears. "That's true. I picked him up and banned him from driving any of the company vehicles until he straightened himself out."

"So how does blackmail come into play?" asked Kate.

"The next day, this dude showed up at work."

"What did he say?"

"Turns out he'd filmed me drinking at the bar and getting into the truck. Told me if I didn't help with shipping something up to Fort Mac at the end of the month, he'd send the footage to airport security, and we'd lose our clearance."

Without security clearance at the airport, most of their lucrative courier contracts with companies around Fort McMurray would dry up. Kate felt the truth of it settle, cold and heavy, in her gut.

Conor took a drag on his cigarette and exhaled; the smoke drifted straight toward her.

"Jesus, Conor." She waved it away. "What did this guy look like?"

"Steroid weightlifter type." He set the cigarette down on the edge of his saucer. "Had a large gargoyle tattoo here." He pointed to his forearm.

"Did you know about this?" Kate asked Brenda.

She shook her head. "Not until Conor showed up at my door this afternoon."

Conor twisted around in his seat to look up at Brenda. "I didn't want you to worry, that's why I went to Henry."

Kate poured herself a cup of tea. He'd spoken to Henry? What was he thinking? "Why not come to me? I'm the one who works with the police."

Conor picked at a callous on his hand. "I couldn't handle one of your freak-outs. And besides, I didn't want to get the police involved."

"But…" Kate said and then stopped herself. "Okay, I get it. What did Henry do?"

"He offered to talk to the blackmailer."

"That doesn't sound like Henry." Her husband was a by-the-book kind of guy. Not the type to get in the middle of something like this. Surely, he would've advised Conor to talk to the police. "And did he meet with him?"

Conor shook his head. "Not sure. I was too drunk yesterday to ask."

She mulled over what he'd told her. "But why did you take off from the house?"

"I panicked."

Sounded familiar; avoidance was her brother's M.O. The blackmail story seemed far-fetched, but why would he lie? Kate brushed aside her doubts. She glanced at her watch. If they left now, they could get to the police station in time. "We need to go. Together. In my car."

"But I've got Mom's—"

"My car. I insist." She wasn't giving Conor any more opportunities to take off.

"I'll bring back your mom's Civic tomorrow," offered Brenda. "My eldest has a hockey game in the city. He can drive me home."

"Thanks. Owe you one," said Kate.

Conor brushed ash off his lap. "Looks like you two have it all figured out." He turned to Brenda. "If I talk to the police, we could lose our security clearance."

Brenda picked up Conor's cigarette and took a long drag before she responded. "You've got to tell the police. What happens with our security clearance is the least of our worries. If they killed Henry as a message to you, you're in big trouble."

"I'm so sorry you got dragged into this," said Kate.

Brenda stubbed out the cigarette. "You're not the one who needs to apologize."

Conor sighed. "You're right. I'm the one. Sorry I screwed up again."

Kate struggled to feel sympathy for him.

She waited until Conor was in her car and they were back on the highway to Edmonton before she brought up her plan. "I think you should go to rehab."

Conor slunk down in the passenger seat and mumbled to himself.

"What did you say?"

"Nothing," he said, "you're right."

"Good." She pressed the phone button on her steering wheel, "Call Second Chance Clinic."

Her brother opened his mouth to speak but she motioned for him to keep quiet. The receptionist picked up on the second ring and Kate asked for the director. "My brother has agreed to take the spot," she said.

"Wonderful. We'll see you both here in the morning."

She hung up and glanced over at him. "What's wrong?"

"You…when…I didn't think I'd be going so soon."

"I pulled some strings." She pursed her lips to keep from saying anything else. Conor was more likely to go along with the plan if she refrained from lecturing him.

"How long?"

"Thirty days."

"I don't know…"

Kate clenched the wheel and took several deep breaths. He had to go, for both their sakes. She needed to focus on Sam and organize Henry's memorial. If he went to rehab, it was one less thing on her plate.

7

Christina's ponytail swung from side to side as she perched on the edge of Erik's desk. "Where are they?" she asked.

"Kate called. They need more time, so I've pushed the interview to six."

"You're too soft on her."

She was right, but he didn't want to talk about it. "Did you call the Saxony?"

"The bartender confirms their story. He called Kate, and about thirty minutes later, Henry arrived at the bar to retrieve Conor."

"Do they have security cameras?"

"Only inside. The one in the parking lot is busted."

"We can work with that."

"They use VHS tapes."

That put a damper on his enthusiasm. Did they even make those anymore? Talk about old school. Any footage they'd find would likely be grainy, especially if the tapes were reused.

He checked his watch. They still had another couple of hours before Kate and Conor's interviews. Enough time to pay a visit to the Saxony.

Before they left, Erik stopped by the washroom to splash water on his face in a futile effort to revive his depleted energy. They'd been working non-stop for almost twenty-four hours now, and he was exhausted. He stared at his reflection in the mirror and rubbed his stubbly chin. He needed a shave, but it was going to have to wait. He pulled a spare suit from his locker, wishing he had an iron to smooth out the creases in the knees of the pants.

Christina met up with him in the hallway, showing no outward signs of fatigue. His partner was fifteen years his junior and she still had the stamina for the job, something he'd lost long ago. She waved a file in the air. "We have notes from the autopsy and an update from forensics."

On the drive to the bar, Erik skimmed through the file. Henry had been strangled from behind with some sort of a metal cable and dumped in the field. Where was he killed? Maybe his car? They still hadn't tracked it down. "Conor could've done it," said Erik.

"Timing wise, yes."

"But based on the witness and footprints, two people dumped Henry's body."

"Kate could've helped. She's tall and strong," said Christina.

Erik shook his head. "I know her. She's not capable of this. Besides, they both have alibis."

"From family members. We need to confirm those."

Erik knew firsthand the danger of tunnel vision. They had to investigate all possible suspects, including Kate and Conor. "You're right. We'll double-check their stories." He looked back down at the file. Forensics had found blood on Henry's cuff. A sample had been sent for DNA testing, along with the glove. Manpreet had pulled viable shoe prints and sent a photo of the treads.

Christina parked their car in front of the crumbling stuccoed entrance to the Saxony Hotel and Bar. Erik shut the file and climbed out of the car, eager to get his hands on the footage from the bar. Inside, they paused to let their eyes adjust to the dimness. The drinking hole smelled of musty carpet and sweaty armpits. The bartender, wiping down the counter with a well-worn rag, looked like an aging punk rocker. They flashed their badges.

"I spoke with you on the phone earlier today," said Christina. "You were going to pull the VHS tape?"

"Yes, I already gave it to one of your officers. Mulvaney, I think. Or Morrison. His last name started with an 'M.'"

The detectives looked at each other. "When was this?" asked Erik.

"Couple of hours ago."

"Was he in uniform?" asked Christina. "Did he show his police identification?"

The bartender shook his head. "No, he wore civvies and I didn't think to ask for ID."

Erik rubbed the back of his neck. "Next time, if someone claims to be a police officer, you might want to ask to see their badge." He pulled out his phone and messaged the investigative team.

Did anyone pick up the footage from the Saxony Hotel? Erik tapped his foot as he read the responses. No one from their team had retrieved it. He drew in slow, steady breaths. Someone had impersonated a police officer and stolen evidence in their murder investigation.

Christina glanced over at him, and he gave her a slight shake of his head. Her eyes widened at the implications. She turned to the bartender. "Can you describe what this man looked like?"

The bartender pushed his straggly grey hair out of his face. His jean jacket reeked of cigarette smoke. "He was middle-aged. Brown hair with grey streaks. Bland suburban type. Wore dress pants." He tilted his head towards a scuffed door at the end of the bar. "I can pull today's footage so you can see him."

Erik rocked on his heels. "Good suggestion."

The bartender led the detectives past a couple of near-empty vending machines and through the door marked "Employees Only." On one side of the windowless room, a VHS machine sat on a battered metal desk. The bartender pressed the eject button. Nothing came out. He opened the tape flap and peered inside. "That's strange. I swore I put one in." The bartender ran his fingers along an array of tapes sitting on a shelf above the desk, each labelled with a different day. "Looks like both Saturday and today are missing," he said.

Erik cursed under his breath. "You brought this man back here when you pulled Saturday's tape?"

The bartender nodded.

"Did you leave him unattended?" asked Christina.

The bartender pointed to an exit door at the back of the room. "Went out for a smoke." He scratched his head, flecks of dandruff rained onto his shoulders. "Didn't think it'd be a problem 'cause he was a cop."

The confines of the windowless room began to weigh on Erik. "He wasn't a cop," he said, his tone sharper than intended. "As I said earlier, you should've asked to see his badge." Erik had no patience left for this idiot.

The bartender took a step back, "I'm sorry, man."

Christina opened the door to the lounge. "How about we go back in the bar to talk?"

The detectives sat at the counter on cracked leather stools and the bartender poured them all glasses of water. "That night, Conor was at the one you're at," he said, pointing to Erik's spot at the bar. "I kept refilling his shot glass with Bushmills."

Erik surveyed the empty room. "How busy was it?"

"Very. On the weekends, the locals come out. Things were a bit heated back there." He gestured to the pool table. "One of the players was accused of bumping the eight ball."

"How drunk was Conor?"

"I've seen him worse. But by the time Henry got here, he was slurring words. I didn't pay much attention though. I was focused on the rowdies at the back. I was on my own. Short staffed."

"Why did you call Kate?" asked Christina.

"When Conor was a regular, she'd given me her number. Asked me to call when her brother got too drunk to drive. After his third refill, I called her number. Still had it by the till."

"How long had it been since Conor was last here?"

"At least a year. Thought he might've got rid of the alcohol demon for good."

"If it'd been that long, why did you still have Kate's number?" asked Erik.

The bartender flashed a yellow-toothed smile. "Couldn't bring myself to take it down. Spent a lot of time thinking about those long legs of hers."

Slimy bastard, thought Erik. He abruptly turned and exited the lounge, leaving Christina to wrap things up with the bartender.

"That was a bust," she said, joining him outside.

Erik surveyed the surroundings for other CCTV cameras, but the Saxony was sandwiched between two busy thoroughfares with the closest building over a block away. "Get him to meet with our sketch artist." He kicked at a pile of grey snow next to the cruiser. He'd been too lenient with Kate and her brother. He should've insisted that they come to the station right away. "We need to find out what Conor was up to this afternoon."

"You think he arranged for someone to steal the tape?"

Erik shrugged. "We've got to consider the possibility." The killer—or killers—were one step ahead of them, covering their tracks.

8

The front desk clerk notified the detectives that Kate and Conor had arrived at the station. Erik watched the camera feeds as his partner directed the siblings to take off their boots and led them into separate interview rooms. Conor was hunched over in his chair, head in his hands, while Kate sat up straight with her arms crossed.

Erik let them stew while he examined their footwear, wrinkling his nose at the scuffs on Kate's brown Blundstones. He compared the treads to the forensic photos of the footprints found at the crime scene. Different patterns, but Conor's shoe size was a match for one of the prints.

The detectives entered Conor's interview room first. The confined space with blank white walls always put Erik on edge, but he'd learned to channel that into his interrogations.

Christina pressed the video record button on the controls affixed to the wall beside the table. "For the record, you have come here voluntarily. You're not under arrest and you're not obligated to talk."

Conor glanced up at the camera angled downwards from one of the corners in the ceiling and nodded.

"You have to say it," said Erik.

Conor cleared his throat. "Yes," he said softly.

Erik raised the pressure with a sharp bang of his fist on the bolted-down table. The crack echoed through the nearly empty room.

"You're hiding something from us."

Conor blinked several times, then his jaw slackened. "You're right. I didn't give you the whole story."

Erik leaned forward. *Confession time.*

"I was blackmailed."

Erik hadn't seen that coming.

Conor told the detectives about the video of him drinking and how he'd gone to his brother-in-law for help.

Erik stood and dragged his aluminum chair around the small table, its legs grating against the concrete floor. He positioned himself beside Conor, their knees touching. Conor tried to inch his chair back, but Erik blocked it, bracing his foot against one of the chair legs.

"Let me get this straight," said Erik. "You were blackmailed because they, whoever *they* are, needed someone with security clearance to deliver their product up north?"

Conor twisted in his seat to look at the detective. "Yes, and when I told Henry, he offered to talk to the blackmailer."

"And did he?" asked Erik.

Conor shook his head. "Not sure."

"And if we talk to your business partner…" Erik consulted his file for the name. "Brenda Laboucane. She'll confirm your story?"

"Yes."

"But she can't really, can she? Did she see this guy, or the video?" said Erik.

"Well…no." Conor wrung his hands.

Erik spotted a cut on Conor's wrist. "When did you tell your business partner and your sister about the blackmail?"

"Um. This afternoon."

Erik raised his eyebrows. "Why didn't you say anything earlier?"

"I'm telling the truth. I didn't kill Henry."

"How do we know? No one else saw you meet with the blackmailer," said Erik.

"He didn't give me his name. But I can describe him. Stocky, about forty years old, with a gargoyle tattoo on his arm. I have his number, but it doesn't work anymore. You need to find this guy."

"Don't tell us how to do our jobs," said Erik. Conor flinched.

"Where did you get that, by the way?" Erik pointed to the cut on his wrist. Conor yanked down his sleeve. "I fell when I was drunk," he said.

"Looks like it needs some antiseptic," said Christina.

Conor crossed his arms. "I'm fine."

Erik didn't push it any further. Instead, he shifted back to questioning Conor about the glove at the crime scene. Conor stuck to his story, insisting he didn't recognize it—even as the pitch of his voice rose and his eyes darted around the room. Erik could tell Conor was lying, but he would wait until the DNA results came back before he questioned him further. “That’s all we have for now. Please don’t leave town while you’re under investigation.”

Conor rubbed his temples. “Fine.”

“Thank you,” said Christina, “and please wait here while we talk to your sister.”

The detectives shifted to the adjacent interview room. This time, Christina led the questioning. “Your brother told us about the alleged blackmail. When did you learn about it?”

Kate scowled. “He told me this afternoon.”

“I thought you two were close. Why did he keep this from you?” she asked.

“He didn’t want to get the police involved, and since I work for them…”

Christina shifted her line of questioning. “Why did your brother lie about the glove? We both know he recognized it.”

“I have no idea what you’re talking about,” she said.

Erik gauged her reaction. She kept her face expressionless—and that was her mistake. She was hiding something. “Why did you delay coming in to see us?” he asked.

Kate straightened out her back. “Like I told you already, Conor needed time to recuperate.”

He stared at her. What was she not telling him? Perhaps Conor was doing something else? Like arranging for someone to steal the VHS tape from the pub?

Christina cleared her throat. “Tell me about Northern Ireland.”

Erik shifted in his seat as Kate glared at him. She’d shared her traumatic childhood experience with him in confidence.

“What do you mean?” Kate asked.

So, she wasn’t going to make this easy for Christina.

“I understand Conor is still a suspect in the death of your cousin.”

Kate pulled at the collar of her shirt. “The investigation was flawed. They’d targeted Conor because he was the last one to see her alive.”

“But there was more to it than that.”

“How the hell is this related to Henry’s murder?”

“As a crime analyst, you should know the importance of patterns.”

Erik shuffled the papers on the table—his signal for Christina to wrap things up.

"One more question," said Christina. "After you and Henry split up, did you have a relationship with anyone else?"

Erik looked over at his partner. *What was she up to?*

Kate narrowed her eyes. "I did, but it ended months ago."

"I'm going to need his name."

"Again, I don't see how this is relevant."

Christina started to speak, but Erik interrupted her. "You're right, Kate. Sorry to invade your privacy. Thank you for coming in to talk to us. You're free to go."

The detectives walked the siblings to the elevator. At the doors, Kate asked to speak with Erik in private.

"Christina, would you mind escorting Conor to the lobby?" he asked.

His partner stabbed at the down button and refused to meet his eyes. Erik didn't need to ask why. He'd cut across her questioning of Kate—and now he was agreeing to a private conversation.

He ushered Kate into his office and closed the door. Her face was pale, dark circles under her eyes. He suppressed the urge to hold her.

She began pacing. "This is crazy, Erik. You're off the mark, there's no way my brother would've killed Henry."

"You know the stats. It's standard procedure to look at the family first." He rubbed his eyes. The lack of sleep was getting to him.

"Why did you tell her about Bridget? I shared that in confidence."

He clasped her hand in his. "You know I had to tell her. It's relevant to the investigation."

"Christina doesn't know about us, does she?"

Erik shook his head. "Don't think so. But she was right to ask if you had an affair. A jilted lover makes a good suspect."

Kate exhaled and leaned into him. He put his arms around her and breathed in her scent. "I'm so sorry, about everything," he whispered in her ear. "I still care about you." Her body stiffened and she pulled away. He wished he'd kept his mouth shut.

"I'm taking Conor to the Second Chance rehab clinic in the morning, and then I need to be with Sam and plan the funeral. Please let me know if you make any progress, okay?"

"I promise."

She gave him a wan smile. He opened the door to his office and came face to face with Miles Schultz, the crime analyst on the case. Miles staggered backwards. "Sorry, sir. Just about to knock."

Knock my ass. *How much had he overheard*? "Well. What is it?"

Miles rapidly blinked his eyes, "Ah…well…I was going home?"

Erik crossed his arms. "You don't need my permission."

His face turned red. "Right. Good night, sir," and he hurried to the elevators. The doors slid open to reveal Christina.

"Hold that," said Erik. Christina used her forearm to keep the door open. "Would you mind escorting Kate to the lobby?"

Kate stood beside Christina in the elevator, more than a head taller. Miles backed into the far corner, as if he'd rather be anywhere else. As the doors slid closed, Christina stuck out her tongue at Erik. He grinned. Good thing she still had her sense of humour.

Erik retreated to his office, shut off the overhead light and collapsed in his chair. His body ached with exhaustion. He stared out the window into the evening darkness. What the hell was he doing? He'd been a fool to think he could be objective. His relationship with Kate made that impossible. The solution was clear: tomorrow he'd withdraw from the investigation.

9

Early Monday morning, Kate circled the room at the private rehab clinic, taking in the oak furniture and scuffed walls. The exorbitant fee she'd paid to get her brother a spot certainly didn't go towards the décor. She sniffed. Eau de Pine-Sol. Who used that to clean anymore? She ran her finger along the top of the chunky headboard. No dust. Dated but neat. Not so bad.

Conor filled the top dresser drawer with the meagre contents of his suitcase. "Might as well make myself at home."

She sat on the edge of the double bed and traced the paisley pattern on the coverlet. Would thirty days be enough time for him to recover? On the wall opposite the bed, a framed poster with the saying *Have an Attitude for Gratitude* hung oddly high on the wall. Her brother followed her gaze. "Cheesy but true. Thank you, sis."

She put her arm around him, his bony shoulder digging into her hand. He'd gotten so skinny. "Promise me you'll take care of yourself."

"Same with you."

She hurried out of the room, not wanting him to see her in tears.

The clinic's syrupy administrator hovered in the hallway. "Don't you worry, he's in good hands."

Kate pulled out a used tissue from her parka pocket and blew her nose. "I hope it'll stick this time."

The administrator cleared her throat. "Before you leave, can I trouble you to fill out the paperwork so Conor can attend your husband's funeral?"

Kate followed her to the clinic's communal room. The lopsided second-hand sofas and mismatched chairs reminded Kate of her childhood playroom. On rainy days, she'd play tag with her brother and Bridget, leaping over the tattered sofa, rolling on the shag carpet.

Kate sat at a table with a chipped edge and completed the day release form. The administrator cleared her throat again. "You might want to refrain from serving alcohol at the reception."

How strange to call it a reception. Wasn't that for weddings? And what kind of sister was she? It hadn't even crossed her mind to ban booze. "Of course," she said. Something about this woman put her on the defensive. As if she were to blame for her brother's situation. In a way, she was responsible for the mess he'd become.

Kate handed the administrator the completed forms and headed back to the parking lot. A black Audi, engine idling, was parked in the spot next to her SUV. What was he doing here? She flushed at the memory of what had happened in the back seat of his car a year ago. If only...she clenched her jaw to stop her racing thoughts. No point going down that rabbit hole.

She opened the passenger door and climbed inside. "What's going on?"

"I'm backing out of the case," said Erik. "Conflict of interest."

She touched his arm. "Please, don't."

He stroked her cheek. "My feelings for you are clouding my judgement."

She pulled away from his touch and chose a different tack. "If you were to back out, what would you tell the inspector? That you had an affair with a subordinate? That's career suicide. And what about me? I'd lose my job too."

He rubbed his bloodshot eyes. Poor man. She was pushing him to do something they both knew was wrong. What was he thinking? Perhaps wondering how he'd ever got involved with such a manipulative bitch.

He looked away and clenched the steering wheel. "It's too difficult to be objective."

She chewed her nails. What could change his mind? "I disagree. Both you and I know that any other homicide detective would take one look at Conor's background and the circumstantial evidence in Henry's murder and conclude he's guilty."

"What if he is guilty, Kate?"

She didn't want to answer that question. There had to be another explanation. "All I know is that unlike some of the other detectives, you'll keep an open mind and consider all the evidence."

"Dropping the case may be risky but so is sticking with it. What if the inspector finds out about us?"

"How could he? No one else at the station knows." She bit the inside of her lip, drawing blood and tears, and leaned in. "Please Erik. I trust you to find out the truth."

His face softened. "You're making it hard for me to say no."

"Then don't." She grasped his hand in hers. "I need you."

He sighed and shook his head. "I hope I don't regret this."

Kate kissed him on the cheek. "Thank you."

With Conor safely ensconced in rehab, Kate drove back to the house and stationed herself at the kitchen island with a full pot of tea and a pile of estate paperwork to review. Thankfully, Henry hadn't changed his will when they'd separated. Everything was now hers, including the house. She could give notice to her landlord at the apartment and move back permanently.

Alma fluttered about, washing counters, tidying up.

"Sit down. Take a break," said Kate.

She pulled up a stool and lifted the teapot, her wrist wobbling as she poured. Kate studied her mother's pale face. She seemed older, frailer. "How are you doing?"

Her chin quivered. "Been better."

Kate reached out, her large hand enveloping her mother's. As a child, Kate had prayed to be petite and small boned like her, but the genetics lottery had divvied that out to her brother, and she'd inherited their father's tall frame, all six feet two inches of it. Kate's eyes stung at the thought of their complicated mess of a father who'd taken off soon after Bridget's death. Last she'd heard he was living in Vancouver. Never in a million years did Kate think she'd end up a single mother. She'd married Henry because he was reliable and stable. Nothing like this was supposed to happen to him.

"We need to properly say goodbye," said Alma.

Kate nodded. Earlier that morning, the medical examiner's office had called. They'd completed the autopsy and released Henry's body to the funeral home. "I've arranged for us to visit this evening," she said.

"Can't we go sooner? Samantha hasn't left her bedroom in two days."

Kate gathered the estate papers and put them back into the folder. "You're right. This can wait." She climbed the stairs, knocked on Sam's door and walked in. Sam lay on her back, staring up the ceiling. Kate pulled up the blinds and cracked open the window to air out the room. Sam flung the comforter over her head. "Don't."

"Sweetheart, time to get up." Kate sat on the end of the bed. "Please. We need to go to the funeral home to say goodbye to your dad." She held her breath, uncertain how her daughter would respond. Sam kicked off the covers, her smudged-mascara eyes red and puffy. Kate wrapped her arms around her. "I know this is hard."

"Fine, I'll go."

Kate sniffed. "How about you shower first?"

Sam pulled away. "Don't feel like it."

"That's fine." Kate rummaged through her pocket for a tissue, spat on it and tried to wipe off the mascara marks under Sam's eyes.

She pushed her hand away. "Ew, Mom, that's gross."

Kate held up her palms. "Sorry. Old habits die hard."

10

At the police station, Erik walked past his team, acknowledging them with a brief nod. He was in no mood to stop and chat. He spotted Miles checking his watch. That twerp was keeping tabs on him. Erik settled in at his desk and logged onto his computer. He needed a few minutes to collect his thoughts before the morning debrief.

Several minutes later, Inspector Barclay poked his head in his office. "Glad you've finally joined us."

"Sorry, sir. Overslept." Compounding the lies. He was having second thoughts about caving in to Kate. She was right about how things would go down if he asked to be taken off the investigation. The inspector would want to know why, and Erik would have to come up with a plausible lie, which he didn't know if he was capable of doing, or else tell the truth and jeopardize both his career and Kate's.

She'd appealed to his ego, insisting he stay on the case because he was the unit's best investigator. But she was in denial about her brother—he knew that much. In all likelihood, forensics would identify Conor's DNA on the glove at the crime scene and his blood on the victim's sleeve. If it came back a match, Erik would have no choice but to charge Conor with murder. And that was what got him second guessing his decision to stay on the case. If Conor was charged, a defence lawyer could spin the case by claiming Erik was targeting Kate's brother out of spite. But would Kate really reveal their affair and give the defence that kind of ammunition? Maybe not, but her brother might. Conor knew about the affair. He'd seen them come out of a motel room.

No use speculating about that now. He had more concrete problems to tackle. He pushed back from his desk and called for the team to gather in the boardroom. He and Christina stood next to the whiteboard and watched the officers and the crime analyst file into the room.

"Sir—" said Miles.

Erik cut him off, palm raised. "Hold on." He wrote "sketch artist" on the whiteboard and waited for the team to settle.

"Hello everyone. Let's get started," said Christina.

"As you may already know," said Erik, "on Saturday, someone impersonating a police officer stole the CCTV footage from the Saxony before we had a chance to retrieve it."

"Could it be Conor?" asked Miles.

Erik clenched his jaw. "Not likely. The bartender knows him."

Miles blushed. "I forgot."

Erik softened his tone, "But you're right, he could've enlisted the help of someone to steal the tape."

"I need to tell—" said Miles.

Erik interrupted him. "Just wait." His gaze swept the room and settled on Yee. "Constable Yee, did you review the security footage from the house across the street from Kate's?"

"Yes, and it confirms her story," said Yee. "She arrived at the family home on Saturday at 10:00 am and didn't leave until early the next morning when you and Detective Wong arrived to tell her about Henry."

Thank goodness Kate's alibi held up. She couldn't have helped Conor dump the body.

"Excellent. This morning, the bartender from the Saxony will be coming into the station to meet with a sketch artist. Constable Yee, I'd like you to be there for that process."

"Miles, did you get the airport footage?" asked Christina.

"Yes, we found video of Conor at the bar drinking."

Erik wrote "airport bar video" on the whiteboard. The blackmailer, if he existed, should be in the footage. "Good. Constable Yee, can you review that as well? See if you recognize anyone in there that might've been videotaping Conor having a drink." If there really was a blackmailer, he might have a criminal record that would help to identify him.

"What about footage at Conor's company, Northern Shipping?" asked Christina.

Miles shook his head. "No luck. Busted camera."

How convenient. According to Conor, the blackmailer had paid him a visit at his office. But without CCTV evidence, they couldn't prove, or disprove, his claim. "And how about you," said Erik, pointing to a young constable whose name he'd forgotten. "Can you look into both Conor and Henry's financial records?"

"Yes, sir."

Christina cleared her throat. "Turns out Henry had a girlfriend. Jennifer MacQuarrie. Worked with him at the university." Erik spun to face his partner. Why hadn't she told him about this before the meeting? "I'll go talk to her," said Christina.

His partner didn't trust him when it came to Kate, that much was obvious. And truth be told, she was right not to. "Good idea," said Erik. "And talk to Henry's other colleagues as well while you're there."

Miles stuck up his hand like he was in a classroom. "Yes, what is it?" asked Erik, keeping his tone steady to hide his irritation. There was something about Miles's personality that rubbed him the wrong way.

"I was trying to tell you, sir. Conor's mother lied. She wasn't home when her son was dropped off. She was volunteering at a church bingo until midnight."

That changed everything. Why would she give a false alibi? Erik pulled up the timeline on his computer and projected it on the boardroom screen for the team to view.

"Henry picked Conor up from the bar around 1:00 pm. Alma claimed he dropped her son off mid-afternoon, but if she was at the bingo until midnight, that gives Conor plenty of time to kill Henry and find help to dump the body."

"Someone should talk to traffic. Tracking down Henry's Volkswagen may be key to solving this case," said Christina.

"I'll do that, ma'am," offered one of the officers.

Erik pointed to the young constable. What the hell was his name? "And you, find out if Conor's company, or any of his friends, owns a—"

"Sir—" said Miles.

These damn millennials had no sense of protocol. He held up his index finger to silence Miles and turned back to the constable. "See if Conor's company or one of his friends owns a black van like the one used to dump Henry's body."

"Yes, sir," said the constable.

"Miles, what is it now?" Erik asked in a cutting tone. The analyst's face flushed as red as his hair.

"Conor was a suspect in his cousin's unsolved murder. Do you want me to put together a backgrounder on that case?"

"Not a priority," said Erik. "The murder happened twenty-five years ago, and Conor was never charged."

"But I think it's important, sir," stammered Miles. A thin film of sweat had formed on the crime analyst's forehead.

Constable Yee raised her eyebrows.

Erik took off his glasses. *Insolent little shit.* "Are you the lead detective on this case?"

"Sorry, sir." Miles wiped his forehead with the back of his hand.

Erik sighed. "Fine. Put together a backgrounder." He dismissed the team and they quietly filed out of the room. Christina remained seated at the table. When the room cleared, she waved her pen at him.

"What?"

"You're too hard on him."

"He irritates me."

She shrugged. "Me too. But I don't show it."

He sank into the chair beside her. "You're right. I'll try harder."

She smiled and gave his arm a quick punch. "Take a chill pill, dude."

"Yeah, whatever." But she was right. This case was getting to him.

"Shouldn't we question the mother about providing a false alibi?"

"No, let's hold off. I don't want them to know we know yet. Conor's in rehab for a month; he's not going anywhere. Let's wait until we have the forensic results. If his DNA is on the cuff and glove found at the scene, we'll have enough for search and arrest warrants."

Erik had several hours of peace and quiet before Miles rapped on his half-open office door.

"Sorry to bother you, sir," he said.

Too late. "What is it?"

Miles handed him a folder. "Backgrounder on the cousin's murder." With his floppy hair and grin, the analyst looked like an eager puppy keen for a pat on the head.

"Right. Thanks." Erik set down the file without a glance. Miles's smile faded. He'd obviously expected a more enthusiastic response, but Erik wasn't in the mood to dole out compliments.

The analyst rocked back and forth on his feet. "Pretty gruesome murder of the cousin."

Erik wasn't amused at the analyst's attempts to ingratiate himself. "Did I ask for your opinion?"

Miles's eyes widened. "I...sorry...but..."

Erik opened the file and began to read. Miles coughed. Why was he still here? "What now?"

Miles pulled back his shoulders and looked him straight in the eye, "I know I have a lot to learn before I'm the same calibre as Kate Heaney."

Erik leaned back in his chair. "Yes, you do. She's the best in the business."

"I welcome any feedback so I can improve. I really want to do my best, especially with this case."

Christina was right. He was too hard on Miles. "Fair enough. Let's meet tomorrow to review the data and charts you've been working on."

"Yes, sir, thank you, sir." Miles backed out of the room.

Erik resumed reading. He didn't get very far before he was interrupted by another knock at the door.

Christina leaned against the door frame. "The sketch was a bust. The artist didn't have enough to work with."

He motioned for her to come in. "I'm not surprised," he said. "The bartender's an idiot. Probably dipping in the sauce at work."

She narrowed her eyes at him. "Everything okay?"

"Just tired," he said. "I'm reading about the unsolved murder of Bridget Heaney, Kate and Conor's cousin. It happened twenty-five years ago, in the spring of 1990, in Northern Ireland. Bridget lived with the family, more like a sibling than anything, and Conor was the last person to see her alive."

Christina plonked down in the chair across from him. "How old was Conor at the time?"

"Fifteen. And Kate was thirteen. Same age as Bridget." He pointed to the file. "According to Conor, he was on his way down at the lake, or lough as they call it there, to go fishing. Bridget had followed him partway, but he'd told her to get lost. When she didn't return for dinner that night, Alma, Kate and Conor went searching and found her body dumped by the lough. She'd been hit in the back of the head. No viable forensic evidence."

"Why did the police suspect Conor?"

"Turns out he'd lied about the fishing. His fishing rod was broken." What Erik didn't tell his partner was that Kate was the one who'd tipped off the police about it being broken.

Christina chewed on the lid of her pen. "That's not much to go on."

"Before the police could interview Conor, he ran away from home, and it took two days to track him down. He never explained where he went or what he did."

"Do you think he could've murdered his cousin?"

"No idea. But even if he did, it doesn't mean he killed Henry. Let's not jump to conclusions. We wait for the DNA results."

11

At the funeral home, Kate ran her hand along the lacquered mahogany coffin on display. No sign of a price tag.

"Dad would be horrified to be buried in something like that," said Sam.

"You're right." Not that she'd ever discussed those matters with Henry. And she hadn't found any directives in his will. But Kate was fairly certain he'd want cremation.

A man in a suit approached, his hands clasped behind his back, and gave a slight bow. "Good afternoon. How may I help?" His voice was low and solemn.

"We're here to view Henry Franzen. I'm his wife; this is my daughter, Sam; and my mom, Alma," said Kate.

He raised his well-groomed eyebrows. "I thought you were coming this evening?"

"Is there a problem?"

"Well..." He glanced over at a closed door marked Viewing Room.

Before the funeral director had a chance to stop her, Kate pushed open the door. Inside, a woman was draped over Henry's body, sobbing.

Behind Kate, Alma muttered, "Jesus, Mary and Joseph."

The woman looked up with tear-soaked eyes. She frowned at Kate, but her expression softened when she saw Sam. "Oh, honey, I'm so sorry about your dad."

Sam bit her lip, gave a quick glance at Kate and said, "Hello, Jennifer."

The girlfriend. And Henry had obviously introduced her to their daughter—a fact Sam had failed to mention. Henry should've spoken to her first before doing something like that. Heat surged through Kate's body and she blurted out, "What the hell are you doing here?"

Sam drew in a sharp breath.

Jennifer backed away from the viewing casket. The funeral director, hands fluttering, placed himself between Kate and Jennifer. "So sorry about this mix-up. How about we let her finish in here while we go and discuss burial options?"

Kate took a deep breath and unclenched her hands. "Yes, let's do that."

They moved back to the display room and Kate reached out to Sam. "Sorry, sweetheart." But her daughter flinched at her touch. Kate sighed and followed the funeral director into his office, leaving her mother to comfort Sam. The director shut the door behind him, apologizing profusely, a sheen of sweat on his face.

"No, I'm the one who yelled. I'm sorry," she said, stifling the rage coursing through her body.

The director sat at his desk. The ornate design matched the deluxe coffin in the display room. A reward for high sales? He gestured for her to take a seat, pulled a handkerchief from his breast pocket and patted his forehead before launching into his spiel about funeral options. He spoke quickly and stumbled over his words, obviously still shaken by the confrontation in the viewing room. She flushed, shamed by her outburst. Although she already knew what she wanted, she let him finish his sales pitch and paused for a moment, pretending to contemplate the options, before she said, "I'll go with cremation, and we'll hold a memorial service here."

"What about a reception?"

"If you could arrange a caterer, we'll have it back at the house."

A soft rap on the door signalled it was their turn to see Henry.

In the viewing room, Sam clung to her grandmother, who stroked her hair and wiped away her tears. Kate stared down at Henry, at a loss for what to do or say. Eventually, she leaned over, kissed him on the forehead and whispered, "I'm sorry, my love."

Jennifer was waiting for them in the display room, the funeral director hovering in the background, wringing his hands. Poor man.

"I want to talk to Sam," said Jennifer.

Kate nodded, not trusting herself to speak.

Jennifer took Sam's hands in hers. "Call me anytime if you need to talk. Understand?"

Sam glanced at Kate. She forced a smile at her daughter in encouragement.

"I will. Thank you," said Sam.

Kate sidled up to her mom. "Can you take Sam back to the car? I need a moment." Alma frowned. "I promise I'll behave," said Kate. She waited until they left before she spoke to Jennifer. "Sorry for yelling, but I was shocked to see you with my husband."

Jennifer's voice was soft; Kate had to lean closer to catch her response. "We were in love. You have no right to take charge of all this."

Kate lashed out. "You two were fucking for a few months. Big deal. Maybe you had plans, but I was with Henry for over seventeen years, and we have a child."

Jennifer stared up at her and burst into tears. "Sorry. I just…it felt like he was the one."

Kate took a couple of deep breaths before handing her a tissue. Jennifer dabbed at her tears.

"I didn't know about you," said Kate.

Jennifer twirled a strand of her long, dark hair around her index finger. "Henry was going to tell you about us that Saturday."

Kate thought back to the brunch, to the moment Henry had mentioned divorce. This woman in front of her was the reason. That same day, he'd asked her to stay with Sam while he was away in Fort Mac. *Make sure to lock the door and set the alarm,* he'd said. At the time, it had struck her as odd. She'd even asked him about it just before he left to pick up Conor. But he'd never had the chance to explain.

Maybe Jennifer knew something.

"Do you have any idea why someone would kill Henry? Was he in some sort of trouble?"

Jennifer shook her head. "No idea. I told the detectives he seemed preoccupied in the days before he was killed. I thought it had to do with prepping for field research in Fort Mac."

"You spoke to the police," said Kate.

"Yes, they also asked about your brother. Something about blackmail."

Kate's pulse quickened. "Did Henry talk to you about that?"

"No, and that's what I said to the detectives."

Jennifer babbled on about how devastated she was by his death, but Kate tuned her out. *Did she really expect my sympathy?* Kate glanced at her phone and pretended to read a text.

"Got to go." She thrust out her hand at Jennifer. "No hard feelings?"

Jennifer nodded and shook her hand. "No hard feelings."

Kate scanned the room for the funeral director, but he was nowhere in sight. Probably avoiding them. She zipped up her parka and stepped out into the cold.

On the drive from the funeral home, Kate kept her mouth shut, knowing anything she said right now would not be taken well by Sam.

At the house, Kate noticed her mom's Civic was back in the driveway, along with an idling Mustang. Brenda, wearing a green hoodie, got out of the passenger seat of the Mustang. Sam rushed over to greet her. "Auntie, you need to wear a warmer coat."

Brenda struck a pose. "What for? My body's built for the cold." Sam giggled as Brenda wiggled her butt. "I've got extra layers."

When Kate joined in the laughter, Sam turned and glared at her before stomping off into the house. Alma gave Brenda a quick wave before following her granddaughter.

"What did you do to piss Sam off?" asked Brenda

Kate rolled her eyes. "Henry's girlfriend was at the funeral home."

Brenda's brows shot up. "What happened?"

"Nothing much. Swore at her."

"You and your brother are a fine pair."

Kate grimaced, annoyed that her friend had lumped her in with Conor. No doubt her life had gone off the rails in past year, but Conor was a whole other level of messed up. "Now I'm back to square one with Sam."

Her friend handed over the keys to the Civic. "Can you really blame Sam for being upset at your outburst?"

Brenda was never one to mince words. "Thanks for bringing back Mom's car."

"Did he go to rehab this morning?"

Kate nodded. "Let's hope it works this time." She peered into the open passenger door of the Mustang. "Hiya, Melvin. Nice new wheels you have." He grinned. Brenda eased back into her son's car.

"Thanks again," said Kate. Brenda gave her the thumbs up and pulled the door closed. Melvin revved the engine and roared off.

As usual, everyone else was picking up the pieces after Conor.

12

A week later, Kate stepped out of the muted light of the funeral sedan and was blinded by the intensity of the sun's rays bouncing off the snow-covered ground. She paused to dig through her purse for her sunglasses.

Alma linked arms with her and Sam, and together they weaved their way around icy patches on the path to the gravesite. They joined Conor and Brenda, who were already standing at Henry's final resting spot. Kate studied her brother's face. Still too thin and pale.

Robins flitted through the leafless branches of the nearby poplar trees. Kate breathed in the crisp winter air. Facing them on the opposite side of the gravesite stood Michael Williams, Henry's long-time research partner and friend. Jennifer, wearing oversized sunglasses and a black wool trench coat, held onto his arm. No doubt about it, that woman got under her skin.

Michael whispered something in Jennifer's ear and made his way over to them. "I'm so sorry," he said to Kate, taking her hands in his.

"Thanks. How are you holding up?"

Michael shook his head. "Doesn't seem real, you know?" He turned to Sam, "How are you doing, kiddo?"

She burst into tears and clung to him. How Kate wished she could take away her child's pain.

Soon, the minister arrived at the gravesite, along with a scattering of Henry's work colleagues and birding friends. "Shall we begin?" he asked.

Michael squeezed Kate's hand. "We'll talk more later," he said, and made his way back to Jennifer's side.

Kate shifted her body so she didn't have to look at Jennifer during the ceremony. As the urn was set in place, Sam read aloud a selection from her father's favourite poem, and Kate held her breath. *Please let her get through this.* Sam managed to finish before breaking into tears. Kate tried to pull her close, but Sam shrugged her off and turned to her granny who said, “Why don’t we go back to the car?”

Kate watched as they walked away, her stomach in knots. She’d made a mess of things with her daughter.

Brenda nudged her with her shoulder. “She’ll come around.” Kate wasn’t so certain. Conor stood nearby; his posture stooped. Brenda and Kate exchanged knowing looks. Something was up with him.

“I’ll let you deal with this,” whispered Brenda, “See you back at the house.”

“You okay, Conor?” asked Kate.

“No, we need to talk.”

Her stomach clenched, anticipating more drama. “How about on the drive to the reception?” He nodded in agreement. “Go on ahead,” she said, “I’ll join you in a moment.”

After he left, Michael approached. “I was here when Henry buried his parents,” he said, “First year university. Terrible time. And now he’s joined them. I can’t believe it.”

“Neither can I.” She tucked her arm in his as they slowly walked along the path towards the parking lot. Jennifer rushed past them, dabbing at her eyes with a tissue.

“In case you’re wondering, she’s a sessional instructor at the university,” said Michael, “That’s how I know her.”

Kate patted his arm. “Thanks. I was wondering.”

Michael tensed beside her, and she followed his gaze. Suzanne, his ex-wife, was standing at the entrance to the parking lot, waiting.

He grimaced. “Sorry, Kate. Can’t deal with her. I’ll see you at the reception.” As he brushed past Suzanne, she gave him a piercing stare. There was no love lost between them.

Kate smiled at Suzanne as she approached. “It means a lot to me that you came.” She leaned in, lowering her voice. “Sorry you two had to cross paths.”

Suzanne had been her dorm roommate and the maid of honour at her wedding. That’s where Kate had introduced her to Michael, Henry’s best friend and groomsman. Over the years, they had drifted apart. Suzanne got a job at an environmental think tank and became increasingly strident in her views. When Kate got pregnant,

Suzanne had criticized her for having a child in what she called "a fucked-up world in denial of climate change." After Suzanne had divorced Michael, Kate completely lost touch with her old friend.

"I'm sorry about Henry," Suzanne said. She glanced over her shoulder before adding, "I need to talk to you. Can we meet up soon?"

How strange. Kate promised to touch base the following week.

At the cemetery parking lot, Kate peered into the interior of one of the two funeral sedans she'd arranged for the day. In the back seat, Sam clung to her grandmother, a wad of used tissues in her lap. "You okay if I ride with your uncle?" Kate asked her.

Sam rubbed her nose with the back of her hand. "Fine," she said, in a nasally voice. "But why does the reception have to be at our place? I don't want to talk to anybody."

I feel the same way.

Alma patted Sam's hand. "That's okay, you don't have to."

The driver turned around. "Are we ready, ma'am?"

"Yes. Sorry. See you back at the house."

Kate joined Conor in the other sedan. The siblings gazed silently out the window as the vehicle wound its way through the cemetery. Kate's stomach growled. When was the last time she ate?

When the driver turned back onto the city streets, Conor closed the curtained partition between the front and back seats and shifted his body to face her. "My therapist suggested I talk to you."

Did this have to happen today of all days? Wasn't she allowed to grieve in peace? She noted him plucking at an elastic band around his wrist. Not a good sign. He's psyching himself up to say whatever the hell it was he needed to say. "What is it?"

He looked her straight in the eyes. "You think I killed Henry."

She rummaged around her purse for a bottle of water and took a sip. "That's not true."

He crossed his arms. "Go on, say it."

She squinted at him. "What do you mean?" But she knew exactly what he meant. "No one can corroborate your blackmail story. And how did your glove end up at the crime scene?"

He rubbed his face. "My own sister thinks I'm guilty."

Same old story. Just like what happened all those years ago with Bridget. He'd lied about the fishing rod, taken off when the police tried to question him, and to this day had never explained why. She closed her eyes and took a deep breath. How dare he bring this up on the day of Henry's funeral!

She slammed her fist against the side door. "Fuck."

Conor flinched.

She hit it again. "Just." Slam. "Leave." Slam. "Me." Slam. "Alone."

For good measure, she kicked the door. Conor shrank back, staring at her, mouth open.

She glared at him, chest heaving. Her whole body vibrated.

From the front seat, the driver cleared his throat. "Ma'am, shall I pull over?"

She yanked open the privacy drapes. "Sorry. No need." She folded her shaking hands in her lap. The sedan turned onto her block. The normally quiet street was lined with cars. How was she going to face all these people?

The driver pulled up to the curb and Conor scrambled out of the car. "Give me a minute, would you?" she asked the driver. She closed her eyes and tried to regain her composure. Her outburst had surprised even her.

Kate unbuttoned her coat as she surveyed the clusters of black-clad guests dotting the living room. Why did she decide to host the reception at the house? Brenda handed her a hanger, a quizzical look on her face.

She loaded on her coat and handed it back. "Don't ask."

Brenda raised her eyebrows. "That bad?"

Kate sighed. "Yes, and I'm in no mood to socialize."

Brenda hung Kate's coat in the hall closet. "That's why I'm on coat duty, to avoid small talk."

Kate craned her neck, trying to spot sight of her mother or Sam. "Where's the rest of my family?"

"Your daughter's in her room, and Alma went to check on her."

Kate understood all too well what Sam was going through. She still remembered how, after her cousin's funeral, she'd hidden under her bed, overwhelmed by all the strangers in their house.

Brenda plunked down on a bench beside the closet. "Do you know I got a visit from the detectives this week?"

Kate joined her. "Erik and Christina?"

"Yes." She nudged Kate with her shoulder. "That Erik, he's good looking in a rugged, aging sort of way but..."

Brenda left the rest unsaid. Kate had confided in her about the affair, but Brenda had never met Erik. She wasn't one to lecture, but Kate could sense her disapproval.

"You do know the police are all a bunch of racists, especially against my kind." She nudged Kate again. "But I like that Christina Wong."

Kate laughed. "May I remind you that I work for the police."

"Yeah, but you're a civilian, not one of those 'stick together no matter what bad shit some officer did' kind of mentality."

Given her experiences as an Indigenous woman, Brenda had every right to distrust the police. "What did they want?" asked Kate.

"I'm not supposed say, but they asked about Northern Shipping, whether the company owned a black van, and for some strange reason my shoe size."

Kate nudged Brenda so hard she almost fell off the bench. "Sorry. I'm excited to finally have some details about the case."

The detectives had shared very little with her about the circumstances around Henry's death. From news reports, she only knew that he'd been found in a snowy field at the edge of town, and his car was missing. That was all. But the detectives' questions to Brenda suggested that a black van might be involved—maybe someone saw the vehicle leaving the scene, or perhaps it was caught on CCTV, though she wasn't sure if there were cameras in that area. If the police were asking about Brenda's shoe size, they must have found footprints. Maybe they were even looking for more than one suspect. A dead body is heavy. Hard for one person to move.

"This better not get me into trouble," said Brenda.

"Don't worry. I won't let the detectives know I know. It's for my own purposes."

Brenda grunted and got up to offer hangers to a couple who'd just come through the front door. Kate had no idea who they were, likely from the university. She bit her nails and prayed they didn't notice her, the grieving widow, sitting on the bench.

Fortunately, they walked right past without a glance.

Brenda rejoined her. "You'd better not be trying to solve this case."

"Of course not," said Kate. "Unless they go after Conor."

Brenda tilted her head towards the living room. "You'd better go mingle."

Kate could've used a stiff drink, but the reception was alcohol-free, thanks to her brother. At least that meant the guests were less likely to linger. She slowly made her way around the room, enduring hugs and small talk from well-wishers. A server held out a tray of hors d'oeuvres and Kate plucked a shrimp-topped canapé and stuffed it in her mouth. She spotted Conor in the far corner of the room, deep in conversation with his rehab escort. What if he'd killed Henry, maybe by accident, and covered it up? Between his strange, uncorroborated story about blackmail and his glove at the crime scene, no wonder the police were suspicious of him.

Conor broke away from his escort and approached Kate, his hands tucked in his pockets. "I'm heading back to Second Chance. I think you need to get some help…" His voice trailed off when he saw her expression.

The nerve of him. She took a deep breath and said, "Thank you for your concern, but—"

Her cell vibrated in her pocket, and she pulled it out to check the number. Unknown ID. She tucked it back in and someone tapped her on the shoulder.

She turned and smiled, "Michael, have I ever introduced you to my brother, Conor?"

The two men shook hands. "Yes, we met at one of your dinner parties."

Right. Now she remembered: when Conor was sober and dating Jeremy.

Michael scratched the back of his head. "Can we talk for a moment?" he asked her.

Conor got the hint. "I have to leave," he said, kissing Kate on the cheek. "Think about what I said."

Kate rolled her eyes and said to Michael, "Let's go somewhere more private." She led him down the hall and into Henry's study. Michael circled the room, examining some of Henry's favourite collectibles.

"He would come into the lab on a Monday morning, all excited about his weekend antique excursions," said Michael. He picked up an intricately carved silver pen off the desk and waved it in the air. "Henry always had a knack for seeing things others didn't."

Kate smiled. Henry loved the rush of finding a hidden treasure. "Yes, he had a great eye."

Michael put his arm around her, and she rested her head on his shoulder.

"When do you want me to pack up stuff at the university?" she asked. Henry's space on campus was even more cluttered than his home office.

He squeezed her arm. "There's no rush. When you're ready. I'll let the department head know you'll need a bit of time."

"Thanks, Michael. You're a good friend."

He stroked his chin. "I was surprised you two split up."

"I was to blame for that."

"Really? I assumed it was because of Jennifer."

"No, I'm afraid I was the one to stray first."

Michael was quiet for a minute, contemplating this news. "He didn't tell me. When I learned he was seeing our new sessional instructor…well, that's something I would do, not Henry." He smiled sheepishly.

He was right about that; Michael's reputation for pursuing attractive young women was well known. Still, she was surprised Henry hadn't told him the reason they'd split up. She liked to think Henry wanted to protect her reputation, but maybe he couldn't be bothered to explain.

"Michael, do you have any idea who could've killed Henry?"

He shook his head. "It doesn't make sense." His phone rang and he glanced at the screen. "Sorry, Kate, it's Tecktronic in Fort Mac. That's what I wanted to tell you. We've had to postpone the research project."

"Sorry to hear that. Stay here and talk? I'll see you back downstairs."

Kate closed the door behind her to give him some privacy. Down the hall, Sam's bedroom door was shut. Broody music played on the stereo. Kate knocked. "Samantha, how are you doing, sweetie?"

"For the hundredth time, it's Sam. Just leave me alone."

Kate sighed and wandered back downstairs. She made the rounds of the room again, forcing herself to make small talk.

By six o'clock, Brenda had handed back all the guests' coats. "Are you all good? I've got to give Melvin a ride to hockey. His Mustang's broken down."

She embraced her friend. "You've been so much help. Love you." Brenda snorted in response but hugged her back. Kate pulled away from her embrace and looked her in the eyes. "Seriously. Thank you."

Brenda opened the front door. "Give that daughter of yours a hug for me."

The caterers from the funeral home had done a quick cleaning before they'd left, but there was still plenty of picking up to do. Kate and her mother collected dirty dishes and napkins that littered the living room and set them down in a big heap on the kitchen counter.

"Let's deal with the rest of this in the morning," said Kate. She opened the cupboard above the fridge and pulled out the pricy bottle of Merlot that Henry had bought on their Okanagan holiday. He'd been saving it for a special occasion; how ironic that turned out to be his funeral.

Alma looked at her with disapproving eyes, but Kate ignored her. What does she think? That I'm going to turn into an alcoholic like Conor? She offered her mom a glass, but she refused and retired to the spare room. *All the more for me.* Kate sat at the kitchen island and slowly got drunk on the contents.

13

Kate woke with a start and clutched her middle. Stabbing pain. She ran to the toilet and threw up. Afterwards, she sprawled on the white tiled floor. The coolness of the porcelain calmed her throbbing head and upset stomach.

Grief hit her like a storm front. Henry never had any intention of taking her back; he'd found someone new. And now he was gone. *Damn him.* She needed his advice. He'd know what to do about her brother…and Sam. She fumbled for her cell and called Erik.

"It's the middle of the night," he said in a groggy voice.

"I'm sorry. I'm sorry. I feel so…" she paused, not knowing what to say.

"Listen, why don't I stop by before work in the morning?"

"Okay. Sorry, I'll go now."

"No, no, don't do that." They were both quiet for a moment. Kate could hear his breathing on the other end of the line. "I miss you," he said softly.

She ended the call, wandered back into the bedroom and pulled aside the drapes. The full moon had transformed the snow-covered landscape into an eerie otherworldly place. Her thoughts went back to that night they'd found Bridget's body, the images and feelings still vivid after all these years. The thump of the helicopter, dogs barking and the shouts of men searching for her cousin's killer. The stern-faced Royal Ulster Constabulary officer clenching a search warrant. And the anger on his bulbous face after learning that Conor had escaped out his bedroom window. "The boy's done a runner," he'd said into his radio. For the millionth time, Kate wondered what'd happened to Bridget. If not Conor, who'd killed her?

Kate's thoughts jumped to her outburst in the funeral sedan. That confrontation had been a long time coming. Her brother wasn't an idiot. He'd rightly sensed her doubts about his innocence—then and now.

Back in Northern Ireland, the police were fixated on Conor, refusing to look at any other suspects. With Henry's murder case, Kate was determined not to let history repeat itself.

She called Conor's ex-boyfriend, Jeremy. Kate had first met him when he'd been hired by the Edmonton Police Service to work on a complex organized crime case. He was an IT expert with top security clearance. When she'd learned he loved hockey, folk music and was gay, she had introduced him to her brother. They'd lasted several years, until Conor started drinking again.

"Is Conor okay?" he asked.

She rubbed her throbbing forehead. "Yes, he's fine. Sorry, did I wake you?"

"No, haven't gone to bed yet. How are you holding up? I'm sorry about Henry. I thought about going to the funeral but then thought it might be best to stay away."

"I'm okay, thanks. Still shocked," She chugged from her water bottle. "Listen, I need your help with something. Do you still have access to the tattoo database?"

"Not exactly, but if you give me a bit of time, I can get in. What do you need?"

She caught herself biting her nails, "Can you search for gargoyle tattoos in black ink on the forearm?"

"You bet. I'll have it within the week."

She'd been reluctant to get involved in Henry's murder investigation, fearful she would discover that her brother was responsible. But now it was time to act. She had to look for other suspects, other explanations, and at least try to prove to the detectives, and herself, that Conor was innocent.

The rest of the household was still asleep when Erik arrived. He sat on one of the stools at the kitchen island and Kate handed him a mug of coffee. He took a sip and stared at her. "I'm sorry to say, but you look like crap."

She inspected her appearance in the hallway mirror. He was right. Her face was puffy and blotchy from the tears, wine, and lack of sleep. She'd pulled back her limp hair in an elastic band she'd retrieved from the newspaper delivered to the doorstep at dawn. Henry had refused to switch to reading papers online. He loved the scent of the ink and the physicality of reading newsprint. Although

Kate and Sam teasingly called him old school, Kate secretly agreed with her husband.

"How's the case going?" she asked.

"You know I can't talk to you about any of this."

"I know. I know. Can you at least tell me how it's working out with Miles?" Crunching the crime data was usually Kate's role in an investigation and she didn't think Miles was up to the task.

Erik smiled at her disdainful tone. "He's sharper than you think, and even discovered—"

"What?"

"Sorry, forgot myself for a moment. You know I can't share any details about the investigation."

She cradled the mug. Erik was keeping up his guard and so should she. He'd flip out if he knew she'd been doing a little digging of her own.

"Why couldn't one of the more experienced crime analysts work on it?" She knew that several of her colleagues might be persuaded to keep her updated on Henry's case, but Miles was not one of them.

"He's the only one who had time in his schedule."

She reached for the sugar bowl at the same time as Erik, and his touch startled her. "Sorry," she said, quickly pulling her hand away. Sugar spilled onto the table.

He grinned. "No worries." Kate was always struck by how his smile could shift his expression from stern and intimidating to boyish and charming. Erik had a knack for focusing intently on people, making them feel heard, and they responded to his undivided attention. She sure had.

He brushed sugar granules off the countertop. "I'm supposed to tell you that your leave has been extended."

Kate stood up. She knew this was coming, but it still stung.

Erik leaned forward and patted the seat. "Sit back down. Please." She clenched her fists but didn't move. He sighed. "You've got to understand from the department's perspective. Your involvement could jeopardize the case."

"You think my brother's guilty, but are you at least looking into other possibilities? What about—"

Erik held out his palm. "Kate, we can't talk about the case." He rose and tucked in his chair. "And I've got to get to work."

She took a calming breath. No use arguing. She accompanied Erik to the front door. "Sorry for putting you in this awkward position," she said, "and for waking you up early this morning."

He kissed her cheek. "Take care of yourself."

"Hello, Detective Jorgensen," said Sam.

Kate swung around to face her. Sam rubbed her eyes, hair astray. Maybe she hadn't seen his kiss?

"Nice to see you again, Samantha," said Erik.

"She's going by Sam now," said Kate. She patted his shoulder. "Thanks for stopping by." She stood on the front step and watched him drive off, rubbing her bare arms to keep warm.

Sam was waiting for her in the front foyer. "Was it Erik you fucked? That explains why no one would tell me who you'd had the affair with."

"Language!" *Fuck*. She'd hoped to keep that a secret. She rubbed her forehead, stalling for time. "Does it matter?"

"He's your boss! And I thought Dad was bad for sleeping with his former grad student. At least he had the decency to wait until after you two separated."

"Jennifer was his student?" Michael hadn't told her that part, only that she was a sessional instructor. Surely there was a rule against a professor having an affair with a junior staff member?

"Mom, stop making this about Dad. It's your fault." She stomped upstairs and slammed the door.

14

A week later, Kate unzipped her suitcase and put away the rest of her clothes in the walk-in closet. She'd finally packed up her rental apartment and was back home for good, but not at all how she'd planned. Picking up one of Henry's favourite shirts, she sniffed the collar, convinced she could still catch a hint of his aftershave. She should deal with his clothes. Maybe next week. The truth was the only reason she was home was because Henry had died. She had thought he would forgive her, that they'd get back together. Instead, he had moved on. If he were still alive, Jennifer might have been sharing the closet with him. Kate closed the door. There was no point dwelling on the past.

She wandered down to the kitchen and stared into the well-stocked fridge, thanks to her mother who'd taken care of her and Sam since Henry's death. She let the cool air calm her flushed face. Damn hot flashes. She'd been getting more of them lately; the stress of the past few weeks had aggravated her symptoms. She opened the jug of juice and drank straight from the container. No one was around to see her. Her mother had moved back to her duplex and Sam had gone to spend the weekend with her. From now on, it'd be up to Kate to handle the household details, and she felt anxious, uncertain she was up to the task. Maybe this time on her own with Sam would help repair their relationship. Her daughter was still so angry with her.

She headed back upstairs, sat cross-legged on the bed and powered up her laptop.

"Yes!" she exclaimed, punching the air in triumph when she spotted Jeremy's email. He'd delivered—dozens of photos and background information, somehow sourced from the police database. She quickly scrolled through the files. Who knew so many criminals had gargoyle tattoos? She meticulously reviewed each file, narrowing down her options. Her heart pounded when she recognized one of the names: Tony Zakreski. Was he the blackmailer? She tried to recall if she'd ever mentioned Conor to Tony—unlikely. But Tony's uncle, Ferenc, was a different story. At some point, she'd confided in her former boss about her troublesome brother.

She needed to show these tattoo photos to Conor. Kate printed Tony's, along with two others that looked similar, and then shut down her computer.

Kate drove out to Second Chance and was escorted to the clinic's common room to wait for Conor. When he came through the doorway, Kate hid her shock at his appearance. In the week since Henry's funeral, he'd gotten even skinnier, as if something was eating away at him. He slid into the seat across from her.

"What's wrong?" he asked, his face full of concern.

I could ask the same of you. She set out the tattoo photos on the table. "Recognize any of these?"

He studied them for a moment, then pointed to Tony's tattoo. "This one."

Kate pulled out three mug shots. Without hesitation, Conor picked out Tony's. "That's him! That's the guy that tried to blackmail me."

Here was the lead she'd been searching for, but if Tony and his uncle Ferenc were somehow involved in Henry's death, this was a whole other level of dangerous. "His name's Tony and he's Ferenc Zakreski's nephew."

"As in the owner of the Ranch? Where you used to work?"

"Yes." She'd waitressed at the Ranch during her university years, but it was only when she started working for the police that she'd learned that the club was a front for Ferenc's criminal activities. Tony Zakreski did most of the dirty work on his behalf.

Conor jabbed his finger on Tony's photo. "You have to show this to Erik and clear my name."

Kate shook her head. "Not yet. It's not enough."

Conor ran his hands through his hair. "What about the airport bar? Tony could be on the CCTV?"

"I'm sure the police already have that footage." She didn't hold out much hope Tony would be stupid enough to be caught on camera. He would've ordered someone else to follow and film Conor, not do it himself.

"Now do you believe me?"

She nodded. "Sorry for doubting you."

He paused and took a deep breath. She braced herself, knowing what was coming next.

"What about Bridget?"

She bit her lip, then finally voiced the question that had lingered in her mind for years.

"Why did you say you were going fishing and then disappear?"

He didn't look away. "Why did you tell the police?" he whispered. "Do you know what they did to me?"

She dropped her eyes. That was the crux of the problem—betrayal on both sides.

"After you climbed out your bedroom window and vanished, they questioned me," she said. "It didn't take much to break me. I was thirteen years old, for God's sake."

"And I was only two years older. The police beat the crap out of me."

Kate crossed her arms. "What do you want me to say? That I believe you're innocent? I'm trying to, I really am. But you've been hiding something about that night."

Conor hung his head. "You don't understand."

No, she didn't. She reached across the table. "I want to understand. Tell me what went on that night with Bridget?"

He clutched her hands, tears streaming down his face. "I have no idea who killed her, but I'm to blame."

She pulled her hands free and folded her arms. "What did you do?"

He rubbed away his tears. "I'm sorry, sis, it's too hard for me to talk about yet. I'm working through it with my therapist."

Her stomach in knots, Kate paused in the lobby of the rehab clinic and rummaged through her purse for an antacid. The conversation with Conor had shaken her. She chewed the tablet, her mouth dry and chalky. After years of avoiding the topic, they'd finally confronted it—yet instead of answers, she only had more questions. Conor insisted he hadn't killed Bridget but admitted he was somehow responsible. What the hell did that mean?

She walked back to her SUV, her boots crunching the ice in the parking lot. In her door pocket she found an old, half-frozen bottle of water and briefly warmed it between her hands before taking a sip. Better. She didn't understand why it was so hard for her brother to talk about what'd happened back home. She now believed him when he said he didn't kill Henry. Maybe she had to trust him about Bridget as well.

She rested the water bottle on her forehead. The coolness calmed her. Enough about Bridget's case. That could wait. She had to focus on proving Conor's innocence in Henry's case. At least she had a lead. Conor had identified Tony Zakreski as the man who'd tried to blackmail him. But how was this connected to Henry's murder? She considered the possible scenarios. Suppose Henry had met with Tony Zakreski, tried to persuade him to back off blackmailing his brother-in-law. But why would Tony kill him?

Maybe Henry found out something about the Zakreski family business that put his life in danger. Or maybe his death had been an accident? Tony was a brutish thug, hopped up on steroids. Maybe he'd gone into a rage and taken things too far. If only she could prove Henry had met with Tony. That might be enough to convince the detectives to shift their focus onto him as a possible suspect.

Her phone vibrated in her pocket. Someone had left her a voicemail. She played the message.

"It's Suzanne. Can we meet? I need to talk to you about Henry's last trip to Fort Mac but can't explain over the phone."

Kate recalled the day of the funeral, when Suzanne had come up to her, expressing a desire to arrange a time to talk. With everything that had unfolded over the past week, Kate realized she'd forgotten to follow up. She picked up her phone and typed out a message:

Can U meet Monday @ 2? Roasters cafe?

The reply came quickly:

Yes CU then.

Suzanne had mentioned Fort Mac, and Tony Zakreski had wanted to use Conor's courier trucks to ship product up to Fort Mac. Could there be a connection?

15

On Saturday morning, Kate called Sam. "Shall I come pick you up from Granny's?"

"No, change in plans," said Sam. "Uncle Conor called. He's getting out of rehab and we're planning a welcome home celebration for him at Granny's house." Kate bit her lip to keep from flipping out. He was supposed to be in Second Chance for another two weeks. Yesterday, when she'd visited him, he hadn't said anything to her about leaving early.

"Auntie Brenda's going to bring him home from the clinic," said Sam. "Can you be here by seven?"

"Sure, and let Granny know I'll spend the night." Kate hung up and tossed the phone onto the bed. What the hell was her brother thinking? Was she to blame? Did her visit stir things up, make him want to leave rehab? All she knew was that he hadn't stayed there long enough to really get his life back on track.

But there was nothing she could do to make him stay. What a waste of money. She'd paid the private clinic thousands of dollars to sober him up. Never again.

Shortly before seven, she pulled up in front of her mother's duplex and got her overnight bag out of the trunk. Fresh snow had fallen that afternoon, but the sidewalk had already been cleared. She let herself in and found Sam in the kitchen decorating a round cake with multi-coloured sprinkles. She'd written *Welcome home (Uncle) Conor!* in blue icing.

"What do you think?" asked Sam.

Kate smiled at the look of excitement on her face. "Delicious."

Outside, a truck horn sounded.

"They're early!" Sam jammed candles in the cake.

Kate peered out the front window as Brenda turned off the engine of her shiny black pickup. Conor eased out of the passenger seat and Brenda slung his duffel bag over her shoulder, brushing away his attempts to take it from her. Her mother joined her at the window.

"That darn neighbour shovelled my walk before I had the chance," she said.

"That's 'cause he's sweet on you, Mom."

"Bah!" She waved her hand in front of her face like she'd smelled something bad. "He thinks I'm an old lady."

But you are. She didn't dare say it out loud.

Sam rushed into the room with the cake. "Where's the lighter?"

"I think I have a box of matches in there," said Alma, pointing to a small side table by the front door. Sam rifled around the drawer, balancing the cake in one hand. Kate cringed, worried it'd fall onto the floor. "Let me help," she offered. Sam held the cake while Kate located the matches and lit the candles.

The flames danced when Brenda opened the front door and plunked down the duffel bag. Conor followed in behind her. "What do we have here?" he said.

Kate stepped aside to reveal Sam holding the cake.

Conor grinned. "It's my favourite niece and my favourite food!"

"I'm your only niece."

"True true."

"You're bringing in the cold," admonished Alma. Conor shut the door behind him. Brenda borrowed Kate's shoulder to balance as she pulled off her cowboy boots.

"Thanks for bringing him home," said Kate.

"No problem. I didn't want to miss out on some delicious homemade cake."

"Uncle Conor, you have to make a wish."

He squeezed his eyes shut for a moment, took a deep breath and blew the candles out. They all clapped and cheered. Sam set down the cake on the hall table and hugged her uncle. He whispered something in her ear, and she laughed.

Kate wiped away a tear. It'd been a long time since she'd seen her daughter laugh.

"Hey, sis, come join in," said Conor.

"Group hug," said Sam. "Auntie Brenda, you too."

"No way." Brenda folded her arms across her ample chest.

Sam beamed when Kate and Conor squeezed her tight. They soon lost their balance and collapsed in a heap onto the floor. Conor helped Kate to her feet. "Nice to see us all smiling."

She leaned in and whispered in his ear, "You're not getting off that easy. We need to talk later."

He snorted and left to join Sam and his mother in the front room. In the kitchen, Brenda cut the chocolate cake into generous pieces while Kate turned on the kettle and dropped a couple of tea bags into her mom's metal pot. "When did you get the new truck?" she asked.

Brenda licked icing off her fingers. "Last week. Pretty fine, huh?" With the success of Northern Shipping, she leased a new one every few years and always chose the high-end model.

Kate tilted her head towards the front room. "Did Conor explain why he left rehab early?"

Brenda shook her head. "Nah. We talked about the new truck on the ride over here."

Kate peered into the blackened interior of the teapot. Once, she'd tried to scrub it clean until her horrified mother put a stop to it. *That's what makes the tea taste so good*, she'd said. And maybe she was right; her mom's tea had so much flavour compared to the swamp water most Canadians made. Kate poured in boiling water, pulled out a black lacquer serving tray and loaded it with mugs and the teapot.

She carried the tray into the front room and set it on the coffee table while Brenda handed out slices of cake. Conor demolished his in seconds. "Things taste so much better when you're sober." No one smiled at his attempt at humour. "Too soon?"

"Afraid so," said Kate.

Conor pushed the crumbs around his plate with his fork. "Wish I could stay longer, but I have a flight to catch."

Sam gasped in surprise and Kate closed her eyes. *Why was he so difficult?*

"But you just got home," said Alma.

Brenda stood up abruptly and brushed the cake crumbs off her wool sweater. "I'm out of here."

Conor followed her to the front door. "I'm sorry, Brenda. I know you were expecting me back at Northern Shipping."

She shook her head. “Enough is enough. We’re swamped at work and now you spring this on me? I don’t want to be partners anymore. I’ll buy you out.”

Her brother looked shaken. But what did he expect? Brenda had been too easy on him for years. “Can you give me a bit more time?” he pleaded. “I have to go back to Northern Ireland to face something.”

Brenda clenched her jaw, her eyes watery. “You’re like a brother to me, but I can’t be in business with you anymore.”

He hung his head. “I have to do this, or I’ll never get better.”

The siblings stood shoulder to shoulder as Brenda slipped on her boots and slammed the door shut behind her. Kate elbowed him. Hard. “What the hell. Erik told you not to leave the country.”

“I’m not under arrest. He can’t stop me.”

They both spun at the sharp intake of breath and faced their mother. “Kate, talk some sense into your brother.”

Here we go again, leaving me to deal with his mess.

Alma turned on her heels and gathered Sam off the sofa, “Wee girl, how about we give your mom and uncle some space.”

Kate waited until they left the room before she asked Conor, “What’s going on in that bloody brain of yours?”

“My therapist says I need to confront my past.”

That bloody therapist again. She’d like to give him a piece of mind about the poor advice he was giving her brother. “You’re running away again.”

“Come on, Kate. Both you and I know that I may not get another chance. Once the DNA results come back on the glove, they’ll charge me.”

“If you leave now, the police are going to think you’re guilty.”

“They already do. But this time, please let me get away before you tell them.”

That was a low blow. Without another word, Conor picked up the duffel bag he’d brought from the rehab clinic and walked out. Kate stood on the front step, hugging herself for warmth, while he loaded his bag into the trunk of a waiting cab and got into the back seat. He kept his eyes averted as the driver made a U-turn and headed for the airport.

16

Erik tried his car door. Frozen shut. He pulled again and his feet slipped out from under him. He grabbed onto the side mirror to catch his fall. Cursing, he penguin-walked around to the passenger side. Overnight it'd rained, and then the temperature dropped below zero. Both his car and the street were covered by a thin layer of ice. Should've parked in the garage. He anticipated a stressful commute to the station this morning.

His phone rang. Christina.

"DNA results are back. It's Conor's," she said. "I've submitted the warrants to the judge."

"On my way." He yanked on the passenger-side handle and the door swung open. He slid across to the driver's seat, catching his hip on the gear shift. He cursed again. The song by the Boomtown Rats "I Don't Like Mondays" sprung to mind. What a start to the day.

Not wanting to end up in the ditch with the dozens of cars there already, Erik resisted the urge to speed. By the time he arrived at the police detachment, everyone was gathered in the boardroom.

"Any word yet on the warrants?" he asked.

"Yes, the judge has signed off," said Christina. The team let out a cheer. Christina held up her hand. "But we can only seize Conor's phone. No other electronic devices."

Damn. He'd wanted to examine Conor's computer. "What about Kate's place?"

"No to that as well."

Erik wasn't surprised the judge had turned down their request to search Kate's house. That'd been a stretch, considering they had little in the way of evidence she was involved.

"Christina and I will head out to the rehab clinic to pick up Conor," said Erik. He pointed to Constable Tang. "You head over to his mother's house. Supervise the search of her place." He assigned another officer to lead the search of Conor's company, Northern Shipping.

By the time they headed out to pick up Conor at Second Chance, the temperature had risen above zero and the ice layer on the roadways had melted. Erik contemplated calling Kate, letting her know about the warrants, but thought better of it. Knowing her, she'd try and warn her brother. He felt a pang of regret. There'd be little chance of getting back together with Kate now that Conor was under arrest. They had a solid case against him. His DNA on the grey glove and Henry's cuff. No alibi. Suspect in the cold case murder of his cousin.

Christina pulled up in front of the clinic and turned to Erik. "Ready?"

Erik took a deep breath. "Ready."

They flashed their badges at the front desk and the woman behind the counter called for the administrator.

"How can I help you?" she asked.

"Can you take us to Conor Heaney?" asked Christina. "We have a warrant out for his arrest."

The administrator brushed her long bangs away from her eyes, an alarmed expression on her face. "He's not here."

"What do you mean?" asked Erik.

"He checked himself out on Saturday afternoon."

Almost two days ago. Heart sinking, Erik glanced at his partner. "Do you know who picked him up?" he asked.

The administrator shook her head. "I don't work weekends."

They rushed back to the car. "I take it we're heading to Kate's?" asked Christina.

"Yes," he said. "No need to panic yet. He can't have gone too far."

17

After Sam had gone to school, Kate set up her laptop on her mother's kitchen table. She'd spent the last few nights sleeping on the sofa, determined not to leave without her daughter. So far, Sam was playing it cool, refusing to come back home with her.

Kate checked her phone for messages. Still nothing from Conor. She had no idea if he'd made it to Northern Ireland, or, if he had, where he might be staying or what he was doing. With a sigh, she set her phone face down on the table. She couldn't understand what was so urgent that Conor needed to leave rehab early and travel back home. He'd claimed he had to confront his past or he'd never get better, but what the hell did that really mean? Why all the secrecy? Was it possible he was lying? The simplest explanation was that he'd fled the country to avoid being arrested for Henry's murder. Yet Kate found it hard to believe Conor could actually do such a thing.

She logged onto her computer and began to research all the open-source data she could find on Ferenc and Tony Zakreski's business holdings. After several hours of digging, she failed to find anything of significance. She held out hope that her coffee date with Suzanne that afternoon might uncover some new information. Perhaps what Suzanne had to share about Henry's last trip to Fort McMurray could help Kate link it to the Zakreskis and provide enough evidence to bring to the police.

But she wasn't sure how much this all mattered now that Conor had fled the country. How was she going to convince the detectives to look at other possible suspects when Conor continued to act suspiciously?

Kate heard a vehicle outside and pulled aside the drapes. A half dozen officers got out of three squad cars. *What the hell?* She flung her coat over her shoulders and rushed outside.

"What's going on?" she asked a stern-faced officer, though she already knew.

"Search warrant," the officer replied, her breath a cloud in the cold damp air as she handed Kate the paperwork.

Kate skimmed the document and saw, just as she had feared, that Conor's DNA had been identified at the crime scene.

She let the officers inside and they fanned out, peering in closets, pulling open drawers. Kate heard a commotion in the kitchen and Alma shouting, "Let me through." Her mother pushed past an officer and stormed into the front room, still wearing her nightgown. As Alma struggled to tie up her housecoat, Kate was startled by how old and frail she looked. "Let me help you with that," she said.

Alma batted away her hand. "I'm perfectly capable."

They huddled together on the sofa as the strangers invaded the duplex. Her mom squeezed her hand and Kate thought back to the day the police raided their house in Northern Ireland. Just like old times.

Soon, Erik and Christina arrived and briefly conferred with the forensics team before coming into the front room. "Where's Conor?" asked Erik, fixing his gaze on them. "We went to Second Chance to arrest him only to learn he'd checked out of rehab early."

Tension left Kate's body. If they were asking, that meant Conor must've made it out of the country without getting flagged.

Her mother kept a tight grip on Kate's hand, but her expression remained composed as she told the detective she had no idea where her son had gone. Impressive.

"Why did you give a false alibi?" Christina asked Alma.

Kate fell back in her seat. *What the hell were they talking about?* Erik looked at her intently, gauging her reaction.

"I don't know what you mean?" asked Alma.

Christina sighed. "Tell us the truth."

"He's a good boy. There's no way he'd hurt Henry."

"We could charge you," said Erik.

Alma stared him down. Erik sighed. "We'd like to talk to Kate in private."

Alma pressed the back of her hand to her forehead as if she were taking her temperature. "Fine." She stood up and headed down the hallway towards her bedroom.

Christina crossed her arms. "Where is he?"

"No idea," said Kate.

Erik hammered home how bad it looked for Conor. "We have his DNA at the crime scene, including his blood found on the cuff of Henry's jacket, and your mother lied about being home when Henry dropped him off."

Kate's eyes widened. She hadn't known about blood evidence. Or her mom.

Erik crossed his arms. "You really didn't know about the false alibi?" She shook her head. "Your mother volunteered at a parish bingo the afternoon of Henry's murder. No way she was home when Henry supposedly dropped Conor off."

Shit. This was really bad. "I'm sure there's some misunderstanding."

"Kate, I have to ask again, did you know your mother lied?" asked Christina.

"Of course not! She's just being overprotective."

"Conor is the prime suspect in Henry's murder, and you're not off the hook either," said Erik.

Should she tell the detectives about Tony and Ferenc Zakreski? A bead of sweat dripped down her back. "I've come up with another possible suspect and I think—"

Erik touched her arm. She flinched and pulled away. "Please leave the investigating up to us."

She got up off the sofa and strode over to the front door. They had no interest in listening to her ideas about the case. "I think it's time for you to leave."

"Please tell him to turn himself in," said Christina as they walked out the door.

Kate slammed the door shut and turned to face her mother who'd joined her at the front entrance. "What were you thinking?" she yelled. "You gave a false alibi?"

Alma put a finger to her lips and moved closer to Kate. "Keep it down. The officers are still out front."

"You could go to jail for lying."

She looked up at Kate, face flushed. "Let them try. I swore I would never again let something happen to Conor without putting up a fight." She took Kate's hand in her own and patted it. "Besides, you know your brother would never hurt Henry. You need to find the real killer and stick it to those detectives."

After dinner, Kate scrubbed the dishes while Alma dried and put them away. They worked in silence, both alone with their thoughts. The police search had shaken Kate, made her question, again, her belief in Conor's innocence. What if he'd made up the blackmail and falsely ID'd Tony Zakreski? Or maybe Tony had helped Conor dump Henry's body after her brother had accidentally killed him? She'd seen how angry Conor could get when he was drunk.

As a crime analyst, she understood why her brother was the prime suspect. Police had identified his blood on Henry's jacket; his glove was found at the crime scene; and his alibi, their mother, had lied. It didn't look good for him. At all. Her brother was in deep shit trouble. And now he'd fled the country. Kate paused her scrubbing but couldn't bring herself to voice her fears.

Alma touched her arm. "I know what you want to say, but you're wrong. Your brother's not capable of murder."

Kate wished she had her certainty. She looked at the clock on the wall. He'd been gone for two days and still no word from him. Kate's phone rang. A U.K. number. "Speak of the devil..." She dried her hands on the tea towel before answering. "Is that you, Conor?" Heavy breathing on the line. "Conor?" Kate's chest tightened.

"What's wrong?" Alma gripped Kate's arm, her eyes wide.

"Can't do this," said Conor, his voice slurred. Muffled laughter and clinks of glasses in the background.

"You're using a pub phone?" Conor had set a record for his shortest period of sobriety.

"Lost my cell."

Of course he had. She patted Alma's hand to reassure her. "Where are you staying?" she asked Conor.

"Um. Can't remember. Wait. I have a card..." She heard a thump, a muffled curse and scratching noises before he came back on the line. "Jurys Inn."

Kate calculated the time in Belfast. Must be around one in the morning. "Listen to me, Conor. Go back to the hotel. Sleep it off. I'll meet you as soon as I can."

Alma shook her head and went back to drying the dishes. Conor agreed and hung up. Kate bit her lip. She should let him figure things out on his own. But what if he really went off the rails? She had to go get him. Hopefully he'd stay put until she got there.

Alma wrung out the dishcloth and drained the sink. "I thought—" her voice broke.

Kate's stomach churned. "It's okay. I'm going to bring him back home."

Alma brushed away her tears and turned on the kettle. "I'll make us some tea. You go book a flight."

Kate bought a ticket on a flight to Belfast. With the time difference and brief stopover in London, she figured she'd be there by late afternoon tomorrow. Kate tossed her clothes back into her overnight bag. She wouldn't have time to go home before heading to the airport.

She checked her text messages and cursed when she read the one from Suzanne. Where were you this afternoon? I waited for over an hour. In all the chaos, Kate had forgotten all about the meeting. She quickly texted her apologies and asked to reschedule the coffee date for the following weekend.

Now she had to tell Sam she was leaving. She hesitated for a moment before she rapped on the door to the spare room. Sam opened it a crack, "What do you want?"

"Uncle Conor's in trouble. I have to fly to Belfast to help him out."

Sam rubbed her eyes, her voice hoarse with fatigue. "What about me?"

"You stay here with your grandmother. I won't be gone long and when I get back, we can spend time together, I promise." Kate reached out to hug her, but Sam pushed her away. "Leave me alone."

"I love you."

"Go."

Kate gently closed the door and heard the click of the lock behind her. So much for repairing their relationship.

18

As a child, Kate dreaded shopping trips to Belfast. Metal barricades ringed the downtown core. British soldiers, guns at the ready, manned the gates. To access the shops, they'd have to stand, arms and legs spread, and get patted down.

On the ride from the airport, what she saw outside the taxi window was unrecognizable. No barriers or military in sight. Pedestrians milled about and car horns bleated. She smiled as a double-decker tour bus drove past filled with *Game of Thrones* fans dressed in medieval gear.

The taxi pulled up in front of the hotel. After paying the fare, she stepped out, flinging her backpack over one shoulder. Her legs felt wobbly as she walked into the lobby.

"I'm here to see Conor Heaney."

The man behind reception peered out over his reading glasses. "You the sister?"

She nodded. "Yes, Kate."

"Told me you'd be coming. Bit of a mess, your brother."

She pressed her palms together. "Hope he didn't cause too much of a disturbance."

He raised his eyebrows and handed her a keycard. "Room 201."

Kate made her way to the room and knocked. No answer. She opened the door with the keycard and wrinkled her nose at the stench. Conor was sprawled on top of the bed covers. Fully clothed. A urine stain on the crotch of his jeans. Mouth wide open. Snoring. And from the smell of it, he'd shit himself as well. Bloody hell. She rubbed her eyes. Jet lag had hit her hard. She shut the blackout drapes, kicked off her shoes and settled back in the armchair.

Kate woke with a start. Heart racing. She looked over at the bed. Empty. She panicked. Until she heard the shower running. She rubbed her stiff neck. How long had she slept? She checked the clock on the nightstand. Six in the morning. No wonder she was sore, she'd spent most of the night in the armchair.

Conor emerged from the bathroom, freshly shaved, and wearing clean clothes. "Thanks for coming," he mumbled, looking everywhere but her face.

She nodded and bit her lip to restrain her impulse to lecture him.

He clutched his stomach and ran back into the bathroom. Kate covered her ears with her hands to muffle the sound of his retching.

"Are we going to talk?" she asked when he re-emerged.

Conor shook his head. "Need coffee first."

"Right. Let me shower and change and then we'll find a café."

At the café, they sipped their coffees and ate toast in silence. When they finished, the waitress placed the bill on the table. "No rush," she said. Conor took some cash from his pocket, set it on top of the bill, and pushed away from the table. Kate followed him outside onto the sidewalk, where she nearly tripped over a sandwich board advertising: *Tour the Murals*. A taxi driver, leaning against his car and smoking a cigarette, waved them over. "I'll drive you there," he offered.

Guess he took them for tourists, Kate thought and turned to Conor. "What do you think? Better than going back to our smelly hotel room?"

He shrugged and pulled up his hoodie.

"Sure, why not?" she said to the taxi driver.

They climbed in the back and the driver headed northeast. He turned onto a road that ran parallel to the Peace Wall, a mishmash of graffiti-filled corrugated iron panels topped with a chain-link fence that divided the Protestant and Catholic areas of West Belfast. A shiver ran down Kate's spine. She'd never set foot in this part of town.

"I'll bring you down the Shankill Road first," said the driver as he turned the corner. "It's the Protestant stronghold." For people like Kate and her brother, this area had once been strictly off-limits—they might have been beaten, or worse, just for entering.

"Can we stop and take a look?" asked Kate.

The driver braked, pitching them forward in their seats, and pulled to the side of the road.

"Follow me," she said to Conor and got out of the taxi. A gust of wind hit her. She shivered and zipped up her windbreaker. She'd forgotten how damp and cold the spring could be in Belfast. She looked up at a giant three-storey-high mural on the gable end of a house. The streetscape scene depicted five men holding AK47s, smiles on their faces. The friendly neighbourhood battalion.

Conor turned to her, his voice tense. "Why are we here?" In the mural behind his head, a massive hand gripped the barrel of a gun.

"It's as good a place as any to talk. Please tell me what's going on. I won't judge."

Conor moaned, "It's—"

A sudden scratching sound startled them. Heart racing, Kate spun around to see the taxi driver standing at the curb, stamping out a cigarette with the heel of his shoe. She shot him a glare and waited for him to get back into the car and close the door before she turned to face her brother again. Conor crammed his hands into his fleece pockets. "Don't want to talk about it right now."

She cursed the driver for wrecking the moment. If she pushed too hard, Conor might flee again.

She reached out to touch his arm. He backed away. "Please. Let me help," she said.

His lips trembled. "I didn't kill Henry or Bridget."

"I know."

He dragged his hands down his face as if trying to strip it off. "I'm here because of Freddy Lynd."

Who? What was he talking about? It took her a moment to place the name. "You mean the youth leader from our village?"

"Yes." His voice was flat. "He's now a priest. Or he was."

Handsome Freddy. The one the girls gazed longingly at. The one who'd led prayer circles and bonfires and long talks about God's love.

"What does he have to do with Bridget?" she asked.

Conor's eyes flicked to the mural, avoiding her gaze. "The day Bridget died," he said, "I was meeting him in the woods."

The sidewalk seemed to tilt. "Meeting him how?"

He clenched his jaw. "The reason I told Bridget to stop following me that day," he said slowly, "was because Freddy and I were planning to have sex in the woods."

It took her half a second. "Oh." Fifteen. Her brother had been fifteen. "But why didn't you just say—"

"Say what?" His voice cracked with emotion. "That I was sneaking off with the church youth leader? In 1990s Northern Ireland?" He gave a short, humourless laugh. "That would've gone down well."

Conor reached for a cigarette. His hands were shaking so badly the lighter slipped. He swore under his breath, tried again. Flame. He inhaled like a man drowning.

"That's why I lied. Said I was fishing." Smoke curled from his mouth. "And then you told the police about the broken rod."

Guilt stabbed through her. "I didn't know."

"I understand." He rubbed his forehead hard. "I panicked. I went to Freddy. Begged him to come with me. To tell them where we'd been."

"And?"

"He said if anyone found out he was"—his mouth twisted—"gay, he'd never become a priest."

She stared at him. "So you kept quiet?"

"What was I supposed to do?" His eyes flashed, wet and furious. "I was fifteen. He was twenty-six. He told me it would blow over. That they didn't have enough to charge me." A hollow shrug. "He was right."

The injustice of it pressed against her ribs.

"Why come here now?" she asked. "Why tell me this after all these years?"

"In rehab," he said, the words sounding scraped out of him. "I told my therapist what happened. He said it wasn't a relationship." He swallowed. "He said it was abuse."

Of course it was.

"He was our youth leader," Conor went on. "He used to tell me he could see straight into my soul." His voice faltered.

"Why not report him now?" she asked, though she already knew the answer.

He looked at her like she was an idiot. "Report a priest? About something that happened thirty years ago?" He gave a dismissive wave of his hand, the cigarette smoke swirling like an incense burner. "To someone who looks like me? The police barely listened when our cousin—who was a young girl—died."

That shut her up.

"You want to know why I started drinking again?" he asked.

She nodded.

"One night I googled him." His voice dropped so low she had to lean forward. "Freddy Lynd."

He took one last drag and crushed the cigarette on the mural wall.

"Molested altar boys," he said, flicking away the cigarette butt.

The words landed between them like something alive.

Kate felt sick. "Don't you dare," she said fiercely. "Don't you dare make this your fault."

He covered his face with his hands, "If I'd spoken up—"

"You were a child."

He looked at her wild-eyed. "I wanted to confront him," he whispered. "But I—"

"We'll go," she said, before she could lose her nerve. "We'll go together.

19

Later that afternoon, Kate and Conor rented a car and drove west of the city, following the contours of Lough Neagh. The same lough where they'd found Bridget's body.

Kate pulled onto a gravel lane lined with a tall hedge and parked in front of a simple whitewashed bungalow. Freddy Lynd's family home. "You ready for this?"

"Not really." He closed his eyes.

"Conor..."

"Just give me a moment."

She pressed her lips together. *I'm here to support him, not boss him around.*

"Let's do this," he said.

Kate held back while Conor rang the bell. When no one answered the door, his entire body seemed to deflate. She caught the scent of barbecued eel and tapped Conor on the shoulder. "Think he's cooking around back." As a child, she loved popping oily eel chunks in her mouth, savouring the rich fatty flavor. Back then, only the country folk ate the eel caught from Lough Neagh. Now, she read that most of it was shipped to the Netherlands where it was highly valued.

They set off around the side of the house where someone had spray painted "Freddy the turd puncher" on the whitewashed wall. Guess the neighbours knew why he was no longer a priest. In the backyard, Freddy stood over a barbecue, turning something with a pair of tongs. When he saw the siblings, the tongs froze halfway to the grill.

Conor stopped dead, mouth open. Kate nudged him with her elbow and said, "Hello, Father Lynd."

Freddy flinched. No wonder. She was certain no one around here was calling him by his priestly title anymore. He made her skin crawl.

Freddy took a step back from the grill, gripping the tongs so tightly his knuckles turned white. "What are you two doing here?"

Conor moved closer, fists tightly clenched. "I read about you in the newspapers." His voice shook. "How could you do that to those boys?" Kate slid an arm over Conor's shoulder, ready to grab him if he tried to punch Freddy. "I should've told the police a long time ago what you did to me."

Freddy set down the tongs and walked towards them with his hands held together like he was praying. Conor took a step back. Up close, Kate could see the dark circles under Freddy's eyes, his pallid skin. "What I did to those altar boys was sinful. And believe me, I'm paying for it. But what you and I had was different."

Conor crossed his arms over his chest. Kate held her breath. *You can do this.* Her brother blurted out, "No, it was the same. You molested me."

Freddy shook his head. "That's not true. You were my boyfriend, Conor Heaney. My first love."

Conor's chin started to tremble, and Kate snapped. "What a load of crap, you manipulative piece of shit." She pushed Conor aside and jabbed Freddy in the chest. He looked up at her, wide-eyed. Sometimes it paid to be tall. "You were our youth leader," she said, her voice shaking with fury, "and you took advantage of my brother, made him keep quiet about the two of you."

Freddy backed away from her, his hands raised like he was under arrest. "If they knew about us, I'd have never become a priest." He turned to look at Conor and said softly, "I would've come forward if the police had charged you."

Conor sucked in a sharp breath.

"But it didn't come to that."

"Are you kidding me?" Conor exploded. "The police tried to beat a confession out of me, and we had to move halfway around the world because the entire village thought I was guilty." His voice cracked. "Still does."

Freddy shrugged weakly. "What does it matter anymore? Your family made a new life in Canada."

Conor snorted with derision. "What life? I'm an alcoholic, trying hard to forget the stuff that happened here."

The two men stared at each other until Freddy hung his head. "I didn't mean for you to get hurt," he whispered. He covered his face with both hands and began to sob.

What a pathetic man.

The odour of charred eel broke the moment. Freddy jerked his head up. "Jesus." He rushed back to the barbecue.

Beside her, Kate could feel the tension drain from Conor's body. She tugged at his sleeve. Time for them to go. They climbed back into the rental, wheels spitting gravel as she floored the accelerator and sped away.

On the drive back to Belfast, Conor, his face a pasty grey colour, whispered, "Stop the car."

Kate gripped the steering wheel and craned her neck looking for a safe place to pull over on the windy country road. "Hold on, there's a driveway up ahead." She took the corner fast and pulled to a stop. Conor bolted from the car and bent over some shrubs to throw up. In the house at the end of the drive, a young woman, baby in her arms, peeked out from behind drapery. Kate waved to reassure her they were harmless, but the woman scowled and turned her back to them.

"Are you okay?" she asked as Conor climbed back in the car.

"Better."

She handed him a tissue to wipe his mouth.

"This is all too much."

"You did the right thing confronting him."

Conor ran his hands through his wavy hair. "I couldn't have done it without you. Sorry for being such an asshole."

"You have been an asshole." She smiled. "Now let's go home."

Conor shook his head. "I'm not going back."

She was afraid he was going to say that. "But—"

"There's a warrant out for my arrest, and I can't bear the thought of being locked up again."

"I get it. But where are you going to stay?"

Conor fiddled with the seat belt. "Don't worry. I'll check out of the hotel tomorrow and book myself a cheap bed and breakfast."

She smiled. He knew her frugal nature.

"And please give my love to Samantha and Mom, tell them I'll come back after things have calmed down."

Shit. Sam. She'd forgotten to check in with her last night. She was about to type her a message when Conor elbowed her. "We have company."

She looked up to see a man wearing a Barbour jacket walking towards their car, a shotgun tucked under his arm. Kate put the car in gear and sped away. She'd forgotten how suspicious people were in these parts.

Conor shook his head. "Damn, what a day."

They returned their rental car on the outskirts of the city and caught a taxi back to their hotel. Kate settled her exhausted brother into his room before retreating next door to hers. She changed into her pyjamas, raided the minibar for a whiskey and a bottle of water, and climbed into bed.

For a few minutes, she pressed her ear to the wall, listening for any sounds from Conor's room. All quiet. She logged onto her laptop, booked a flight back to Edmonton, and then searched for an inexpensive bed and breakfast where Conor could lie low until things got resolved.

With that done, her thoughts turned to Bridget. She'd never looked into her cousin's murder, too afraid of what she might uncover. But now, knowing what had happened to Conor—sure that he hadn't killed Bridget—maybe it was finally time to examine the evidence in Bridget's case. First, though, she had to ensure Conor wouldn't be arrested for Henry's murder. Somehow, she had to persuade the detectives they were off the mark.

The next morning, Kate and Conor checked out of Jurys Inn and took a taxi to a cheap bed and breakfast on the edge of the city that didn't ask for ID. Kate suspected it was only a matter of time before Erik and Christina realized that Conor had left the country. Once they figured it out, she knew the detectives would contact the Belfast police for assistance.

She pulled Conor's bag out of the trunk and tucked some money in his coat pocket. "For food. No more drinking. Please."

"I promise."

"And don't use your credit card."

"I know. I'm not stupid."

She wasn't so sure about that. She helped him register under an alias and hugged him goodbye. "Love you."

At the airport, Kate sent a message to Sam, apologizing for not being in touch sooner and sharing her return flight information. Once on board, she checked her messages one final time before switching off her phone. She smiled when she noticed a reply from Sam, but her smile faded as she read the text: Take a cab. I don't want to C U.

20

Maybe it was time to retire. Erik leaned back in his desk chair and closed his eyes. He rubbed a crick in his neck. Kate had lied to him—she claimed not to know where her brother had gone. Yet, shortly after, she'd flown to Belfast, presumably to meet him. What a fuckfest. Now he had to contact the Northern Irish police and convince them to track down Conor and keep him in custody until arrangements for his extradition could be made.

Christina barged into his office, hugging a folder close to her chest. "We've messed up."

"Looks like you're having the same kind of morning as me." He filled her in on his conversation with the Canadian Border Service.

"Damn. I've heard the extradition process is a bureaucratic nightmare."

Erik jabbed at the computer's escape button with his index finger. "Got an alert from the airline. Kate's booked to arrive home later this afternoon. I'll go meet her at the airport. Maybe she'll tell us where her brother is hiding out."

"Good luck with that." Christina clung to the folder.

"What's your bad news?"

She slapped the folder down on the desk and pulled out a telephone toll analysis chart showing Henry's cellphone calls. "We've missed something big."

The chart resembled a centipede, with Henry's cellphone at the centre and red and blue arrows branching out to represent incoming and outgoing calls. This visual layout highlighted the frequency and duration of calls in the days before his murder, making it easier to spot any unusual activity.

"I recognized a number that should've been flagged," she said.

"Whose is it?"

"Someone from the Ranch called Henry two days before he was murdered."

Erik's left eye twitched. *Damn*. More evidence of his sloppiness; he'd forgotten to go over the chart with Miles. He called the analyst's extension and ordered him to the office.

Miles stood, arms crossed, in front of Erik's desk.

"Remember when I promised to review the phone chart with you?" asked Erik. Miles nodded. "When you didn't hear back from me, why didn't you follow up?"

He shrugged. "Figured it was all fine."

Erik spoke slowly, enunciating every syllable. "Never. Make. Assumptions."

"Yes, sir."

Erik pointed to the chart. "Did you check this number?"

Miles glanced down. "Yes, a brief call from a country-and-western place called the Ranch."

"Are you familiar with the owner of the Ranch, Ferenc Zakreski?"

"No, should I be?"

Erik looked over at Christina, eyebrows raised. *What the hell were they teaching kids these days?* "Detective Wong, can you please enlighten Miles?"

"The owner's nickname is Teflon Man because nothing bad sticks to him. But we believe he heads an organized crime group involved in drugs and weapons smuggling."

Miles blinked rapidly. "Oh."

Erik addressed this partner. "If Ferenc's involved, this case got a lot more complicated."

He logged back into his computer and started searching the police database for background information on the Ranch's owner. Miles cleared his throat. Erik glanced over at him. "Why are you still here? Get back to work."

"Yes, sir." He fled the room.

"What an idiot."

"He's young, doesn't know the history of this city," said Christina.

She was right. He was too hard on Miles, and as the lead investigator, he should've reviewed the chart earlier. "Right. Glad you saw this. Let's refocus, figure out how Zakreski's group is involved."

Christina pulled up a chair. "What's the connection, if any, between Henry, Conor and Ferenc?"

Erik knew of at least one. He ran his fingers through his hair. "Please don't jump to conclusions."

"What is it?"

"Kate worked as a cocktail waitress at the Ranch all through university." It had to be a coincidence. They'd already ruled out her involvement. At least directly.

Christina shook her head and a strand of hair fell out of her ponytail. "We can't eliminate Kate as a suspect. She could have recruited her brother and one of Ferenc's men to kill Henry."

"What's the motive?"

"Henry had a new girlfriend. Maybe jealousy." Christina tucked the loose strand behind her ear. "Or maybe a drunk Conor killed Henry after the drive home from the bar, and either he or Kate called Ferenc for help to cover up the murder."

He could see that as a possibility: Kate coming to her brother's rescue.

He steepled his fingers, studying her. "What if Conor was telling the truth about the blackmail?"

"You're suggesting Ferenc might've been behind it?"

Erik nodded. "What if Conor refused to be blackmailed, just like he told us, but then, for whatever reason, he killed Henry and went to Ferenc for help?"

Christina chewed on her loose strand of hair. "A quid pro quo. Conor agreed to ship drugs up north in exchange for help with disposing of Henry's body. But if he was working for Ferenc, why would he even mention the blackmail to us in the first place?"

Erik shrugged. "No idea."

Christina stood up, her ponytail swishing. "In any case, I think we should make a surprise visit to the Ranch."

"I need a coffee for the road. You want one?"

Christina shook her head. "Meet you out front."

In the lunchroom, Erik pressed the grinder, releasing the pungent aroma of freshly ground coffee beans. Their unit had recently pooled their money to buy a high-end automatic espresso machine, but word had spread, and officers from other sections were now using it. The nerve, Erik thought. Someone had even taped a sign to the cupboard that read, "For Homicide Unit use only!" Hopefully that'd stem the tide.

As he waited for the coffee to brew, his thoughts turned to his partner. Christina was the best he'd ever worked with—smart, tough, and always by the book. He'd managed to keep his affair with Kate a secret from her, and he couldn't risk telling her now. What he'd done broke the rules, and if he got caught, at least she'd have deniability. The last thing he wanted was for her to get pulled into his mess.

The whoosh of steam announced the coffee was ready. He poured milk into a travel cup and added the espresso shots and several heaping teaspoons of sugar. Travel cup in hand, he rode the elevator down to meet Christina, who was waiting out front in their unmarked car. She glanced over at him before pulling into traffic. "You certainly know a lot about Kate's personal life."

He tried to decipher her expression as she drove southwest towards the nightclub. What was she implying? Had she figured out he'd had an affair with Kate? He sipped his coffee before responding. "She worked in this unit for a long time."

21

In the daylight, the Ranch looked derelict. Debris from the club-goers lay strewn about the parking lot: empty beer cans, the pointy heel of a woman's shoe, a torn condom wrapper. Erik detected the rancid smell of urine as they climbed the cracked concrete steps to the back door. He pressed the intercom button and waved his badge at the security camera. A few moments later, the metal-reinforced door, plastered with country music promo posters, swung open. A square, steroid-enhanced frame blocked the way into the club.

Erik recognized him as Ferenc's nephew, Tony. As he ushered them inside, a server hurried past, head down. She wore one of the club's infamous outfits: High heel booties, cowboy hat, short skirt, and plaid top with plenty of undone buttons. Erik shook his head to rid the thought of how Kate, with her long legs, must've looked in the outfit. Bet she'd made a mint in tips.

"Officers, what can I help you with?" asked Tony.

"We'd like to speak to your uncle."

Tony narrowed his eyes. "He's not available right now."

Christina put her hands on her hips. "Not available or doesn't want to talk to us?"

Tony stared at her, refusing to answer her question.

The officers shared a look. Time to ramp up the pressure on Tony. "Do you know someone named Conor Heaney?" asked Erik.

Tony shrugged. "Nope."

"Are you sure about that?" asked Christina. "We have information that suggests otherwise."

Tony gazed up at the ceiling like he was deep in thought, and then slowly nodded his head. "Oh yes, now I remember. We considered hiring his courier company, but their rates were too expensive."

Erik's pulse quickened. This idiot just admitted he knew Conor.

"And what about Henry?" asked Christina.

"Who's Henry?" Tony's eyes darted back and forth between the detectives.

Erik studied him, trying to decide if Tony was nervous or genuinely confused. "Henry Franzen, Conor's brother-in-law. His murder was all over the news. His body was dumped in a field."

"Do you know anything about it?" Christina added.

Tony thrust out his chin, his muscles straining against his too-tight T-shirt. "You need to leave."

"Tell your uncle we'd like to talk to him," said Erik.

Tony glared and hustled them out of the club, slamming the door behind them. "Did you notice the tattoo on his arm?" Erik asked.

Christina nodded, a preoccupied expression on her face. "Maybe you're right. Conor was telling the truth about the blackmail."

The best lies have an element of truth, thought Erik. "Even if he was blackmailed, that doesn't mean he's innocent in Henry's murder. Like you said earlier, maybe Conor enlisted their help to dump the body."

"I'll arrange for surveillance," said Christina. "Let's see what Ferenc and Tony do next."

22

Kate passed through the sliding doors into the arrivals area. A twenty-something bearded male in a pink ski jacket held up a piece of cardboard with "Turner Family" on it. An elderly woman in a hijab burst into tears at the sight of a weary couple with a toddler. The woman squeezed the toddler's cheeks and hugged the young woman.

No one to meet me. Kate sat on a bench by the luggage return and called her mother.

"Why didn't you let us know when you were coming back?" asked Alma. "We could've picked you up from the airport."

Guess Sam hadn't told her grandmother about the text. "Can I talk to Sam for a moment?"

"I'll go get her." After several minutes, Alma came back on the line. "Sorry, sweetheart, she doesn't want to speak with you."

The man in the pink ski jacket strode past her, followed by three teenage boys and their parents. The youngest of the boys stumbled over Kate's outstretched legs. "Sorry," he mumbled, his face flushed in embarrassment.

"Why don't you take a few days to recover from the jet lag?" Alma suggested. "I'm sure Sam will be more reasonable by the weekend." Her mother's tone sounded frustrated—Sam must have been giving her a hard time. After a brief pause, Alma asked, "How's Conor?"

That was a tough question to answer. "He's going to be fine. Staying put in Belfast. I'll fill you in when I swing by on the weekend." She ended the call and flung her backpack over her shoulder. Her body ached with fatigue; she'd barely slept on the flight, and it was only mid-afternoon in Edmonton. This was going to be a long day. Coffee—that's what she needed. She queued at a kiosk and studied the massive *Bush Pilot in Northern Sky* mural on the nearby wall.

"Get me one as well, won't you?"

Kate startled and turned.

Erik stood next to her, so close she could smell the musky scent of his bodywash.

"You found me."

"I wasn't exactly hunting," he said.

She ordered herself a double shot of espresso and an Americano misto for Erik, raising her eyebrows as he stirred in three bags of sugar. She thought he'd cut back on the sweets. They settled on the metal seats in the food court.

"You've been keeping things from me," said Erik.

"So have you."

"Where's your brother now?"

"Don't know. Somewhere in Northern Ireland."

Erik folded his arms across his chest. "I know you're lying. Police are looking for him there. It's only a matter of time before he's arrested."

Kate hoped Conor would keep a low profile at the bed and breakfast. "You might find this hard to believe, but Conor went back home to deal with personal matters related to my cousin's case."

"You're right. I do find it hard to believe."

Kate downed her espresso, savouring the intense flavour.

It was Erik's turn to raise his eyebrows. "How can you drink that straight up?"

She shrugged and set down her empty cup. "I don't know who killed my cousin, but I can now prove that it wasn't Conor. And he's also innocent in Henry's murder."

"What kind of proof?"

She told him about the church youth leader, Freddy Lynd, and why Conor had kept it a secret all these years.

"Even if that's true about your cousin, it doesn't change the facts in Henry's case. Your brother's DNA was found at the crime scene."

"What if he was set up?" she asked. "I think Ferenc and Tony Zakreski may be involved."

Erik stirred another packet of sugar into his coffee. "How did you come to that conclusion?"

She rummaged through her purse for the tattoo photos, thankful she'd left them in there and handed one to Erik. "Conor ID'd Tony Zakreski as his blackmailer. See his gargoyle tattoo?"

Erik examined the photo. "How did you get your hands on this?"

She grabbed it back. "That's not the point."

The intensity of Erik's gaze unnerved her. What was he thinking? Had she convinced him there was something more to Henry's case? She shifted in her seat, resisting the urge to look away. Finally, he shook his head and reached for his briefcase. "I shouldn't be showing you this, but—" He pulled out a telephone toll analysis chart and asked her if she recognized any of the numbers.

"This is from Henry's cell?" she asked.

"Yes, his phone was found in his coat pocket."

Why hadn't the killer destroyed Henry's phone before dumping his body? It didn't make sense. Kate scanned the chart and zeroed in on the calls with a northern Alberta area code.

"All Fort Mac numbers," said Erik. "We've identified most of them. Some to a company called Tecktronic, a few to and from the Gusher Hotel. And a couple to an out-of-service cell."

"Tecktronic is funding Henry and Michael's research on migratory birds," she said. "It's a company that maintains oil sands tailings ponds." But why had Henry called the Gusher multiple times? He wouldn't have stayed at that seedy downtown hotel. He always booked in at the Radisson when he travelled to Fort Mac. She decided to keep that information to herself.

"This number looks familiar," said Kate, pointing to one with an Edmonton area code. Erik didn't answer straight away.

She glanced up and caught the odd look on his face.

Oh. This was a test. He was waiting to see whether she'd recognize it. Whether she'd admit to it. But why did she know that number? Then it clicked.

Damn. Of course.

She looked back at the screen. "That's the Ranch's number, right?"

Erik nodded.

"This proves Conor was telling the truth about the blackmail."

Erik rubbed his chin.

Was she getting through to him?

"How?" he asked.

She spelled it out for him. "Conor was threatened by a man with a gargoyle tattoo on his forearm. He had to lend them his company truck, which has airport security clearance, or the tattooed man, who we now know is Tony Zakreski, would release the incriminating video of Conor driving drunk."

A woman walked past their table carrying a tray loaded with takeout food and trailed by three giggly children. Kate waited until they'd passed, then continued: "Conor went to Henry for advice and Henry offered to talk to the blackmailer."

Erik brushed sugar off the tabletop. "We tried the alleged phone number of the blackmailer that Conor gave us. It didn't work. Besides, that number isn't on Henry's phone chart."

"Must've been a burner phone," said Kate. She tapped the chart. "But at some point, Tony or Ferenc Zakreski called Henry using the Ranch's number. Maybe that's what got Henry killed—he figured out Tony, crime boss Ferenc Zakreski's nephew, was behind the blackmail."

"We're already looking into the Zakreskis' involvement, but that doesn't mean Conor, or you for that matter, are in the clear. Conor could've enlisted the help of the Zakreskis to dump Henry's body. And you worked at the Ranch while you were in university."

Kate stared at him, exasperated. What was it going to take to convince Erik that Conor was innocent?

23

Kate jolted awake. Her cat had attacked her foot. She glanced at her alarm clock. 11:45 pm. She'd only been asleep for a few hours. Sighing, she lay back and stared at the ceiling, stroking her cat behind the ears. He turned his head away and resumed grooming. Not the most affectionate creature in the world.

That's when she heard the noise. Someone moving around downstairs. Could it be Sam? She grabbed her cellphone from the side table and crept down the stairs. On the landing, she caught a whiff of men's cologne. *I know that scent.* Hands shaking, she reached for the canister of bear spray she stored in the front closet. Missing. *Shit.* She shouted out, "Ferenc, did you take my mace?" and heard a hearty chuckle from the living room.

"Kate, you never fail to impress me. How did you know I was here?"

"Your cologne. Still wearing the same fragrance, heavy on the sandalwood. Aramis, I think?"

"Ah, yes, it's the habits that get you caught, isn't it?"

Kate flicked on the lights. The owner of the Ranch sat at the far end of the grey sectional, meticulously dressed in a tailored suit and cradling the black canister in his hands.

She pointed to the bear spray. "Are you going to use that on me?"

"Of course not, my Amazonian. I took this for my protection. Wouldn't want you to accidentally pull the trigger. I'll tuck it down here for safekeeping." He placed the canister on the coffee table and patted the seat beside him. "We need to talk."

She weighed her options: run out the front door or hear him out. Curiosity got the better of her. She took a few steps towards him. "You broke into my house."

"Easy to do. The alarm was off."

Damn jet leg had made her mind fuzzy. "Why are you here?"

Ferenc pressed his fingertips together. "Your police boyfriend paid a visit to the club earlier today…"

How in the hell did he know about her affair with Erik?

"I think I've surprised you, no? We like to keep an eye on the police, see what they're up to in their private lives. When my guy told me about you two…" He grinned. "You naughty girl."

Kate scowled. "Why are you telling me this?"

"Please ask your boyfriend to back off. It's difficult getting business done.

"Are you threatening us? What are you going to do if Erik doesn't back off?"

"You don't want to find out."

"I'd like you to leave now," she said.

He held up a well-manicured hand. "Hold on. It wasn't us. We didn't murder Henry."

Kate put her hands on her hips. "Why should I believe you? Either you or Tony spoke to him two days before he died, and Tony tried to blackmail my brother."

He stroked his purple paisley tie. "I will admit, only to you, that Tony might've put the squeeze on Conor, but backed off after we found out he was your brother."

Kate got a fluttery feeling in her stomach. "You admit you talked to Henry?"

"Yes, and once I knew of the family connection, I assured Henry we'd leave Conor alone. And we did. We found someone else to ship our product up north. There was no need to hurt Henry. Besides, civilians are off limits."

How noble. A crime boss with principles. "Then who killed Henry?"

"Are you sure it wasn't your brother? The police seem to think so."

"Absolutely not."

Ferenc rested his ankle on his knee. "One more thing. Henry asked what I knew about the Fort Raiders."

Feeling dizzy, Kate leaned against the wall. Why would Henry want to know about a Fort McMurray gang? "What did you tell him?"

"That they're very dangerous, not to be messed with."

How ironic, coming from a drug kingpin.

Ferenc stood up and buttoned his suit jacket. "Don't forget to talk to your boyfriend. Take care of yourself, my Amazonian."

After he left, Kate collapsed on the sofa. Was he telling the truth about Henry? She picked up the phone to warn Erik that Ferenc knew about their affair but had second thoughts and shut it off. No damn way she was going to let Ferenc interfere with the investigation into Henry's murder.

24

On Saturday morning, Kate drove to her mother's. Sam answered the door. *What the hell?* She'd pierced her septum and wore a nose ring like some fucking Swiss cow. But it could've been worse. Ear spacers. Drugs. Or a druggie boyfriend. Kate took a deep breath and held it for five seconds before letting it go. "Did Granny know about that?"

"Didn't find out until afterwards," shouted Alma from the kitchen.

"It's not like you've been around to ask," said Sam.

Ouch. "Fair enough. But I'm here now. Promise that next time you'll run something like this by me first?" But, please God, no next time with the piercings.

Sam pulled on her nose ring. "Why are you here?"

"Jennifer called; they need your dad's office emptied for the new professor. I have to pack up his things and I could use your help."

Sam's chin quivered. Had Kate made a mistake suggesting this? Maybe it was still too soon. "Okay, I could do that," said Sam.

"Since we'll have to bring the boxes back to the house, why don't you pack your bag? You can stay overnight. Or even come back for good? Auntie Brenda is stopping by for dinner, and she'd love to see you."

Sam narrowed her eyes. "Don't push me, Mom."

"I'm sorry, sweetheart. You have every right to be mad. But I hope you know that you're the most important person in my life, and I love you." Kate saw a faint smile forming at the corners of Sam's mouth.

"Stop. Enough."

While her daughter collected her belongings, Kate plunked herself down at the kitchen table. Alma poured her a cup of tea and whispered, "Well handled. She might not show it, but Sam missed you."

Kate sipped on the hot tea and scalded her mouth. That's when it hit her: the parallels with her own childhood. She closed her eyes, remembering the stinging tears and aching loneliness, her mom's attention focused on Conor. But what else could she have done? Conor had needed his mother more back then. And how hard that must've been, a newly single mother, deserted by her husband, with two teenagers. Somehow, she'd managed to move her family halfway around the world to find a better life.

Kate wanted to do right by Sam, give her the attention she deserved.

"Now, what is going on with your brother?"

Biding for time, Kate gulped her tea. She spluttered and coughed when some of it went down the wrong way. "We decided it's best if he stays put for now," she said. "Got him a place to stay under a fake name."

Alma patted her hand. "You did well."

Kate felt a sense of relief. Her mother didn't seem to suspect there was more to the story, and Kate planned to keep it that way for now. Eventually, Conor might choose to tell her about Freddy Lynd—or he might not. That decision was his to make.

At the university, Kate pulled on the wood-handled doors to the Biological Sciences building. The exterior resembled a multi-sized cluster of stark, 1960s-Soviet-style apartments fused together.

Sam paused at the entrance. "This is going to be hard."

Kate put her arm around her daughter. "Yes, it will."

They climbed the north wing staircase to the third floor. Jennifer was waiting for them inside Henry's office.

"This place brings back a lot of happy family memories. Thanks for letting us pack up his things," said Kate.

Jennifer looked like she was about to cry. She pointed to empty boxes piled up beside Henry's oak desk. "You can use those, and we have more if you need them."

"We can take it from here," said Kate.

Jennifer turned and fled the room.

"Mom, you didn't have to be so blunt."

Kate felt a pang of guilt. "Sorry."

"You need to say that to her."

"Fine. After we finish up here."

Kate scrutinized the ornithological specimens that lined Henry's shelves: a great horned owl in a glass case, eggs on little stands arranged largest to smallest, a collection of nests. Sam, tears streaming down her face, stroked the feathers on her favourite, a tiny Saw-whet owl mounted on wooden base. Years earlier, Sam had named the mottled-brown bird, and it'd become the family tradition to greet him whenever they visited Henry's office.

"Hello, Witty." Kate gave the owl a little pat on the head. The stand wobbled, so she tilted it to investigate. Strange—something was stuck to the bottom. Kate used her nails to pry off a piece of masking tape. Underneath was a key. She turned it over in her hand; the number 469 was engraved on the key's head.

"What's that?" asked Sam.

"No idea." Kate flattened the tape and squinted, trying to decipher the words written on it. "Can you read this?"

Sam leaned in. "'It says, 'Look in the duck.'"

Kate's mind started whirring. What did the message mean? Why would Henry hide a key in such a way? They scanned the shelves but couldn't find anything resembling a duck. Kate tucked the key and message in her jeans pocket.

"Let's keep quiet about this until we figure out what's going on."

Sam's eyes widened in surprise or fear—Kate wasn't sure which one. "Could this be connected to his murder?"

"It's hard to say. It's been a while since we've been here. Who knows how long it has been tucked under Witty."

"Should we call the police?"

"Not yet. Let's first see if we can find out what it opens."

Kate glanced at her watch as Sam placed the lid on the last box. They'd packed up Henry's office in less than two hours. "I guess that's it," she said, her voice echoing in the now empty room. All signs of him had been removed, and it broke her heart.

Jennifer reappeared at the doorway and Sam waved her in. "Mom, I think you should ask her."

Sam had put her on the spot; Kate didn't fully trust Jennifer.

"Sorry about being so blunt earlier."

Jennifer nodded, her eyes glistening. *Shit, she's going to cry again.* In an effort to stave off the waterworks, Kate pulled the key from her jeans pocket and asked, "Do you know if Henry had a storage locker or safety deposit box? We found this packing up."

Jennifer examined the key. "No, I don't, sorry." Her face crumpled.

Sam handed her a tissue. "Would you like something from Dad's office?"

Jennifer dapped at her teary eyes before pointing to a brass desk lamp. "Henry and I found it at an antique shop. We had such a lovely day together."

Antique shopping. *That used to be our thing*. Kate noted Sam glancing at her and gave a resigned sigh. "You can have it."

Jennifer started to cry again. "Thank you."

There was a rap at the open door. Michael leaned against the doorframe. "Thought I'd check in on my favourite ladies."

"Nice to see you," said Kate. "What are you doing in the office on a Saturday?"

"I'm not here for long. Just needed some papers."

"Hi, Uncle Mike." Sam gave him a hug.

Michael picked up a box. "Let me help carry these out."

A cold breeze cut through Kate's jacket as they loaded the boxes into her SUV. She should've worn a warmer coat. "Guess who I'm seeing tomorrow for coffee?"

Michael shook his head. "No idea."

"Suzanne." Kate had rearranged her coffee date for the following afternoon.

Michael raised his eyebrows. "Didn't know you were still friends with my ex."

"We reconnected at Henry's funeral." Michael grunted. Kate loaded in the final box and closed the trunk. She gave him a warm smile. "Thanks for your help."

"Anytime." He scanned her up and down. "And remember, I'm just a phone call away." *Was he flirting with her*? Typical Michael.

Sam put on her seat belt and cranked up the heater. "When the hell is spring going to arrive?"

"Watch your language," said Kate.

Sam laughed. "Seriously? You're the worst offender."

She did have a point about the swearing. And the weather. Bloody dreary. Leafless trees, dirt-crusted snow, drab sky.

Kate pulled in front of the house just as Brenda arrived in her pickup. Kate popped the trunk and they began unloading boxes. Brenda joined in and when she spotted Sam's new nose ring she asked, "Doesn't snot get caught in there?"

"That's gross." Sam dashed up the stairs, two steps at time, carrying one of the boxes.

"Leave it in Dad's office," shouted Kate.

After they finished, Kate and Brenda sat at the kitchen island. "Are the boys with their dad this weekend?" asked Kate.

"Yup, and I'm darn happy about not having to spend my spare time at the rink watching their hockey tournament."

Kate laughed. "I miss spending time with you and the boys."

Brenda raised one eyebrow—the look Conor always called her signature "You're an idiot" expression. Kate figured she deserved it. Over the past year, she'd gone off the rails: banging her boss, destroying her marriage, and neglecting the people who mattered most—Sam, Brenda and her boys, and her mom. What if… She stopped herself. There was no sense in playing the "what if" game now. All she could do was try and fix things going forward.

"We miss you," said Brenda.

"I'm sorry I've been such a self-absorbed bitch this past year."

Brenda shrugged and they burst out laughing.

Sam came into the kitchen holding her red portable speaker. "What's so funny?" she asked.

"Nothing," Kate and Brenda said in unison.

While Sam tried to find a music selection they'd all agree on, Kate sautéed kale, garlic and spicy sausage and Brenda boiled pasta. Sam's first song choice, a jarring cacophony of screeching vocals and heavy guitar, received a hearty NO from both women.

Sam smirked at their reaction. "Just joking. How about this one?" Kate didn't mind the dark lyrics, but Brenda shook her head.

"Okay, I think our tastes intersect with this band," said Sam. Kate scratched her head. Since when did her daughter use words like "intersect"? She's growing up too quickly.

The beats of "Sisters" by A Tribe Called Red filled the kitchen. Brenda pumped her fist in the air. "Now we're talking. Turn it up." Sam blasted the song on the portable speaker, and they bounced around the room. Her beaming daughter made Kate's heart soar. It'd been too long since she'd seen Sam smile.

The ting of the stove timer signalled an end to the dance session. "Pasta's ready," said Brenda.

Sam plated the food and Kate grated Parmesan on top. As they ate, they reminisced about Henry, his passion for birds and his crazy collecting habits. "Remember the time he came home with a replica British telephone box?" asked Sam.

Kate laughed. "He'd wanted to put our landline phone inside it."

"What happened to it?" asked Brenda.

"I thought it was a great idea," said Sam, "but mom made him drive it right back to the junk shop.

"The bright red didn't quite fit in with our décor," said Kate, "and it was almost seven feet tall."

It wasn't until they'd cleared the dinner dishes and retired to the living room that talk shifted to Conor. Brenda rested her palms on her thighs. "Tell me about Northern Ireland. Did you track down your brother?"

Kate recounted her eventful trip. Both Sam and Brenda's eyes widened when she mentioned Freddy Lynd. "Your granny doesn't know yet," she warned Sam.

"A bloody priest, huh? I should've known," Brenda said.

"Conor kept it well hidden. It wasn't until this last stint in rehab that the therapist pulled it out of him and helped him work through it."

Brenda stood up and began pacing. "I've got to talk to him. Tell him I'd still like to be business partners."

"Are you sure?" Kate asked.

"Can't abandon him now that I know what he went through."

Sam's face brightened. "Will this help convince the police that Uncle Conor is innocent in Dad's case?"

"Sorry, sweetheart. They still consider him a suspect."

Sam's hands clenched into fists. "There's no way Uncle Conor hurt him."

Poor child, Kate thought. She should find her a therapist after all she'd been through.

"You're right," she said. "And the police will soon realize that, don't you worry." She shivered and pulled the edges of her knit cardigan tightly around herself. She still couldn't explain how Conor's blood and glove found their way to the crime scene. She changed the topic: "Tell Brenda what we discovered this afternoon."

Sam explained how they'd found a key taped under a stuffed owl in Henry's office. "Dad had written 'Look in the duck' on the tape, whatever that means."

"Any idea what the key opens?" asked Brenda.

"Haven't a clue," said Kate. Her eyes wandered over to the mantelpiece, home to several of Henry's most treasured knick-knacks, including a small, roughly carved wooden duck he'd purchased during a birding holiday in Peru. At his urging, they'd all written out a wish on slips of paper and tucked them inside the duck's false bottom.

"I wonder…" said Kate.

She crossed to the mantel, lifted the fist-sized carving, and turned it over in her hands. Her pulse quickened as she slid open the secret compartment in the base of the duck. Two items lay on top of the folded wishes: A piece of paper creased neatly in half and an orange plastic tag with an NS symbol and the number 469. Kate pulled out the tag. Her breath caught. She held it up.

"I know what the key opens!"

The NS was for Nisku Storage, a facility near the airport. NS had come up in a case Kate had worked on the previous year. She didn't typically discuss her work with Henry, but after she'd woken up four nights in a row screaming, her fatigued husband implored her to tell him what was going on.

"Henry must've chosen Nisku Storage because he knew I'd recognize the logo."

She explained how she'd gone to Nisku Storage to help the detectives document items in a locker connected with a missing persons case. When the staff had opened the door, the stench emanating from the six-by-six-foot room suggested they'd just found their missing person. Inside a large metal trunk were the grisly decomposing remains. It was something she would never forget.

"That's terrible," said Sam.

Kate hesitated, wondering if she should have kept that detail from her daughter. But it was too late now. She unfolded the piece of paper. Written in black marker were the letters: R-M-S.

"Henry's handwriting?" Brenda asked, leaning in for a closer look.

Kate nodded. "But I haven't the faintest idea what it means."

"You have to tell Erik," said Brenda. "Arrange to meet him at Nisku Storage."

"You're right."

Kate dug in her pocket and pulled out the key that they'd found under Witty the owl.

"Put it with the rest of your keys so you don't lose it," said Sam.

"Good idea." Kate rummaged through her purse for her keychain and added the storage locker key onto it.

Brenda unfolded her bulky frame. "I've got an early start tomorrow. Got to get on the road." She gave Sam a high five and hugged Kate. "Promise me you'll take Erik with you to the storage unit. Don't go on your own."

Kate handed Brenda her brown leather bomber jacket. "I promise."

"Auntie, you need a warmer coat," said Sam.

Brenda pulled out her keys and pressed the automatic starter for her truck. "What do I need a big coat for? I have a heater and seat warmers."

While Sam turned on the dishwasher, Kate called Erik.

"Please, keep an open mind." She explained to him about their discovery at the university and the bird carving at the house. "I'm certain Henry hid something in his storage locker that might lead us to his killer."

"How do you know the key was for you? Maybe he'd left it for Jennifer."

"It was our family tradition to pet the owl. No one else would do that, and it was only after we touched it that we noticed the key taped to the underside." She was met with silence on the line. "Please. This could solve the case."

"Fine. I'll meet you there first thing in the morning."

After she spoke with Erik, Kate went into Henry's office and rummaged through his filing cabinet.

Sam poked her head into the room. "What're you doing?"

"Looking for any mention of RMS in your dad's papers." Kate shut the cabinet drawer and slumped down in his office chair. "But I'm not having any luck."

Sam walked over and kissed her on the cheek. "I'm off to bed."

"Night night, sweetheart." Kate sighed and absentmindedly fiddled with a loose pull on the desk drawer. She couldn't recall Henry ever mentioning anything with the initials RMS. What did it mean, and why had he hidden the key and messages in the first place? It'd been pure luck that they'd come across it under Witty. Maybe he'd planned to tell her where he'd placed the key but was killed before he had the chance.

Kate opened the desk drawer and surveyed the contents. An organizational tray held a pile of sticky notes and a jumble of pens. She flicked through sticky notes. All blank. She was about shut the drawer when she noticed the edge of a piece of paper sticking out from under the plastic tray. Curious, she pulled it free and began reading the typewritten message addressed to Henry.

`Stop collaborating with dirty oil or face the consequences.`

That sounded like a threat. She read the rest of the brief note. It was no surprise he got angry messages. Lots of people, herself included, were upset when Henry and Michael had accepted research funding from an oil industry company. Still, the anonymous, typewritten note felt particularly ominous.

She tucked the note in her handbag, planning to show it to Erik when they met at Nisku Storage in the morning. Before heading to bed, she pulled out her laptop and googled "RMS," curious to see what would come up. The results included Royal Mail Service, Risk Management Systems, and a beauty supply company. Frustrated by the lack of context, she realized she would need to wait for the storage locker's contents to shed any light on her questions. Her eyes ached with fatigue, so she shut down her computer and fell asleep.

Kate woke to her cat sitting on her chest, staring at her with his wide blue eyes. Second night in a row. She scratched behind his ears, and he gave a loud meow.

"What is it, buddy?"

A faint clunk echoed somewhere in the house,

Her cheeks flushed. She lay still, listening. Where had that come from? Must be Sam. Or—God forbid—another visit from Ferenc. But she'd made sure to set the alarm before heading to bed. She nudged the cat away, grabbed her cellphone and slid her hand under the bed for the bear spray before remembering she'd left it downstairs.

Damn.

Hugging the wall and keeping her steps light, she peeked in Sam's room. Her daughter was lightly snoring, her comforter in a bunch at the end of the bed. Kate exhaled—but only slightly.

She crept downstairs to the front foyer and flipped open the cover on the alarm. Blank. No lights on at all. *Oh shit.*

A sudden, explosive pain shot through the back of her head.

And then everything went dark.

25

Monotonous strip malls and big box stores lined both sides of the highway on the drive to Nisku Storage. Damn depressing. As Erik told Christina about the phone call from Kate, his work partner drummed her fingers on the steering wheel.

"A hidden key and message. A bit far-fetched, don't you think?" she asked.

"Why would Kate lie?"

Christina gave him a sideways glance. "I can think of a reason—to divert attention away from her and Conor."

"Let's see what's in the locker first before we jump to any conclusions."

"Agreed." She scratched the bridge of her nose. "I know you're close to Kate, but you have to consider the possibility she's involved."

Was he reading too much into the way she'd emphasized *close?* Maybe she suspected there was something going on between him and Kate. "As I said, let's not jump to conclusions."

Christina shrugged her shoulders, "You're right. We both need to watch out for tunnel vision."

She parked in front of a squat building with a neon Nisku Storage sign. They got out and walked over to a row of large garage-door-style units. Erik consulted his notes. "All these begin with 5; we're looking for number 469," he said. "Must be inside."

Christina opened the entrance door, and an electronic ring announced their arrival. Their footsteps echoed on the concrete floor in the spartan space. As they approached the reception desk, the attendant, swallowed in a too-big uniform, did a double take. He clearly didn't get too many visitors. His cheeks flushed, and he quickly set his cell face-down on the counter.

"Need some help?"

Christina flashed her badge. "Can you tell me where we can find unit number 469?"

The attendant's acne-covered face flushed an even deeper red when he saw her badge. Stepping out from behind the counter, he gestured towards the storage units. "It's a storage locker—one of the small ones over there."

While the attendant's back was turned, Erik peeked at the phone on the counter, curious what flustered him when he saw Christina's badge. A porn site. No wonder he was nervous. He quickly returned the phone and glanced at his watch.

Kate should here by now.

After twenty minutes passed with no sign of her, Erik tried calling but she didn't answer her home phone or her cell.

They gave it another twenty minutes before Erik tried her numbers again. No luck. Who else could he call?

"Do you still have Brenda's phone number?" asked Erik. They'd interviewed her about Henry's case a few weeks earlier and Christina had taken notes.

"Why?"

"Last night, when Kate called, she told me Brenda had come over for dinner and was there when they found the message in the bird carving on the mantle. Maybe she knows what's going on."

Christina flipped through her notepad until she found Brenda's contact information.

Erik entered Brenda's number as Christina paced the room. "Do you know if Kate is on her way?" he asked.

"She should have arrived by now," Brenda replied. "Something's wrong."

Christina stopped mid-stride and looked at Erik, a flicker of concern crossing her face. "Should we be worried?"

"Brenda seems to think so."

That was enough. Without a word, they bolted for the car and tore out of the lot, the vehicle's rear end fishtailing on the icy tarmac.

26

Kate regained consciousness slowly, like the tide coming in. Clarity came in waves. Her eyes flickered open. Why was she lying on the floor? A throbbing pain at the back of her head made it difficult to think.

She struggled to make sense of what had happened. She could remember coming downstairs to check on a noise—and then everything went dark.

She tried to move and felt a burning in her wrists and ankles. Rope. Adrenalin rushed through her body. She tried to shout out for Sam but choked on the gag covering her mouth. She willed herself to slow her breathing. *Please God, let Sam be okay.* Tears slipped down her face.

Turning her head, she spotted her cell on the hallway floor a short distance away. Maybe she could reach it. She rocked from side to side, trying in vain to loosen the bindings and cried out at a sharp pain in her side. No use. She closed her eyes and prayed.

After what seemed like hours, her cell rang. Then her home phone. More time passed as she faded in and out of consciousness, then the doorbell rang followed by a loud smash as someone broke down the door.

"Kate." Erik rushed over and untied her gag as Christina worked on her wrists and ankles.

"Sam," she croaked, struggling to speak.

Erik asked Christina to call for backup and rushed up the stairs. Once Kate's bindings were undone, Christina helped her to her feet and advised her to stay put. Kate ignored her and stumbled up the stairs. Her body wasn't cooperating, but fear for her daughter propelled her forward. Erik stood in the upper floor hallway, his gun drawn, and entered Sam's room. Christina, then Kate, followed behind and gasped at the sight of clothes and furniture strewn about the room.

No sign of Sam.

Her heart began to race when she noticed the dresser shoved in front of the closet door. The detectives strained to push it out of the way, then reached for the handle. Kate squeezed her eyes shut, terrified at what they'd find inside.

"She's okay," shouted Erik.

Kate rushed to the closet, where Sam was cowering in the far corner. She gathered her daughter into her arms as the detectives worked quickly to untie the bindings around Sam's wrists and ankles. The moment she was free, Sam clung to her, sobbing into her shoulder. Kate felt something warm and wet at the back of her head. She reached up, touched it, then stared at her fingers. Blood. Sam was saying something, but Kate couldn't make sense of it. The room tilted. Her vision blurred at the edges.

Then everything went black as she crumpled to the floor.

"Mom, what's wrong?" Sam and the detectives leaned over Kate, their brows furrowed with concern. Kate tried to sit up, but a sharp pain forced a cry from her lips. Erik gently propped a pillow under her legs and wrapped her in a blanket.

Kate struggled to speak, her tongue thick and heavy in her mouth. "I'm fine," she managed to say.

"No, you're not," Erik said. "We've called an ambulance."

Sam held her hand as they waited for the paramedics to arrive. Kate shut her eyes and listened to the wail of the sirens. She heard the clang of the stretcher being pulled from the ambulance and the low voices of the paramedics as they entered the house and climbed the stairs. When they reached her, they greeted her, asked a few questions, and examined her head wound and ribs.

Kate refused to be loaded onto the stretcher. "I can walk." The paramedics assisted her down the stairs and into the ambulance. "I want my daughter with me." She didn't want to let Sam out of her sight.

"I'm right here," said Sam, climbing in to join her for the ride.

At the hospital, the paramedics wheeled Kate straight into a room where a nurse retook her vitals and checked her head and ribs. After he'd finished, he turned to Sam and said, "The police want me to collect the material under your nails."

A surge of heat flooded Kate's body. *What had the attackers done to Sam?* She looked into her daughter's eyes, searching for answers.

"I know what you're thinking, but don't worry," said Sam. "I scratched one of the men, that's all. They're trying to get some of his skin cells to run a DNA test."

The tension drained out of Kate. They were safe. She rested her eyes and listened to the clicking of the nail trimmers.

A touch on her shoulder startled her. She looked up at a woman in a white coat, stethoscope dangling around her neck. "I'm Doctor Lufte," she said. "I'd like to take a look at your pupils." She clicked on a penlight and peered into Kate's eyes. Her breath smelled of coffee.

The doctor wrote something in a chart and asked Kate to describe her symptoms.

"Dizzy. Fuzzy brained. Tired." She winced in pain as she tried to shift her position. "And sore ribs."

The doctor tucked the penlight in her pocket and pulled up a chair. "You have a concussion, and I'd like to keep you in for observation."

Kate nodded, resigned to spending the night in the hospital.

"Let's check your ribs." The doctor gently pulled up Kate's shirt. She flinched when she saw the left side of her torso had turned shades of purple and flinched again as the doctor probed the area. Kate couldn't remember how she'd gotten the bruise, but the shape looked suspiciously like a boot print.

"Don't think you've broken a rib, but we'll send you for an X-ray." She wrote some more notes on the chart. "Why don't you get into a gown and settle in? The nurse will give you something for the pain."

"Thank you," said Kate, her voice shaky.

After the doctor left, Sam helped Kate change into a gown and snuggled beside her in the hospital bed. Kate kissed Sam's cheek and tucked back a strand of her rambunctious hair that had fallen into her lovely face. Her daughter was safe, that was all that mattered.

27

Kate woke to the sound of her mother calling her name. She kept her eyes closed, not certain if she could handle her right now.

"Maybe we should let her sleep?" asked Brenda.

Kate opened her eyes and a grin spread across her friend's face. "Welcome back to the land of the living."

"Why are you two hovering at my bedside?" she asked.

"Came to check in on you," said Brenda.

Kate scanned the room. A pale light shone through the small window of the stark semi-private. Her heart raced. "Where's Sam?"

"With the detectives," said Alma. "They're doing a walk-through at the house."

When Kate tried to sit up in bed, a sharp pain radiated down her left torso. "Fuck."

"Kate. Language," said Alma.

"Sorry. Where's the thing to adjust the bed?"

Alma handed her a remote control. Kate pressed the button and the top third of the bed slowly tilted up. A wave of dizziness hit. She took deep breaths to steady herself.

Alma opened her mouth to speak, but Brenda beat her to it. "Good thing you're so hard-headed."

Kate rolled her eyes. "Very funny."

Alma wore her usual coral lipstick and power pantsuit but the concealer under her eyes failed to mask the dark circles. "How are you feeling?" she asked Kate.

"Better. How about you?" asked Kate.

Alma patted her arm. "I'm fine."

As usual, her mother was doing her best to keep up appearances and conceal how she really felt. She had mastered this after Bridget's murder, when rumours and gossip circulated accusing Conor of being the killer. That was when their father walked out—leaving just when they needed him most. Still, their mother carried on, steadfastly ignoring the stares and the finger-pointing.

She adjusted Kate's sheets. "I hate to bring this up now—"

Here comes the lecture.

"—until the police find who's responsible for the home invasion, I think you and Samantha should come stay with me."

"You're right."

Alma tilted her head, surprised that Kate agreed with her. "Sam should go with you, but I'm staying put," Kate said.

"Your daughter needs you," Alma protested. "Why don't you both move in for the time being?"

"After what happened, she's safer without me around," said Kate.

Brenda piped in, "You can't blame yourself."

Kate noted her mother's frown. She certainly blamed Kate.

Brenda's phone rang. She held it out for Kate. "Your brother. He's been calling every hour to see if you've woken up yet."

Kate took the phone and looked around before answering. "Hope you're using a burner phone," she said to her brother.

"Thank God you're okay."

"Belfast police are on the lookout for you."

"Don't worry about me. Do you know who attacked you and Sam?"

"Not sure, maybe Ferenc's men."

Conor's voice broke. *Was he crying?* "I'm coming home."

"Don't. They'll arrest you at the airport."

"Mom!" Sam entered the room, followed by the detectives.

"Got to go," Kate said and hung up. The last thing she wanted was the police finding out she was in communication with her brother.

Sam grinned and rushed to Kate's bedside. "You're awake."

Erik cleared his throat. "Sorry to interrupt, but we need to ask you a few questions."

Kate smoothed her hair, wishing she'd had a chance to brush it or put on some makeup.

Alma glared, her nostrils flaring. "Can't it wait?" she demanded.

Kate wasn't sure if her mother was upset because she thought Kate needed more time to recover, or because Erik—Kate's ex-lover—stood in the doorway.

"Sorry, it can't," Erik replied, ignoring Alma's pointed looks.

Brenda put her arm around Alma and guided her and Sam from the room. "Let's get a cup of tea while Kate talks to the detectives."

Christina stopped them on the way out the door. "Brenda, we need you to come down to the station after we're done here," she said.

"What for?"

"To talk to you about your visit with Kate and Sam on Saturday evening."

Brenda rolled her eyes. "Fine. But first I need to take these two for tea and doughnuts."

After they left the hospital room, Christina shut the door and sat down on the arm of the chair facing Kate. "Glad you're okay," she said.

Erik stood at Kate's bedside and took her hand. She felt warmth rush to her cheeks. "You gave us a quite a scare," he said.

Kate caught the look on Christina's face and quickly pulled her hand away. She shifted in bed and winced in pain. *Damn.* She kept forgetting about her ribs. "I guess you want my account of what happened?"

Christina opened her notebook and took notes as Kate explained that she'd gone downstairs after hearing a noise, discovered the power to her alarm had been cut, and was struck on the back of the head before she could call for help.

"We did a walk-through at the house with Sam," said Erik. "Your keys are gone, along with your laptop. Nothing else."

Kate stared at him, struggling to process what he'd said. "My keys?" She shivered. "I don't understand. Why my keys?" She pictured her key ring—the house key, the car key, her gym fob—and the storage locker key. Her stomach dropped. "But how in hell did they know about the Nisku Storage key?"

Erik shook his head. "Not sure."

"At least they didn't get into the locker." The grimace on Erik's face suggested that she was mistaken. "You're telling me," she said, her voice rising, "that those fuckers, whoever they are, got into it?"

"Keep your voice down," said Erik.

"Whatever," she said, massaging her throbbing forehead. A nurse poked her head into the room. "Sorry for yelling," said Kate.

When the nurse closed the door, Erik said, "When you didn't show up at Nisku Storage, we went looking for you. That's when they got in the locker."

"Why didn't one of you stay behind and guard it?"

Christina shrugged, "No way we could've predicted this would happen."

But Kate knew the real answer—they hadn't taken her story about the key seriously, which is why they hadn't considered it. Well, to hell with them. Their best chance of solving Henry's murder had vanished. Whatever had been stored in that locker got Henry killed—Kate was certain of it. She took solace that at least the home invaders wouldn't be able to access her computer. She had set it to automatically erase all her data after three incorrect password attempts.

"Did you check the security cameras at the storage place?" she asked.

"Yes," said Erik. "But whoever they were knew what they were doing. They wore a hoodie and kept their face averted from the cameras."

"Could you tell what they took?" asked Kate.

Erik quickly glanced over at his partner before he answered. "Looks like a file folder."

Christina crossed her arms, obviously annoyed that Erik had revealed that information.

Erik cleared his throat, and Kate could already anticipate the question he was about to ask—the same one she'd been asking herself: "Who did you tell about the key?"

She shifted in bed, wincing at the pain in her ribs. "Jennifer and Brenda. But I trust Brenda with my life. Jennifer, who knows, but what's her motive?"

"What about your brother?" asked Christina.

Always back to him. "No way he's involved. He'd never do anything that could hurt me or his niece. Besides, he's probably still in Northern Ireland."

Christina shut her notebook. "We've asked both Brenda and Jennifer to come to the police station to be interviewed."

Brenda wasn't going to be happy about that. Her friend mistrusted the police, and for good reason. "Like I told Erik, I think Ferenc Zakreski is behind all of this," she said.

"How did you come to that conclusion?" asked Christina.

Kate held up her index finger. "First of all, Conor told Henry he was being blackmailed."

"Allegedly blackmailed," interrupted Christina, "We only have Conor's word on that."

"Let's assume Conor's telling the truth," said Kate. She held up two fingers. "Secondly, based on Conor's description of the blackmailer's tattoos, we were able to identify him as Tony Zakreski, Ferenc's nephew."

"Yes, Erik told me. How convenient," said Christina.

"Please hear me out," said Kate. "We also know that Henry offered to talk to the blackmailer, and from his cellphone records, we know someone from the Ranch called him two days before he died."

"We have no idea who he spoke with at the Ranch or the topic of the conversation." Christina turned to Erik. "How did Kate know about the phone call to the Ranch?"

"Let her explain."

"When Ferenc paid a surprise visit to my house, I knew I was on to something," said Kate.

"*You* talked to Ferenc?" Chistina rose suddenly, sending her notebook to the floor

Before Kate had a chance to respond, Christina turned to her partner, "Did *you* know?"

Erik held up his hands. "No, I didn't know about the visit."

Both detectives fixed their gaze on Kate. "So," Eric said, "what did he say?"

Kate reached for the bed remote, silently cursing her bruised ribs, and pressed the button to raise her bed higher. Better. She wasn't used to people looking down at her.

"Ferenc confirmed that Henry had called him about my brother but denied that he or Tony had anything to do with Henry's death. I think his exact words were, 'civilians are off limits.' But his late-night visit convinced me that he's lying. He's involved somehow."

Christina bent to pick up her notebook. "Why do you think that?"

"Henry was a smart man." Kate spoke softly; her head was pounding. "He would've realized that he'd need some sort of leverage to persuade Tony and Ferenc to back away from blackmailing Conor." She paused for a moment and took a sip of water. "Now this next part is supposition, but what if Henry found something, some sort of incriminating evidence against Tony or Ferenc to get them to drop the blackmail?"

"That's what you think Henry had stored in the storage locker?" asked Erik. "Some sort of leverage against Tony or Ferenc?"

"Yes, maybe he found proof of criminal activity. But, in any case, it backfired for Henry. Instead of persuading Ferenc and Tony to back down, it ended up getting him killed. And ever since his murder, they've been trying to get their hands on this leverage before we did."

Christina shook her head. Kate could tell she wasn't buying it.

"Interesting theory," said Erik, "But you have nothing concrete to back it up. Besides, how would they know about the key?"

"Maybe he bugged my house."

Christina laughed. "Sounds far-fetched. Besides, your brother's DNA was found at the crime scene. Have you considered that he may be working with Ferenc?"

Kate seethed. They were still trying to connect her brother to the case. "You know how cunning Ferenc is. What if he planted that evidence? Conor makes the perfect fall guy."

The room fell silent as an aide entered, pushing a food cart through the door.

"Lunchtime," he announced, placing the tray on the table. Kate ignored the unrecognizable meat and instead lifted the lid on the green Jell-O.

Christina's phone buzzed, and she glanced down at a text. "Jennifer's on her way to the station."

Could Jennifer be involved? She knew about the key; Sam had told her about it when they were packing Henry's office at the university. But it didn't make sense. As much as Kate disliked her, Jennifer had no motive to kill Henry.

"Just give me a minute," Erik said to Christina. "I'll meet you at the car."

Christina shrugged and left the room.

Kate finished the Jell-O and licked her spoon clean. "I'm a big girl. What do you want to ask?"

"You're holding something back."

Erik was always good at reading her. "Ferenc knows about us."

"How?" he asked.

"Not sure. Implied he had inside sources."

Erik clenched his fists. "What does he want?"

"To leave him alone."

Erik crossed his arms. "Not going to happen."

"He's going to try to blackmail us."

He took her hand in his. “I’ll handle it. You need to let this go, focus on healing.”

She’d been mistaken; Erik didn’t understand her at all. No bloody way she was going to let this go after what they’d done to her and Sam.

“Take care of yourself.” He kissed her on the forehead and left the room.

Kate shifted in bed and groaned. She’d forgotten about her bruised ribs. Again.

Soon after the detectives had left, the nurse returned to tell her that she might be released from the hospital.

“When?” asked Kate.

“The doctor wants to see you first.” He inspected the bruising on Kate’s ribs. “How’s that feeling?”

“Still sore.”

He wrapped a towel around an ice pack and pressed it to the bruising. “Ice it as often as possible over the next few days.”

After the nurse left, Kate swung her legs over the side of the bed and slowly pushed herself upright. She shuffled to the suitcase of clothes her mother had brought and dragged it closer. When she tried to lift it onto the bed, a sharp pain shot up her left side.

“Where do you think you’re going?

Kate flinched at the voice behind her. “Hey, Brenda.” She steadied herself against the mattress. “Where’s Mom? And Sam?”

“They’re still at the café.” Brenda glanced at her watch. “But I’ve got to get to the police station for my interview.”

“I’m coming with you.”

Her friend put her hands on her hips. “You can’t leave the hospital.”

“Nurse told me I might be able to go after the doctor takes another look at me.”

Brenda checked her watch again. “I’ve got to leave right now if I want to make it in time.”

“Go on then,” said Kate, “and when I’m given the all-clear, I’ll cab it over to the station.”

Brenda smiled. “Thanks, my friend. I could use your support.”

Last year, Brenda had ended up in custody overnight after she was pulled over by a traffic cop and she accused him of racial profiling. The traffic cop put her in handcuffs and hauled her into the station, making up some bullshit story about an attempted assault on a police officer.

"I'm sorry you got sucked into all of this," said Kate, "Just remember, it's Erik and Christina you'll be speaking with, not some dumb-shit racist officer."

"Right," said Brenda, the word edged with apprehension.

"I'll be there as soon as I can."

Soon after Brenda left, the doctor rapped on the door, "Kate, I hear you're eager to leave us."

Kate smiled. "I'm getting restless."

"I've reviewed your chart and think you're fine as long as you take it easy, get plenty of rest."

After the doctor left, Kate changed as quickly as she could, given the circumstances. She wanted to leave before her family came back from the café. Her mother would insist that she go home, not rush off to the police station.

An orderly wheeled her to the front entrance. Given her concussion, Kate was supposed to have someone accompany her home. She got out of the wheelchair and waved to a stranger parked in an idling vehicle at the pickup zone. "There she is," Kate said to the orderly. "I can take it from here, thanks."

She waited until he'd gone back inside the hospital before she carried her suitcase over to the taxi stand. She waved at the driver, and he popped open the trunk but didn't bother getting out to help. *No tip for you.* She slung in her suitcase and had to lean against the car until the dizziness subsided.

"Main police detachment please," she said as she settled in her seat. She sent a quick text to her daughter and mom to let them know where she was headed.

Alma responded right away. Go home and rest!!

Kate smiled at Sam's text. U r a good friend tell auntie to stay strong

Kate typed: I'll see you both tomorrow xo

She hated the idea of leaving Sam right now, but she also understood that things would be difficult for her friend at police headquarters. At least Brenda wouldn't have to face the officer who had harassed her. He'd been suspended, albeit with pay, as Brenda had angrily pointed out, pending a disciplinary review.

The driver pulled out into traffic and then glanced in the rearview mirror. "Are you a cop?" he asked.

"Nope."

Ordinarily, she liked chatting to taxi drivers, hearing their stories. Today she craved quiet. Feeling slightly nauseous, she closed her eyes. That's when she remembered Suzanne. *Damn.* She was supposed to have met her on Sunday afternoon, but with the attack and all that had followed, she'd forgotten to touch base. Given that Suzanne hadn't reached out either, Kate figured she must be upset at being stood up a second time. Hopefully, she would understand once Kate explained what had happened. She called Suzanne's number and left another message.

Kate put away her phone as the taxi stopped at police headquarters. She paid the fare, retrieved her bag, and headed inside. Reaching for her key card, she remembered she didn't have one anymore. Instead, she used the ticket machine, which spat out a number 25 ticket. The sign above the plexiglass booth read, "Now serving number 24." She took a seat in one of the well-worn chairs and, when her number was called, she spoke with a woman she didn't recognize with the name tag "Paisley" pinned to her fitted sweater.

"How can I help you?"

The policing community was a close one, and although Kate was a civilian, she'd always felt like one of the team. Speaking with this new employee made Kate feel disconnected. "My name is Kate Heaney, and I am here for Brenda Littlechild. She's being interviewed by Detectives Erik Jorgensen and Christina Wong."

Paisley called and spoke to someone in the Major Crimes unit. She hung up the phone and said, "The interview's still underway. You're to wait here."

Banishment. Kate sat back down. She was of no help to Brenda here. Paisley kept glancing over at her. She must've clued into her identity. The crime analyst with the murdered husband and suspect brother. Would things ever return to normal?

She tried to find a more comfortable position in the chair, but every time she shifted, a sharp pain radiated through the left side of her body. On top of that, her head started to throb again, and a wave of heat washed over her as if someone had cranked up the thermostat. This was getting biblical. A hot flash on top of everything else. Sweat dripped down her back and pooled at the waist of her pants. Could this day get any worse? She closed her eyes and tried to meditate.

Kate opened her eyes at the drone of the elevator approaching the lobby. When the doors glided open, Brenda and Erik stepped out. Erik spotted her first. "Kate, why aren't you in a hospital bed?"

"I got released and wanted to provide emotional support to this gal," she said pointing to Brenda.

Paisley watched from behind the plexiglass partition and Erik glanced her way before speaking. "Brenda is free to go. We're satisfied for now that she had nothing to do with this latest unfortunate incident." Kate chose not to take his impersonal tone personally. He was just being cautious for both their sakes.

Brenda offered to drive Kate home. As they climbed in her truck, Kate asked, "How did it go in there?"

"I survived," she said. "Thanks for coming."

Kate shrugged. "Not that I did much."

"Just glad I had a friendly face waiting for me in the lobby." Brenda glanced over at Kate. "I get why they wanted to talk to me. I'm the only one who knew about the key and the locker at Nisku Storage."

Kate pointed out that Henry's girlfriend, Jennifer, knew about the key.

"But she didn't know about the location of the locker." Brenda kept her eyes on the road, one hand steady on the steering wheel. With her free hand, she reached over and opened the glove compartment. "What if someone was listening to our conversation at your house last night?"

When Kate saw the bug detector, she threw back her head and laughed, then cringed at the pain. "You think my place is bugged? That's unlikely."

"Maybe, but I'm excited to try this baby out." Brenda had studied electronics at college before she'd gone into business with Conor. She was a technical genius and had a garage full of wires, circuit boards and all sorts of gadgets.

Kate fidgeted with her parka's zipper. "What if Ferenc bugged my place?"

Brenda gave her a quick glance. "If he did, we're all in big trouble."

28

Brenda stood in the middle of Kate's living room. "That night Ferenc showed up here, where did he sit?"

"Over there." Kate pointed to the far end of the sectional sofa.

"Shut off your cell." Brenda waved the black RF signal detector in the air. "This picks up any type of wireless signal."

She powered down her phone and set it on the kitchen island countertop. Brenda started her sweep at the sofa where Ferenc had sat and methodically waved the handheld device up and down the furniture and walls. At one point, the detector gave a loud beep, startling Kate. "Did you find something?"

"Nah, just your Wi-Fi booster."

After what seemed an eternity, Brenda finished her sweep of the house. "Nothing here."

"You sure?"

"If you had a bug, this thing would've found it." Brenda picked up Kate's cell from the kitchen island. "Maybe it's on here?"

Kate was skeptical her phone had been tampered with. "I rarely let this out of my sight, but—"

She ran her thumb over the power button. That night of the attack, she'd had it with her when she'd gone downstairs to check the house alarm and had been hit over the head. When she'd come to, she'd been surprised her attackers hadn't taken her phone. Maybe it was because they knew it was bugged and wanted to keep monitoring her?

"We need Jeremy's help," said Brenda.

Jeremy worked out of his *faux*-Craftsman-style home. The exterior's heritage look belied the high-tech interior, fitted with the latest security devices—motion sensor lights, cameras, fingerprint entry and a remote door opener. He buzzed them in and descended the cherrywood staircase to greet them at in the front hallway.

"Nice to see you again," he said to Brenda. "Surprised you're working with the police after what happened last year." Brenda tightly squeezed his outstretched hand. "Ouch," he said, shaking it out. "Sorry for bringing it up."

Brenda had filed a complaint about being racially profiled by the traffic cop and he'd been suspended. Then she started getting anonymous threatening phone calls.

"I'm helping Kate, not the police," she said.

Jeremy nodded in understanding, "Hard to say no to her, isn't it?" Kate elbowed him. "What brings you two here?" he asked.

"Would you mind looking at my phone? I think it might be bugged." She handed it to him. "I've turned it off just in case."

"Follow me." He guided them to the basement and unlocked the doors with a fingerprint scan. "This room is a giant faraday cage and blocks out any signals. It'll be safe to power it back up in here."

He pulled out a stool from under the table that spanned one side of the room. "Conor called me from Belfast," he said as he powered up the phone.

"He'd better be careful or he's going to end up in jail there," said Kate. "He's supposed to be hiding out, not calling everyone he knows."

Jeremy shrugged. "I'm not everyone."

Good point. Before Conor had messed up everything with Jeremy, their years together had been happy ones. Maybe things would be different now that her brother had confronted his past. But first she had to make sure he didn't get arrested for Henry's murder.

"Conor told me he ID'd Tony Zakreski by his tattoo. You think Tony or his Uncle Ferenc bugged your phone?"

"Possibly."

"Be careful, Kate. The Zakreskis are dangerous men."

He rolled up the sleeves and plugged Kate's phone into his computer. "This could take some time. Make yourself comfortable. Grab a drink." He pointed to a mini-fridge in the corner of the room.

Brenda pulled up a seat alongside Jeremy to watch him work. Kate grabbed a Perrier and stretched out on his sofa. She still felt off kilter. Her ribs ached and her head throbbed.

Less than an hour later, Jeremy shouted, "Gotcha!"

Kate dragged herself off the couch to see what he'd found.

"It's really quite ingenious," he enthused, "a virus turned the cell receiver into a microphone. You can listen in on phone conversations and tune in to anything that is going on within a certain radius."

How surreal. Henry murdered, a home invasion and now her phone turned into a listening device. On top of everything, her stomach issues had kicked in. She poked at the burning spot. *Fuck.* Not a good idea when you have bruised ribs. She checked her pockets for antacids but came up empty.

"Can you figure out who placed it on my cell and when they did it?" asked Kate.

"No, unfortunately. Either someone had access to your phone and installed it manually, or you accidentally clicked on a link that triggered a remote installation."

Kate knew she would never click on a suspicious link, and she couldn't remember ever leaving her phone unattended. Regardless of how the virus was installed, she now had proof that someone—most likely Ferenc—had been eavesdropping on her conversations. "It's time to call in the detectives," she said.

Within the hour, Erik and Christina arrived at Jeremy's house with a police IT specialist in tow. The IT expert whistled at the sight of Jeremy's workroom. "Nice digs." He verified the virus on Kate's cell and inspected Erik's phone, but it was clean.

Armed with evidence that Kate's cellphone had been compromised—and her account of Ferenc's late-night visit—the detectives determined they had enough grounds to bring Ferenc in for questioning. Christina called for police backup to meet them at the Ranch.

As they walked towards the front door, a terrible thought struck Kate. She nudged Erik with her elbow. "I need to talk to you," she hissed.

"Give me a moment," he said to Christina.

"Don't take too long," she said, glaring at Kate as she left the house.

What was that look for? Kate wondered, as Erik touched her arm. "Sorry I didn't believe you about the bug," he said.

She readied herself for confrontation. "You can't interview Ferenc. He's going to say something about us." She took a step closer. "Please."

He took her hands in his. “I’m sorry, Kate, but no, we have to question him. Odds are, he’ll lawyer up and refuse to talk anyways.”

Kate’s heart lurched when she realized Brenda, Jeremy and the IT specialist were all gathered at the top of the staircase, their eyes locked on her and Erik. Embarrassed, she quickly pulled her hands away from his, the heat rushing to her cheeks. Without a word, Brenda turned on her heels and strode out the door. Kate fumbled to pull on her jacket, then rushed to catch up with her. “Brenda, please. It’s not what you think,” she called out, her voice tight with desperation.

“Are you two still a thing? asked Brenda.

Kate forced a laugh. “No.” But Brenda’s sideways glance said it all. She didn’t believe her.

“Seriously, it’s long over. He was just comforting me.” She realized over-explaining her actions made her sound guilty.

Brenda gave her signature one raised eyebrow. “Whatever you say, Kate. I’ve got to get the boys to hockey practice. You can figure your own way home.” She climbed into the driver’s seat and slammed the door shut.

As Brenda sped away, Kate wondered how she was going to get home. She noticed the detectives’ car still parked in front of the house, so she walked over and rapped on the passenger window. Erik rolled it down.

“Can I catch a ride with you two?” she asked.

Christina shot her a quick look, then began typing a message to dispatch. “We’re not a cab service.”

Kate took a step back. “No problem. I understand.”

Erik shifted uncomfortably in his seat. “What my partner is trying to say is we’re heading straight to the Ranch to pick up Ferenc.”

“Let me know how it goes.” She gave a half-hearted wave as they pulled away from the curb and out of the cul-de-sac. What the hell had she done to piss off Christina Wong? Kate kicked at a snow pile. *Bet she knows too.* Her affair with Erik Jorgensen hadn’t been worth all the harm it’d caused.

“I can give you a ride as far as the detachment.”

Kate turned around. She’d forgotten all about the IT specialist.

“That’d be great, thanks.”

As he drove along the meandering residential road, Kate caught him glancing over at her. *He knows too.* He pulled onto the rush-hour-clogged Anthony Henday Drive, and Kate leaned against the passenger door. She groaned at the pain in her side.

"You okay?" he asked.

She rifled through her purse for her meds. "I bumped my bruised ribs."

She popped a Tylenol 3, leaned back and closed her eyes. Her mind kept turning to the detectives' impending interview with Ferenc. Would he follow through on his threat if they didn't back off? Even if Ferenc mentioned the affair during his interview, it probably wouldn't matter. Who would believe him? And even if he did have an incriminating recording from her bugged phone, he couldn't use it without implicating himself.

"Shit," said the IT specialist. Kate opened her eyes and braced herself as he manoeuvred through three lanes of busy traffic to reach the off ramp. He glanced at her again. "Sorry, almost missed the turnoff."

He pulled into the headquarters parkade, and Kate thanked him for the ride. "I'll call a taxi from inside," she said. Once inside the lobby, she waved to Paisley, who was behind the plexiglass, and carefully lowered herself into a chair, mindful of her sore body. How had she ended up sitting in this depressing police station lobby twice in the same day?

Paisley glanced around before stepping away from the reception desk. "What are you doing back here?"

"Waiting," Kate replied.

"Do you want me to call up to someone?"

"No, don't bother. I'm calling a taxi." Kate pulled out her phone, ignoring Paisley. She wasn't in the mood to explain her presence at the detachment. *Nosy busybody.* Paisley shuffled back to the reception booth.

Kate began to key in a number but had second thoughts and pocketed her phone. Instead, she sent Erik a text message: I'm at the detachment. Can I catch a ride home after your interview with Ferenc?

She shifted around in her seat in a failed attempt to find a comfortable position and questioned her motives. What did she want from Erik? She could tell he wanted to pick up where they'd left off, but is that what she wanted?

A few minutes later, Miles entered the lobby and headed toward the elevators. *Please don't let him see me.* He spotted her and stopped in his tracks. Kate smiled and gave a half-hearted wave. Miles walked over to where she was sitting. Looking down at her with a frown, he asked, "What are you doing here?"

Ignoring the stabbing pain in her torso, Kate stood up and looked down at him. "Ferenc's being interviewed right now about Henry's murder."

He jammed his hands into his pockets. "I know. That's why I was called in. But that doesn't explain why you're here."

Kate changed the subject. "This case must be a big learning experience for you."

"Not really."

"How do you like working with Detectives Wong and Jorgensen?"

He narrowed his eyes at her. "You don't belong here."

She met his gaze. "That's not up to you."

"We'll see about that." He turned on his heels and walked off towards the elevator.

29

The detectives stepped into the interrogation room. Down the hall, their colleagues gathered around a screen to watch the interview. Ferenc, dressed in a grey suit and purple tie, lounged back in his seat. What a cool customer, thought Erik—acting like he doesn't have a care in the world. Christina began the recording. Erik lobbed Ferenc several innocuous questions before asking, "Why did you break into Kate's house?"

"I didn't."

Erik leaned forward. "Why did you send your men to rough up and rob Kate?"

Ferenc rested his forearms on the table. "I have no idea what you're talking about."

"Did you put a listening device on her phone?" asked Christina.

"That's ridiculous. Did Kate tell you that? She's lying."

"Why would she lie?" said Erik.

Ferenc shrugged. "Maybe you should ask her. She had her reasons to get rid of Henry. Maybe it had something to do with her boyfriend," he said with a wink at Erik.

Erik's stomach churned. Kate was right; if he continued to interrogate Ferenc, the crime boss would reveal Erik and Kate's affair. But what else could he do?

Several minutes later, a fresh-faced constable entered the interrogation room and whispered in Erik's ear, "The inspector wants a word."

"Right now?" he asked. The constable pursed his lips and nodded. This didn't bode well. Erik shut off the camera. "We're pausing the interview, please remain seated." He left the room, followed by Christina.

"What's going on?" asked his partner.

Erik shook his head and lied. "I have no idea."

Inspector Barclay's face was even more flushed than the constable's who had come to fetch them. This was going to be a rough ride. The inspector's anger was rare, but when it surfaced, it was enough to unsettle even the most hardened detectives.

"We are waiting for one more person," he said while Erik and Christina stood ramrod straight.

After the young constable reappeared with Kate, Erik's worst fears were confirmed. The inspector barked at the constable to leave and close the door behind him. At the click of the latch, the inspector pointed his finger at Christina.

"Detective Wong, were you aware what was going on?"

"No, she wasn't," said Erik. "I kept it a secret."

The inspector snapped at him, "I asked her the question, not you." He swung around to look at Christina. "Well?"

"I don't understand what's going on, sir."

"You didn't know about the relationship between these two?" He gestured to Kate and Erik.

Christina's eyes widened. She shot Erik a quick glance, then turned back to the inspector, "No, sir, he didn't tell me."

Erik held his breath. Will the inspector accept Christina's circumspect response or dig further? "Then you may leave."

Christina bolted from the office. Erik closed his eyes in relief—at least his partner wouldn't get pulled into his mess.

"But sir, it was over a long time ago," protested Kate. "And I transferred to a different unit."

The inspector's face turned a deeper shade of red. "When a murder suspect knows all about your past relationship and tried to use it to his advantage, it matters. We have a rule against fraternizing. Period. End of story."

He took a deep breath and lowered his voice. "Detective Erik Jorgensen, you are suspended with pay, pending an internal investigation. Kate, your employment with the Edmonton Police is in jeopardy. I suggest you contact your union representative."

With that, the inspector walked over to the window and stared outside, his back to Kate and Erik. They'd been dismissed.

Erik opened the office door and nearly collided with a startled Miles, who had to grab the doorframe to steady himself. "Listening in again?" Erik asked.

Now things made more sense. Miles must've told the inspector what Ferenc had revealed during his interview. The crime analyst had also eavesdropped outside Erik's office the night he'd spoken with Kate.

Miles stammered something about it being Erik's fault.

He glared at him. "What did I do to deserve your disloyalty?"

"Plenty," Miles shot back, spinning around and darting down the hallway.

30

The young constable escorted them to the front doors, then hurried off. As Kate and Erik stepped outside, sleet fell from a darkening slate sky. They stood on the brick-clad promenade, silent and shell-shocked by what had just happened inside

Across the street, at a construction site, a tattered white tarp snapped in the wind. Kate opened her mouth to speak, but Erik raised a hand.

"Sorry, Kate, can't talk about this right now. I'm afraid I'll say something I'll regret."

He walked away, leaving her beside one of the blue pylons installed after Nine-Eleven to protect the police station from van bombs—an unlikely threat in Edmonton, or so she once would have thought. Before Henry was murdered, she would have scoffed at that idea, too.

Kate dug through her purse and pulled out her cell. The screen was blank. Shit, she'd forgotten to charge it. Erik soon drove past her in his Audi. He slowed down at the stop sign, spun his tires as he struggled to get traction on the slippery street and then sped off. She closed her eyes. *Shit. Damn. Fuck.* She had to go back into the police station and ask Paisley to call her a taxi. How humiliating. By now, the entire station would know what'd happened.

When she opened her eyes again, Erik was pulling up to the curb. He must've driven around the block.

"Get in. I'll give you a ride," he said through the open passenger window.

Kate wondered what'd changed his mind. "I'm sorry you've been suspended," she said as she climbed into the passenger seat.

"Me too."

They didn't speak for the rest of the drive. At her house, he got out and walked her to the door. That's when she realized she didn't have keys. The home invaders had taken them. She fumbled in the darkness to locate the spare one hidden inside the front lantern.

Once inside, Erik helped her take off her coat, gently pulling off one sleeve at a time, his hand lingering on her arm. "Thanks," she whispered. She bent down to remove her boots and steadied herself against the wall.

"You need to rest," said Erik.

"You're right." She wanted to say more to him, but now wasn't the right time. It'd been a brutally long day, and she was utterly spent. "Thanks, Erik. I'm sorry."

He kissed her lips. "So am I."

Kate locked the door behind him, headed straight for her room and collapsed on her bed, too exhausted to even change.

Kate awoke to the smell of bacon and the voices of her family. What were they doing here? She dragged her sore body out of bed and rinsed her face in the sink. She gazed at her reflection, taking in her wrinkled blouse and stringy hair. *Whatever.* She downed two pain pills and made her way into the kitchen. "What a pleasant surprise."

"We thought you might need a proper breakfast," said Sam.

Alma handed Kate a mug of steaming coffee. "Why didn't you let us know you got home safely? I tried to call yesterday evening but your phone was off."

In the whirl of events that had unfolded the previous day, Kate had completely forgotten to plug it in.

"Sorry. I was so exhausted that I went straight to bed."

"Erik told me. I called him when I hadn't heard from you."

Shit. What else did he say? She figured he must've kept quiet about the bugged phone and their suspension from the police department because there was no way her mother would be this calm if she knew. And Kate planned to keep it that way. She would flip out if she learned that Kate may have lost her job.

"A penny for your thoughts?" Kate asked, putting her arm around Sam, who was standing over the stove pushing bacon around in the frying pan.

Sam pulled away.

Now what had she done to upset her daughter? "Why don't we have a chat in your room?"

Sam nodded and led the way. In her bedroom, she shot a quick glance towards the closet door.

"Sorry, sweetheart, that was insensitive of me to suggest we come in here."

Sam sat cross-legged on her bed and hugged her one-eyed teddy bear. "I tried to call you last night, but you didn't answer your phone. I was really scared something had happened."

Kate opened her mouth to respond, "But—"

"No ifs, ands, or buts. Isn't that what you say? Promise me you'll stop investigating Dad's case? Please? It's too dangerous."

"You're right," said Kate, sitting on the edge of the bed.

What she didn't say was that it might be too late to stop. The home invasion made it clear to her that she was in the middle of it whether she liked it or not. Sam chewed on Teddy's arm, reminding Kate of what she'd been like as a toddler, one of Teddy's limbs always in her mouth like a pacifier.

"How are you coping with all of this?"

Sam shrugged, Teddy's arm still caught between her teeth. Kate's heart broke at everything her daughter had been through.

"Until I know it's safe, can you please stay with Granny?"

Sam pulled the arm from her mouth. "Fine. But you need to call me more. I worry too, you know."

Kate reached out and lightly squeezed Sam's arm. "May I remind you the last time I tried calling, you told me to find my own way home from the airport?"

Sam rolled her eyes.

"Seriously," said Kate. "I know I'm not in the running for Mother of the Year, but it's not all on me. Can you give me a break, stop getting so darn angry at me?"

"But..." Sam paused, hugging Teddy to her chest. "Fine."

When they returned downstairs, they found Erik sitting at the counter, devouring one of Alma's famous breakfasts and discussing the best place in town to buy real back bacon.

Sam turned to Kate and whispered, "What's he doing here?"

Kate tucked her stringy hair behind her ears and smoothed out her shirt. She tugged on Sam's arm and murmured, "Be nice."

Erik looked up as they settled on stools at the counter. "Good morning." He gestured to his heaped plate of food. "I certainly timed my visit well."

Why was he so chipper this morning? Kate's stomach rumbled at the sight of Erik biting into a piece of thickly buttered soda bread. She couldn't remember the last time she'd had proper food. Alma plunked down two plates full of back bacon, eggs and toast in front of her and Sam.

Pouring herself coffee, Sam announced, "I'm going to watch TV." Plate in one hand, mug in the other, she turned and walked away before anyone could object.

Alma shook her head and helped herself to some bacon. "Are you done going after my son, Detective Jorgensen?"

Kate swallowed a mouthful of eggs. "Mom, leave it alone," she said.

Erik wiped his lips with his napkin before responding. "Well, ma'am, I'm sorry, but I can't say too much about the investigation."

They ate the rest of the meal in silence, and after they were done, Erik thanked Alma for breakfast. She gave him a tight smile and left the room.

"Sorry about my mother and Sam. They can be blunt."

Erik laughed. "Runs in the family."

She crumpled up her napkin and tossed it at him. "Why are you here?"

"I—"

"Never mind. Glad you came. You can take me to Nisku Storage."

31

"I'm suspended, remember?" said Erik.

"But the staff at the storage place don't know that."

Erik shook his head. "I should've known you'd keep digging."

"It's too late to back out," said Kate. "I'm not about to let these people threaten me and my daughter and do nothing about it."

"What do you want at Nisku Storage?"

"If we know when Henry rented the locker, we can go to the university and ask Jennifer to check those dates on his work calendar. I know she has access. It might help us figure out what he was up to."

Erik sighed and muttered, "This could get me fired." But he did as she'd asked and drove to Nisku Storage. Inside, behind the reception desk, a young attendant in an ill-fitting uniform did a double take when he saw them and turned his phone face down.

Kate leaned in and whispered, "I take it he recognizes you?"

"Yes, same kid as before."

She shrugged off her bulky coat and approached the reception desk. Smiling, she extended her hand to the attendant. "I don't think we've met yet. I'm assisting Detective Erik Jorgensen." The attendant blushed and limply shook Kate's hand. His hand felt warm and clammy in hers, and Kate resisted the urge to wipe her hand on the front of her jeans. She gave him as dazzling a smile as she could muster. "Would you mind providing us with the date the victim rented the storage locker?"

The attendant scratched at a zit on his forehead. "I already gave that to the other officer—Wong, was her name, I think."

Kate leaned on the counter. The attendant's eyes darted around, avoiding her gaze. She lowered her voice and spoke in a conspiratorial tone. "Detective Wong is in a meeting, and we urgently need to verify the date."

He checked the computer. "February 14th."

She rested her hand on top of his, "Thank you, you're a life saver." The attendant giggled.

"What an awkward kid," Kate remarked as they drove away.

Erik shifted in his seat. "Last time we were in there, I caught him looking at a porn site called MILFs. Bet you he was up to the same thing today."

Kate wrinkled her nose. Gross.

Kate led the way through the Biological Sciences building.

"Henry loved pointing out its quirks," she said. "Did you know there's a classroom entered through a closet and a stairwell that leads to nowhere?"

Erik studied a map posted in one of the hallways. "Confusing design."

"Supposedly, it's because of infighting within the building team. They all just did their own thing, no coordination, and this mess is the result."

"What are you implying?"

Kate shrugged. "We need to work together."

They climbed the north wing staircase to the third floor and knocked on Jennifer's office door. She opened it, her eyes widening at the sight of Kate.

"How's Sam doing?" she asked. "The poor girl must've been so frightened."

Kate frowned. How did she know about the home invasion?

"Detective Jorgensen and his partner questioned me about the key," Jennifer explained. "That's how I found out."

"Sam's fine," said Kate, her voice brisk.

Jennifer led them inside her office. "Come in. Sorry for the tight quarters. I share with three other instructors."

Her desk stood like a beacon of organization in a sea of messiness, the surface clear of papers, books lined up neatly on a shelf. Kate leaned in to read the titles and noticed they were ordered alphabetically.

"Didn't Henry's clutter bother you?" It'd certainly been a source of tension in their marriage.

Jennifer straightened out a pile of papers on her desk. "Funnily enough, that's how we started dating. I'd offered to organize his messy office, and he asked me out."

Kate dug her thumbnail into the palm of her hand. *You've got to be kidding me.* She'd always refused to pick up after her husband.

Jennifer flashed her a smile. "I knew that was going to be our biggest challenge when we moved in together."

What the fuck. Living together? Henry had certainly moved on quickly. Kate unbuttoned her coat. Damn hot flashes.

"Sorry, I shouldn't have told you that," said Jennifer

Bet you're not sorry at all. Kate forced a smile and dismissed her with the flick of her hand. "No big deal."

Erik cleared his throat. "We're wondering if you can show us Henry's work calendar for February?"

"Certainly," said Jennifer. She pulled it up on her computer. "Do you have a specific day in mind?"

"Saturday, February 14th."

Jennifer clicked on the date and bit her lip.

"What is it?" asked Kate.

"That's the day I picked him up from the airport. He'd been in Fort Mac to discuss the field study with Tecktronic."

Jennifer fiddled with an antique gold ring that Kate suspected had been a gift from Henry. Its style closely resembled the jewellery Henry used to buy for Kate, even though she herself seldom wore any. It seemed he had finally found someone who truly appreciated his gifts.

"Anything about that day stand out to you?" asked Erik.

"Yes, it was Valentine's Day, and we had our first fight," she said. "I'd driven all the way out to the airport to pick him up with the understanding we were going to spend time together. But when he got in the car, he asked me to take him home. Said he had something to do but wouldn't elaborate. I got upset."

Kate shared a look with Erik. That's when Henry must've rented the storage locker.

"Do you know where he stayed in Fort Mac?" asked Erik.

"That was the other strange thing," said Jennifer. "He'd booked in at the Gusher, which is a really grungy hotel. Usually, he stayed at the Radisson."

"Did Michael go with him on that trip?" asked Kate.

Jennifer twirled the ring. "No. He was supposed to but got sick with the flu."

"Thanks for your help," said Erik.

He and Kate left the office, closing the door behind them, and conferred in the hallway. "In Henry's phone records," he whispered, "there were several phone calls from the Gusher the day before he died."

Kate pointed down the hall. "We should talk to Michael while we're here. Find out what he knows about Henry's last trip to Fort Mac."

Just outside Michael's office, Erik's phone rang. He glanced at the screen and told Kate to go ahead without him. She knocked on Michael's door and tried the knob. Unlocked. She stepped inside and found Michael immersed in his work at his desk. Kate had only visited his office a few times and was reminded how much his style differed from Henry's. The space was minimal yet elegantly decorated, featuring a large abstract landscape on the far wall. Clearing her throat, she startled Michael. When he looked up and saw her, his face broke into a grin.

"Kate, so nice to see you." He got out from behind his desk and gave her a hug. "How are you and Sam doing? I heard about the home invasion."

"How did you find out?" she asked, surprised he knew.

"Jennifer told me," said Michael.

Jennifer had a big mouth. "I'm okay, but the police want it kept quiet since it's an ongoing investigation."

"My lips are sealed," he promised.

Erik rapped on the door and joined them inside.

"Have you met Detective Jorgensen?" asked Kate.

"No, I haven't." Michael shook his hand. "Nice to meet you."

"You too. I believe my partner, Detective Christina Wong, spoke to you soon after Henry…"

"Yes, it's so shocking…"

Kate turned to gaze out his office window, taking in the view of the river valley. "Your space is quite a contrast to the sessional instructors'."

Michael laughed. "As you know, it's one of the perks of being a tenured professor." He gestured for them to take a seat. "I take it you have some more questions for me about Henry?"

"What can you tell us about his trip last month to Fort McMurray?" asked Erik.

"Not much. I was supposed to go with him but came down with the flu."

"Do you recall anything unusual that Henry did or said after returning from that trip?"

Michael stroked his chin. "Not that I can recall. Why?"

"We're putting together a timeline of his activities in the month leading up to his murder," said Kate.

"Back then, we were working out the details for our research project," said Michael. "That's why Henry travelled to meet with Tecktronic."

"That day of the funeral reception," said Kate, "you'd mentioned the research project was in jeopardy. What's happening with it now?"

Michael smiled. "I'm pleased to say that Tecktronic is back on board."

"Henry would be happy about that," said Kate, although she wasn't thrilled that the research project was going ahead. Henry had enjoyed a distinguished career as an ornithologist, but she feared he'd now be remembered as the researcher who accepted funding from the oil industry—a clear conflict of interest, in her opinion. That was when she recalled the threatening letter she'd found in Henry's desk drawer. She rummaged through her handbag, unsure if it was still there, and discovered it crumpled up in the corner of the front pocket.

"That reminds me, do you know anything about this?" She smoothed out the paper before handing it over.

Michael read it and shook his head in disgust. "Not another one of these?"

"You've had more?"

He thrust the note back at her. "Oh, yes, for some reason, those crazy eco-terrorists latched on to the fact we're getting money from Tecktronic. But how else are we supposed to fund our research these days?"

"You weren't worried?"

"Nah." He scratched his head. "You don't think they killed Henry, do you?"

Kate tucked the note back in her bag, "Sorry, Michael, can't say too much. We'll let you get back to work."

Kate chose a corner seat in her favourite café in the Strathcona neighbourhood. The purple padded panels lining the walls muffled the hissing from the hard-working espresso machine and the conversations of other patrons. She craved a coffee; weeks of restless sleep were taking their toll. Erik laughed as he set her drink down in front of her.

"Your eyes lit up at the sight of this," he said.

After a few sips, Kate set down her drink. "Who called you earlier?"

Erik cradled his mug. "My union rep. They want to meet with me tomorrow morning and go over our strategy."

She'd been putting off calling her union. What would she do if she lost her job? No use thinking about that now. Better to focus on Henry's case.

"Interesting what Michael said about the threat letters," said Erik. "He and Henry should've reported them to the police."

Kate pulled out the letter. "I'd forgotten I had it. Found it in Henry's desk drawer the night of the home invasion."

Erik read it through and handed it back to her. "What are your thoughts?"

She reread it several times before she spoke. "Look at the unique syntax, *Collaborating with dirty oil* and *Big Green gives it away*. I bet the writer has used the same wording before."

She pulled out her phone, typed the two phrases into Google and skimmed through the results, selecting the ones that looked intriguing. After some digging, she discovered both phrases in a post on a Facebook Business page called "The Grimy Reality of the Oil Sands." She scrolled through comments. "Got something," she said. "Look at this guy. Bertrand Mickleford. He likes and comments on all the posts." She showed Erik her screen. "I'll bet you that he's the owner of the page."

"Looks promising."

Kate took her phone back and spent the next hour combing through open-source data for details about Mickleford. Bertrand called himself an environmental freelance writer based in Fort McMurray and his articles were critical of the government and mainstream environmental groups, accusing them of selling out. He'd also written stories advocating the use of violence, if necessary.

All signs pointed north. She shut off her phone and said, "We need to go to Fort Mac."

32

The following afternoon, Kate gazed out the window of the half-full, fifty-seater turboprop. The clear day provided a panoramic view of the boreal forest landscape: scrubby blue spruce and jack pines interspersed with snow-covered muskeg and frozen looping rivers. Kate glanced over at Erik in the aisle seat beside her, hunched over a book, headphones in his ears.

They'd scored the emergency exit row, but despite the extra legroom she struggled to get comfortable. She crossed and uncrossed her legs and surreptitiously undid the waist button on her jeans. No use. Her unsettled mind was the problem. She couldn't stop thinking about the text her daughter had sent just after they boarded the flight: U lied to me!!

That's all Sam had written. What did she mean by that?

Have I lied?

Worried for her safety, Sam had wanted her to step away from the case, but here she was, off to Fort Mac. But she'd never promised Sam she'd stop. Kate thought Sam would understand why she had to continue with the investigation, but obviously she'd been wrong. She vowed to make things right with Sam after she got back.

Kate reclined her seat and closed her eyes. She was certain Fort Mac held the answers to solving this case. Ferenc and Tony had tried to blackmail Conor into running drugs up to Fort Mac. After his last visit to the northern city, Henry had rented the storage locker, and Bertrand, the author of the threatening letter, also lived there. And then there was Suzanne, who claimed she had information about Henry's final trip to Fort Mac. But when Kate last tried to call Suzanne, her number was out of service. She must have changed it.

Kate reflected on the day Henry was murdered, trying to remember exactly what they discussed during brunch. She had agreed to stay at the house while he was in Fort Mac. That's when he'd reminded her to lock the doors and set the alarm before leaving.

He must've known something was wrong at that point. But what? Why hadn't he confided in her? She wished she'd asked him more questions that day.

As they boarded the aircraft, Erik had confided that he hated planes. "Please don't ask me to talk. If I listen to music and distract myself with something to read, it makes it more bearable."

She hadn't known Erik was afraid of flying. It struck her how little she truly understood about his personal life, despite having worked with him—and slept with him. *That first kiss.* She shook her head, dispelling the memory. Not the right time or place. She glanced at his phone, curious about what he was listening to. Something decent, she hoped. She leaned closer and saw it was Vampire Weekend. Not bad. She tapped his open book. Erik looked up, removing one earphone.

"Sorry to bother you. Just curious to know what you're reading."

He used his index finger as a bookmark and flipped the book closed so she could read the front cover. *Nemesis* by Jo Nesbo. She smiled and gave him a thumbs-up. He replaced his earphone and resumed reading. Why would he want to read about murder after working on homicide cases all day?

After the flight landed, Kate bickered with Erik over who should drive the rental vehicle. Erik acquiesced, muttering something about women with control issues. Kate ignored him, certain she was the better driver.

Fort McMurray's downtown core reminded her of a grizzled oil worker wearing a new suit. Shiny new shops were interspersed with rugged frontier town offerings like the Gusher. Kate pulled the grey Toyota Corolla in front of the hotel. The exterior, clad with *faux* rock, a garish yellow neon sign and dusty windows, had seen better days. "Cheap and cheerless" was an apt description for the place. What had motivated Henry to stay here? He loved buildings and objects with character and history, but this hotel was plain ugly.

The lobby lived up to the promise on display outside: faded carpeting, a scuffed and battered front desk, and a musty scent in the air. A plump lady with a perm perched behind the counter, eyes darting back and forth between Kate and Erik, making sure that they wanted separate rooms on the same floor. "Sorry, thought you were a couple. On business, are ya?" she asked.

"Yes," said Erik, giving her a warm smile. She glowed at his attention and didn't ask any more questions.

They skipped the elevator and took the stairs to their second-floor rooms. Kate checked the mattress seams for bedbugs—none found. She set up the collapsible suitcase stand by the TV, though one leg wobbled. Still, it was safer than placing her bag on the threadbare carpet where all sorts of tiny crawly creatures could be lurking.

Curious about the clunking sounds in the hall, Kate poked her head out and saw a cleaner loading her cart. On a whim, Kate showed her a photo of Henry and asked if she recognized him, but the cleaner spoke very little English. Undeterred, Kate pointed to the walkie-talkie on the cart and asked, "Can I talk to the manager?" The cleaner picked up the two-way radio and spoke in another language—possibly Tagalog.

"Malou here soon," the cleaner told Kate and wheeled her cart down the hall. Kate leaned against the scuffed peach-coloured walls and waited.

Erik opened the door to his room. "What's up?" he asked.

Before Kate could respond, the elevator doors across from their rooms slid open and what she assumed to be the cleaning manager stepped out. The stout woman carried a two-way radio in each hand, and a ring of keys jingled at her waist. "You wanna talk?" she asked.

Kate showed her the photo of Henry. "Do you recognize him?" To their surprise, the manager nodded vigorously.

"I remember. Such a nice man. Always say hello and left a big tip." That sounded like Henry.

"Who're you?" she asked Kate.

"Henry's wife."

"Oh." Malou's demeanour changed. Her eyes darted every which way, trying to avoid eye contact.

"Kate, do you mind making that phone call now? I can finish up here," said Erik.

"Right. I'll do that. Thanks for your help," she said to Malou and went back into her room to wait for Erik.

Kate flicked on the TV, settled on a Food Network baking competition, and tried to concentrate on it. As the judges announced the winner, Erik knocked. She let him in. On screen, a young woman from Halifax jumped up and down and waved to her family in the audience.

“Good, I was rooting for her,” she said.

“What’s that?”

“Never mind. Trying to distract myself. What did Malou have to say? Something she didn’t want me to hear.”

Erik rubbed his temples. “Well…”

“Just break it to me.”

“The last time he was here, Malou saw Henry talking to one of the regulars at the bar downstairs. Malou described her as a thirty-something-year-old woman with short spiky black hair. They got into the elevator together.”

“What do you mean by a regular?”

He cleared his throat. “Sex worker.”

Right. Henry sleeping with a prostitute. She’d never expected that.

33

An hour later, they left to make an unannounced visit to the writer of the threat letter. When they got to the car, Erik held out his gloved hand. "Give me the keys."

Kate was too upset to argue. Henry wasn't the type to sleep with a prostitute, or so she thought, but what wife does? She knew from her work as a crime analyst that many johns were married with kids and their partners were clueless about their extracurricular activities.

Erik glanced over at her and then reversed the car out of the parking lot. "Let's refocus—decide how we're going to question Bertrand."

She sat quietly in the passenger seat as he navigated north through the city. Fort McMurray was still in the firm grip of winter and the roads were icy. They inched along over the bridge across the Athabasca River. Most residents drove trucks or vans, dwarfing their compact rental vehicle.

"Fucking hell," swore Erik. Kate smiled.

"What?" he said.

"You rarely swear. Are you okay?"

"I feel so damn claustrophobic in this tiny vehicle. And you usually do enough swearing for both of us."

Very true.

As they drove, signs advertising new developments lined both sides of the road. They stopped in front of a recently built two-storey house on the town's outskirts.

"He lives here?" asked Erik.

"Fancy house for someone like him," said Kate. She'd assumed Bertrand didn't have much money. In addition to writing for various left-wing blogs and websites, the political science graduate worked at a local electronics store. And even though the oil boom had slowed down, rents and housing prices were still astronomical.

They rang the bell and a woman in her early thirties holding an infant answered the door. Erik flashed his badge, surprising Kate. He should've handed it in when he was suspended. "Hello, Miss, we'd like to speak with Bertrand Mickleford."

"Oh, he rents the garage around back. Has he done something?"

They assured her that it was nothing serious, explaining they just had a few questions related to a case. She gave them a tight smile and shut the door. They followed a well-trodden path to the backyard.

"Why do you still have your badge?" asked Kate.

Erik had a guilty look on his face. "It's an old expired one. Never got around to turning it in and thought it'd come in handy on our trip."

Kate knocked on the garage door. She could hear someone moving around inside but no one answered.

"Bertrand, we know you're in there." Erik raised his voice. "I'm Sergeant Jorgensen of the Edmonton Police and my partner Kate Heaney."

"We need to talk to you about the letter you wrote to Professor Henry Franzen," said Kate.

The door slowly opened to reveal a skinny man in his late twenties with pale, almost translucent skin and short black hair. He had the pinched, myopic look of someone who spends long periods of time in front of a computer screen. He narrowed his eyes and stared at Kate.

"You look familiar," he said.

"Can we come in?" asked Kate.

Bertrand sighed and opened the door wider. "When I heard Dr. Franzen had been killed, I figured it wouldn't take long before you tracked down the"—he flexed his fingers in quotation marks—"crazy environmental activist."

Bertrand gazed past them, prompting Erik and Kate to turn and see what had caught his attention. In the upper window, the woman from the house was watching, still holding her infant. Bertrand waved to her and said, "Come on in. I don't want the landlady thinking I'm some sort of criminal. I can't afford to rent anywhere else in this godforsaken city."

They followed him into his cramped quarters. The garage had been converted into a rental unit, with a small kitchen at one end and a twin bed at the other. Every bit of wall space was covered with photographs and articles about oil sands projects—aerial shots of tailings ponds, the maze of above-ground pipes transporting bitumen to storage facilities, and images of industrial-looking buildings.

"Have a seat." He gestured to the couch next to the entrance. Erik perched on the arm and Kate brushed crumbs off the cushion before she sat down.

"I've just boiled the kettle. Anyone for tea?"

They both refused the offer and watched as he added a heaping spoonful of loose-leaf into a tea ball strainer and plunked it in a chipped mug full of freshly boiled water. Bertrand carried the mug in one hand and used his other to drag over a chair from the kitchen table.

"Ah, now I know who you are." He jutted his chin toward Kate. "You're the wife. I read somewhere that you worked for the police." He sat down on the chair. "What do you want to know?"

"Why did you write the letter to the professor?" asked Erik.

"Too many scientists are taking oil industry money, compromising their work. The professor was a sell-out. He'd made a deal with the devil."

Bertrand rose and crossed to the wall of photographs, launching into his philosophy. The longer he spoke, the more animated he became. Kate's head ached; she struggled to listen.

"Bitumen extraction uses arsenic and mercury and tons of water. What's left is a toxic slurry dumped into tailings ponds. Millions of migratory birds fly through this region. Some land on those ponds and die. Henry's work to keep them away just prolongs the use of tailings ponds. We need to shut them down entirely."

Every so often he'd yank a photograph from the wall waving it for emphasis.

They let him vent. When he stopped talking, Erik started grilling him. "Why the anonymity? If you believe in this, why not put your name behind it?"

Bertrand returned to his chair. "Scare tactics work, they get people to back off. I was hoping to intimidate him, make him think twice." He dunked the tea ball several times. The scent of ginger and fennel filled the air. "It's scarier if you don't know where the threat is coming from. Besides, I didn't want to get a visit from the police."

He pulled out the tea ball and set it beside his cup. "But I guess that didn't work out too well."

"Henry was back in town in mid-February. Did you talk to him then?" asked Erik.

Bertrand took a sip of tea before answering. "I followed him to the Gusher parking lot. I was going to talk to him, but a woman beat me to it. They spoke for a few minutes and then she got in his car, and they drove off."

Kate leaned forward. "What did this woman look like?"

Bertrand looked over at Erik and then back to Kate. "I could be wrong, but I think she was, and I'll use the politically correct phrase, a 'sex worker.' She had long blonde hair, which looked like a wig, and a pink fluffy coat."

"How old?" asked Erik.

"She looked really young. Maybe even underage. Sorry." He glanced at Kate, his eyes filled with pity, which made the situation even more humiliating. "A lot of men behave up here in ways they'd never consider back home," he added.

The last thing Kate wanted was sympathy from the likes of him. She changed the topic. "How did you learn about Henry's work in the first place?"

"Not sure." He took another sip of tea.

She was about to accuse him of lying when Erik touched her shoulder. He wanted to handle this. "Can you tell me where you were on Saturday, February 28th," he asked

Bertrand slumped in his chair. "Listen, I know this doesn't look good. I was in Edmonton that weekend. Our group held a day-long strategy meeting."

"And what was discussed? asked Erik.

Bertrand squirmed. his face shiny with perspiration. "Look, paying celebrities like Leonardo DiCaprio to fly in and denounce the oil sands doesn't work. More extreme measures are needed to stop the expansion."

Kate and Erik exchanged glances. Bertrand had tried to confront Henry during his last visit to Fort Mac. He was also in Edmonton the weekend of Henry's murder to meet with a group of like-minded environmental extremists.

Erik crossed the room in three strides and stopped in front of Bertrand. "What kind of measures?"

Bertrand took a slow sip of tea.

He's stalling, Kate thought.

Erik grabbed the mug out of Bertrand's hand. Tea sloshed onto the floor.

Bertrand cowered in his seat. "Look, it was all talk. We weren't going to follow through on these things, okay?"

Erik set the mug down hard on the table beside him and loomed over Bertrand. "You need to tell me exactly what was discussed and who was there."

Bertrand used the back of his thumb to wipe off the sweat above his lips. "Okay, okay. We talked about sabotage."

"Define sabotage." said Erik. His voice sharp.

"Physically damaging the pipelines or equipment, hacking into their servers to spread viruses, that type of thing," said Bertrand. "For the record, I disagreed with those methods. Too much chance of things going wrong and causing more environmental damage."

"What methods did you advocate? Killing people?" said Erik.

"No way! We didn't kill Henry. We only wanted to threaten him and his partner. That's why I wrote the letter."

"Who brought up the idea of hacking the servers?" said Erik.

Bertrand shook his head. "I'm not going to name names, but we have a few guys who are computer geniuses. Like, they even do stuff as part of Anonymous."

Kate raised her eyebrows. Anonymous was a loose online collective that prided itself on embarrassing corporations and governments. "You're one of them, aren't you?" she asked. "You work at an electronics store. You must know your way around a computer."

Bertrand snorted. "I know a few things, but I'm not in the same league as those guys."

Erik pulled out his notepad and pen and set them down on the kitchen table. "Give me the names of everyone at this meeting." Bertrand hesitated, then crossed to the table and wrote down a list of names.

He'd caved in quickly under pressure, thought Kate.

Erik picked up the notepad and examined it. "You claim you didn't kill Henry. So who did? Was it someone on this list?" he asked, waving the notepad in the air.

Bertrand wiped his forehead. The armpits of his shirt were stained with sweat. "Like I said, we're just talk and no action. I don't think any of these guys would commit murder."

"You wrote a threatening letter." Erik reminded Bertrand. "That was action."

"Yeah, but it's a long way from murder."

"What time did the meeting end, and where did everyone go after that?"

"We met Saturday morning at Aaron's. The others left after lunch, not sure where they went. Aaron and I spent the rest of the day playing video games, then I crashed at his place."

Kate did the math. Henry had been killed in the afternoon and his body was dumped in the field around 10:00 pm. It fitted the time frame. Could someone on the list be responsible?

"Is there anyone besides your friend who could verify you were at Aaron's?" asked Erik.

Bertrand thought for a moment. "Yes, actually! Aaron's girlfriend showed up mid-afternoon. She was pissed he wasn't answering her texts. I answered the door 'cause Aaron was busy on the PlayStation."

"What did she say?"

"She told me to tell Aaron it was over. She was sick of him ignoring her, that he paid more attention to gaming and activism than her. The thing is, Aaron already had his eye on some other enviro chick, so he was kind of relieved. He's the good-looking one."

"We will need her number as well."

Bertrand shrugged. "Fine. I'll track it down for you."

Erik handed back the notepad and pen. "One more thing. Write down the name of the person who told you about Professor Henry Franzen's research work."

"Oh, man, she's going to kill me," groaned Bertrand. "I'm not saying that literally," he added when he saw the look on their faces.

Kate looked over his shoulder as he wrote down the name: Suzanne Morton. *Why the hell was her old friend involved with Bertrand and his buddies?*

34

On their way back to the hotel, they stopped at a Chinese takeout with decent online reviews. Erik dashed inside the restaurant to pick up their order while Kate remained in the idling rental car.

She found herself wondering how Suzanne had gotten mixed up with the likes of Bertrand and his eco-gang. After her friend got the job at the environmental think tank, she had become more strident in her beliefs. But associating with a group that advocated violence was a whole other level. Kate thought back to the day of Henry's funeral when Suzanne had approached her at the gravesite to offer condolences. She'd wanted to talk, but the first time they'd arrange to meet, Kate had to rush to Northern Ireland to chase after her brother, and the second time, Kate had been recovering in hospital from the home invasion. And now Suzanne's number was out of service.

Erik returned, holding two large paper bags. "We ordered too much."

"We need to track down Suzanne," said Kate. Her friend had some explaining to do.

Back at the hotel, they carried the takeout to Erik's so-called suite, which was slightly larger than Kate's room. In addition to a queen bed, the suite featured a small table with chairs, a mini-fridge, and a sink. They dug into the oily food and reviewed their visit with Bertrand.

"Do you think he could've killed Henry?" asked Kate.

"Doubt it, but we need to talk to the others in his group. If they're involved in Anonymous, and talked about more extreme measures, we have to take it seriously."

"But why would they bug my phone and stage a home invasion to steal the storage locker key?" asked Kate.

Erik snatched a piece of broccoli with his chopsticks. "No idea. Maybe Henry got his hands on some incriminating evidence about a planned attack by the group?" He popped the morsel into his mouth. "They probably have the technical skills to do it." He tucked into a spring roll and then helped himself to some noodles. "Why aren't you eating?"

She crinkled up her nose. "Lost my appetite." *How could Henry sleep with a prostitute?*

"I know what you're thinking, but don't jump to conclusions," he said.

"Easier said than done." Kate reflected on the happier days she shared with Henry during their marriage and wondered if he had been involved with prostitutes at that time.

"For all we know, he was just questioning them."

"What do you mean by 'them'?" asked Kate. "You think there was more than one?"

Erik rested his chopsticks across a plastic bowl of wonton soup. "Yes. We have two distinct descriptions. The cleaner described her as a woman in her late thirties with short black hair. Bertrand described her as blonde and underage."

After dinner, Kate returned to her hotel room to change for the bar. She dressed in jeans, a plain black tank top and cowboy boots. After she was done, she headed back to Erik's suite. He was standing in the middle of the room ironing a T-shirt, wearing only a pair of fitted jeans that showed off his muscled torso. He flashed a smile. "Sorry, needed to get out the wrinkles."

"I'll just meet you there." She stumbled over the threshold as she hurried out of the room. Too dangerous to stay and watch him.

The bar's inhabitants stared as she walked into the dimly lit room. She was tall and female in a town where men outnumbered women ten to one. The place was a packed and noisy multicultural hub. The oil industry attracted workers from around the world. Big wages in a city in the middle of nowhere meant money for drugs, drinks, and women.

She sat on a bar stool and ordered a glass of house red from the bartender. A group of Chinese businessmen sat at a booth in the corner, speaking Mandarin and drinking Scotch. Young males with baseball caps on backwards flirted with the scantily clad servers. On the far side of the room, apart from the main crowd, a gang of noisy bikers played darts. A few sported black leather jackets, others wore vests with Fort Raiders badges on the back. Kate thought back to the night Ferenc had shown up in her living room. He'd said that Henry had asked about the Fort Raiders. What if Ferenc had been telling her the truth?

One of the men, lean and tall, with a greying beard and skull tattoo on his neck, broke off from the group and headed her way. She regretted not waiting for Erik. He sidled up to her and said, "Can I buy you a drink?"

She showed him her glass. "Thanks, but I already have one."

"You have some impressive long legs, woman," he said, putting his hand on her thigh.

You've got to be kidding me. His buddies watched to see what would happen next. "Move your fucking hand—now!" she snapped. With her black belt in judo, she was confident she could take him down, but then she'd have to contend with his friends.

"Oh, she's feisty." He laughed, withdrawing his hand from her leg. "Just giving you a compliment."

Kate held his gaze, willing herself not to look shaken, lifting her chin in defiance.

"Whatever, lady." He rolled his eyes and rejoined his friends. They erupted in laughter. A couple of them nudged their buddy, teasing him about Kate's brush-off. He shrugged them away with a scowl, grabbed a dart and hurled it at the board.

Her hand trembled as she picked up her wineglass to take a sip. That could've been much worse.

"Sorry for that," the bartender said quietly to Kate. He sported a sleeve of tattoos and multiple piercings. "Jeff and his friends are regulars here and know the owners. It's a bit of a tightrope trying to keep the peace, if you know what I mean."

"It's not your fault." She took a deep breath, then seized her chance: "There's a woman who comes in here often, dark spiky hair. Do you know if she's open to seeing couples?"

Before the bartender could respond, a server shouted out a drink order, pulling him away. He turned to the bar and began pouring beer into a pint glass, then concocted a cocktail with rum and fruit juice.

Erik plunked down beside her. "I saw the tail end of your encounter with the biker. Well handled." Registering her tense expression, he added, "Sorry if I was too flippant. You okay?"

"I can't stand guys like that." She set down her glass. "And this wine tastes like vinegar!"

Erik caught the bartender's attention and ordered a beer. After pouring the drink, the bartender scribbled something on a napkin and surreptitiously slid it to Kate before leaving. She glanced down at it: *Crystal. Room 321.*

Erik downed his beer and set forty dollars on the counter. "Thanks. No need for change," he said, clearly tipping for the bartender's help with the room number. He wrapped an arm around Kate's waist, glancing over his shoulder as they left the bar together. She sensed the stares, but no one followed. They entered the stairwell, which smelled of *faux*-citrus-scented carpet cleaner and wet dog, and climbed to the third floor. They located her room and Erik knocked on the door.

"Who is it?" asked a woman through the closed door.

"Hello, Crystal," Eric replied. "The bartender gave us your name."

She opened the door and studied them. Long fake eyelashes and heavy make-up failed to hide the dark circles under her eyes and the wrinkles around her lips. Crystal patted her shag haircut. "A couple will cost you double."

Did Henry really have sex with her? Kate grabbed onto Erik's arm. "I can't do this," she whispered.

Erik pulled her into the room and closed the door behind him. "Double is fine," he said to Crystal.

Crystal held out her hand. "Let's see the money upfront."

Erik pulled out a bunch of twenty-dollar bills from his wallet and handed them to her. She tilted her head towards the bed, and they perched on the edge while she counted the money. Once satisfied, she tucked it away in a side-table drawer.

"What do you want?" she asked.

"We'd like to ask you some questions," said Kate. She pulled out a photo of Henry from her clutch bag. "Do you recognize him?"

Crystal's eyes widened and she shot a look up at the ceiling. They followed her gaze.

Damn. Was there a security camera or listening device hidden in the fire alarm?

"Get out—now! Or I'll start screaming."

Kate reached out her hand. "Please, I didn't mean to scare you. We need your help. He was my husband."

Crystal crossed her arms and looked away.

"Sorry to bother you, ma'am," Erik said, grabbing Kate by the elbow and pulling her out of the room. As Crystal slammed the door shut, he hissed, "Quick, give me one of your business cards."

What the hell is he up to? Kate pulled one out of her wallet. He snatched it from her hand, pushed it under Crystal's door and then briskly walked away. Kate rushed to catch up with him.

"Wait. What are you—" Erik shook his head and put a finger to his lips.

When they entered Erik's room on the second floor, he systematically checked for hidden devices—looking under lampshades and the bed, then using his multi-tool to unscrew the light switches and electrical outlets for a closer inspection. He dragged a chair from the kitchenette, stood on it, and examined the fire sprinkler. Afterwards, he turned on the radio, tuned it to a country music station, and sat down on the couch. She sat down beside him.

He whispered in her ear. "You saw the camera in her room? Kate nodded. "That type can record audio as well. Don't think there's any in here but just to be safe, let's make it look like we're whispering sweet nothings to each other." He grinned but she couldn't bring herself to smile.

"What the hell is going on, Erik?" she hissed.

"I'm not sure."

"Crystal looked really scared when she saw Henry's photo. And she kept looking up at the camera."

"Yes. Two possible reasons the camera was installed in the room. It could be there for her safety, or…"

He paused and she finished his thought. "Blackmail."

The bartender had said the Fort Raiders in the bar were friends with the owner. What if the gang was running the bar or the entire hotel? She narrowed her eyes. "Do you think they were blackmailing Henry because he slept with Crystal?"

"Maybe. Sorry." He rubbed his hands together, looking more excited than sorry. He was in detective mode, and they'd just uncovered some sketchy activity.

What if Ferenc had been telling her the truth—that Henry had asked him about the Fort Raiders? And if he'd told the truth about that, what did that mean? Could he have also been telling the truth when he said neither he nor Tony had killed Henry? She shivered and shifted her body closer to Erik. "Why did you give Crystal my business card? Do you really think she'll contact me?"

"Yes, she might, when she feels it's safe."

Kate checked the time. Midnight. She leaned closer and spoke softly. "Shall we call Brenda or Jeremy? See if they can find out who owns the hotel?"

Erik shook his head and whispered into her ear. "Too risky to call in the room. Let's get some rest and wake up early, make those calls from the car."

His soft voice sent tingles down her spine. "I'm too wired to sleep."

"How about some TV?" Erik stretched out on the bed and pressed the power button on the remote.

She had something else in mind. She opened the mini-bar and selected four tiny bottles of vodka. She unscrewed the caps and offered one to Erik. He smiled and tapped the side of her bottle with his. "Cheers."

She downed the vodka and said, "I'll be right back."

In the bathroom, she soaked a washcloth with cold water and rinsed it out. She sat next to him on the bed, cloth in hand.

"You okay?" he asked.

"Would you mind pressing this against my bruised ribs?" she asked. "It helps reduce the swelling."

"Are you sure?" he asked, his breath getting shallower.

Henry had moved on, so why couldn't she? She whispered in his ear. "Yes."

Erik set down his drink, gently pulled off her tank top and dropped it on the floor. Kate had a fleeting thought about bed bugs in hotel carpets, but his gaze pulled her back to the moment. He held the cold cloth against her torso and gazed at her breasts in her lacy black bra. "After I'm done with the cloth, shall I put your shirt back on?"

Kate shook her head. "No."

35

Kate woke to the ping of a text and reached over to the side table, cringing at the sharp pain. Fuck. Forgot about the ribs. She looked at her phone. A text from Crystal: Not safe to talk now. Janelle will get in touch.

Who's Janelle?

Erik stirred next to her and stretched. Kate showed him the message.

"Might as well get up now and make those calls." He swung his legs out of bed. "What time is our meeting with Tecktronic?" he asked.

She rubbed her eyes. "Ten o'clock."

Erik buttoned the shirt he'd ironed and laid out the previous evening. "We should get ready for that now, just in case."

Kate groaned. They'd only had a couple hours of sleep, and the vodka hadn't helped. She dragged herself to the shower. By the time she got out, Erik had retrieved her suitcase from her room and had set it on the bed. "We should stay together for safety reasons," he said. Kate wasn't going to argue. Biker gangs and surveillance cameras. What was going on in this hotel?

She gripped the towel wrapped around her torso with one hand and unzipped her bag with the other. How awkward. She selected her clothing and went back to the bathroom to change. She pulled on black leggings, a tunic, and her favourite booties with a two-inch heel. When she emerged from the bathroom, Erik gave her an admiring look.

"I love that you wear heels," he said.

"Why wouldn't I?"

He kissed her on the lips. "Good point."

Kate had reached her full height by the age of sixteen. Like many self-conscious teenagers, she'd slouched in a futile effort to make herself less conspicuous. It was her short, tough volleyball coach that said, "Fuck what people think. Own your height. Use it to your advantage."

Kate had taken that advice to heart.

Concluding it was too risky to make calls in the room, they drove to the nearest twenty-four-hour Tim Hortons for takeout coffee and settled back in the car with the motor running and heater cranked. Erik called Jeremy and put him on speaker phone. He answered on the second ring and sounded alert for the early morning hour. "I haven't gone to bed yet."

Kate could hear laughter in the background. "Where are you?" she asked.

"With someone."

Guess he'd moved on as well. Her poor brother. "We need your help. Can you go somewhere private?"

"Hang on." They waited until Jeremy gave the all-clear before they filled him in on what had happened in Fort McMurray.

"We suspect the Gusher Hotel and Bar is run by the Fort Raiders, but we need to get a name, find out who's in charge," said Erik.

"I'm on it, but I have to tell you, if they're as organized as it sounds, they'll hide behind a numbered corporate entity. It may be difficult to get a name, but I bet Brenda could help."

"How?" asked Kate.

"You said they had cameras in the rooms, right? Well, Brenda knows most of those guys that sell corporate surveillance equipment. Bet she could convince them to share information about the owners."

"Thanks, Jeremy. We'll call her next," said Erik.

Unlike Jeremy, Brenda had been fast asleep and wasn't too pleased about being woken up at five in the morning. "Couldn't you have waited?"

"Sorry." Kate explained what they needed.

"I'll ask around. Can't promise anything. By the way, thanks for giving me the heads-up you two were suspended," she said.

Shit. She'd forgotten to share that information with her friend. "Sorry. Who told you?"

"Detective Wong," Brenda snorted. "Watch out, Erik. Somehow, she's found out you're in Fort Mac. She's pretty pissed. And Kate—she told Alma that you've been suspended."

Double shit. That was supposed to stay under wraps until they got back home. Her mom must be furious. "Thanks for the warning," said Kate. She planned to avoid her mother's calls.

"Are you two sure you know what you're doing?" asked Brenda. "I don't want you to end up dead like Henry."

No, not really, is what Kate wanted to say. "Don't worry, Brenda. Erik's got my back."

"Right. Well, I'll let Alma know I spoke with you."

Next, Kate texted her daughter: Learning some interesting things up here. Don't worry about what Christina Wong said. I'm fine. Love you.

Sam responded immediately. What was she doing up so early? Grannys mad, me 2. U cld lose yr job!

A police car, lights flashing, pulled up alongside them in the parking lot.

"Get rid of Crystal's text," said Erik.

In her haste, Kate dropped the phone and it landed by the brake pedal. Bloody hell. She strained to reach it.

"Hurry."

She managed to pick it up and erase the message before the officer rapped on the driver's side window. Kate lowered it and a stern-faced policeman shone a flashlight in her face. "Hello, officer. Can I help you?" she asked.

"Please step out of the car," he demanded.

"Why?"

Erik touched her arm. "Careful, Kate. Do as he says."

They undid their seat belts and got out. The shock of cold air took Kate's breath away. She reached back inside to grab her coat when a second, more junior officer got out of the patrol car and shouted, "Don't move."

She raised her arms, parka in one hand, phone in the other. The junior officer grabbed the arm with the phone and snatched it away from her.

"You can't do that," shouted Kate, rubbing the red mark left on her forearm. Tears stung her eyes.

The officers handcuffed them and roughly pushed them into the back of the police car. Kate cried out as pain shot through her ribs.

"We're taking you to the station," said the senior officer.

Erik leaned closer to Kate and whispered, "You okay?"

She bit her lip. "Yeah."

"Don't worry, it'll all get straightened out."

Kate wasn't so sure about that. The officers had no grounds to seize her phone or hold them, but they'd done it anyway.

After a brief drive, they were led into the station and left alone in an interview room. "Not the place to talk," warned Erik.

After what seemed to be an interminable amount of time, the officers sauntered into the room. "Sorry to keep you waiting."

Kate folded her arms. They didn't look very sorry.

"What you're doing is illegal," Erik said. "Charge us with something or let us go free."

"We have reason to suspect you two are engaged in police work without the proper authority," said the senior officer.

So that's what it was all about. "We're here as private citizens," she said.

"You've been misleading people."

"Not true," Erik responded.

The junior officer who'd taken Kate's phone piped up, "That's not what Mickleford told us."

The senior officer shot him a withering look. It was clear he wasn't meant to reveal that detail.

"You're going to take the word of that man?" said Kate, wondering how they'd found out about Bertrand. "Unbelievable."

The senior officer fixed them with a stern look. "My advice? Leave town as soon as possible."

Erik spoke firmly. "Unless you have valid grounds to charge us, I insist that you let us go."

Kate added, "And I want my phone back."

A plainclothes detective entered the room and signalled to the officers to join him. They huddled near the door, speaking quietly so Kate couldn't make out their conversation. The patrol officers' faces turned red, and the junior officer pulled Kate's phone from his pocket, handing it to the detective. She walked over to Kate, handed her phone, and said, "You're free to go."

Outside, Erik called for a taxi to take them back to their rental car. Kate zipped up her parka. "What the hell was that all about?"

"Not sure," Erik replied. "Those patrol officers weren't playing by the rules."

A few minutes later, a taxi drove past them, slammed on the brakes, and paused for a moment before backing up. Kate realized she'd been holding her breath, worried he'd take off. As they climbed into the back seat, the driver studied them carefully in the rear-view mirror, likely assessing the risk of picking up two strangers outside a police station at this early hour.

"Where to?" he asked.

"Tim Hortons off Hardin Street," said Kate.

On the ride back to their rental car, they discussed what'd happened. "Who alerted the local police we were here? Christina?" whispered Kate.

Erik shook his head. "No way."

"Maybe the inspector? But how did he find out?"

They looked at each other and said in unison, "Miles."

But Kate thought there was more to it than that. Why had the patrol officers seized her phone and hauled them in? What were they looking for? Whatever it was, it hadn't been sanctioned. The plainclothes detective had ordered her phone returned. Could they be crooked cops? If so, who were they working for? And what about Miles? How did he know they were in Fort Mac? Was he tracking them? And why? So far, their trip up north had only added to their long list of questions.

The taxi pulled into the coffee shop's parking lot where a black Mercedes-Benz sedan with tinted windows sat idling next to their rental car. The taxi driver's eyes darted to the sedan and back at them. God knows what he was thinking. As soon as Kate and Erik stepped out, he sped away.

The window of the sedan rolled down. In the back seat, a middle-aged Asian man in business attire greeted them. "Good morning, Kate and Erik," he said, his voice carrying a Chinese accent. He looked familiar to Kate. Where had she seen him before?

"Join me," he said, patting the seat beside him. "I have some information that might prove useful to you."

36

Erik climbed into the back of the sedan. *What the hell?* Kate had been ready to turn and run. She peered inside. The man pulled open the front armrest to reveal a small cabinet containing crystal glasses and a bottle of Scotch. "Would either of you like a drink?"

She shrugged. "Sure."

Crazy. Getting into a stranger's car. In the dark. No witnesses. And yet, she reasoned, if he was going to harm them, why would he sit beside them in the back seat? And offer a drink? Maybe he planned to poison them?

She squeezed in beside Erik and accepted a glass of Scotch. The man poured one for himself as well. Kate waited until he took the first sip before she tried hers.

The man bowed his head in greeting. "My name is Mr. Lam."

Now she remembered where she'd seen him. "You were at the Gusher yesterday evening with some of your associates."

"Yes. Very observant. I am told you are an excellent analyst."

How did he know about her? Businessman, my ass. She'd recently read how foreign governments were infiltrating private companies and stealing proprietary information. Maybe that was his game.

Getting straight to the point, Erik asked, "What do you want?"

Mr. Lam handed him a file folder. "I came across some information that may be of help in your investigation."

"Why are you sharing it with us?" asked Kate.

"If you solve your case," he said, "it will be of benefit to my company."

Erik shuffled through the papers and then handed them to Kate.

She quickly looked through them. Financial documents. "Are these Tecktronic's?"

"Yes," said Mr. Lam.

"How did you get them?"

He ignored her question and consulted his Rolex watch. Their cue to leave. She downed the rest of her Scotch. "Thank you for the information and the drink." They got out of the sedan and clambered back into the rental. Kate bumped her forehead on the door frame. Why the hell hadn't they rented a bigger vehicle?

Erik rubbed her thigh. "You okay?"

She brushed his hand off her leg and turned on the ignition. "Fine. Just tired." She was clumsy at the best of times, and the lack of sleep made it worse. She checked the dashboard clock. 7:00 am. No chance to get any more rest. They had too much to do before their morning meeting with the Tecktronic executives.

"You want me to drive?" Erik asked. "Remember, you've also had a drink."

She ignored his comment and pulled out of the parking lot.

At the hotel, they packed their suitcases and checked out. The front desk lady patted her permed hair and smiled at Erik. "Hope you enjoyed your stay at the Gusher."

Kate pulled onto the highway and drove north of the city towards Tecktronic. She tried to figure out how an eco-activist, a prostitute working out of a bar run by a biker gang, a Chinese spy, and two dirty cops were connected. "What the hell did Henry get mixed up in?"

Erik was reading the financial documents Mr. Lam had given them. He looked up. "Bit of a puzzle."

Kate wasn't sure if he meant Henry's death or what was inside the file folder. "Can you make any sense of those papers?"

"They're a bunch of spreadsheets listing the funds coming in and going out of Tecktronic." He pulled out his cellphone and took a photo of each page. "What does Tecktronic do?" he asked.

"They provide tailings pond management consulting services to oil sands companies."

"What does that mean?"

Kate snorted. "Not exactly sure. All I know is that Tecktronic is funding Henry and Michael's research and got them access to a tailings pond."

"Why do they need a pond?"

"They're testing a new way to keep migratory birds from landing on the toxic pits. Why do you ask?"

"The big numbers here don't make sense." He typed out a message on his phone. "I'm sending the photos to a forensic accountant friend of mine."

As they drove northward, the boreal forest gave way to an industrial landscape: barbed-wire-topped chain-link fences with "Keep Out" signs, mazes of pipes and steaming smokestacks, and glimpses of snow-covered tailings ponds.

They pulled up in front of Tecktronic's gates and the security guard waved them through. A grove of spruce trees buffered the nondescript metal-clad building from the stark landscape.

Erik's phone rang. "It's the forensic accountant. That was quick!"

"But they're waiting for us inside."

"Go on without me. Tell them I had to take a call."

Kate stepped out of the car and buzzed to gain entrance to the building. The receptionist led her to the boardroom. On the far wall, an enormous landscape painting of rolling foothills dotted with oil wells caught Kate's eye.

"Impressive, isn't it?"

Startled, she spun around.

A lean, well-dressed man with a toothy smile stuck out his hand. "Sorry. Didn't mean to surprise you. I'm Lyle Sabey, the chief financial officer."

As she shook his hand, he gave her an appraising look. She met his gaze, noting his unusual grey-blue eyes. Instead of averting his gaze, Lyle winked at her. Of all the nerve. Before she could respond, a cherubic-looking man sauntered into the room. "Kate, so nice to meet you. I'm Charles Mayberry, president of Tecktronic."

"Thanks for taking the time to talk with me. Detective Jorgensen had to take a work call and said to go on without him." As they settled around a glass-topped table, Kate surreptitiously pressed record on her cellphone.

Charles offered his condolences. "We're shocked by what happened to Henry."

"Thank you," said Kate.

"How can we help?" asked Lyle.

"I'm retracing Henry's steps in the weeks before he died. Why did he come up here in mid-February to meet with you?"

"We had to discuss logistics for their field research," said Lyle. "We don't own the tailings pond; we are contracted to maintain it, so we had to negotiate access times with the oil company."

"Did Henry seem off or behave differently?" asked Kate.

Lyle shifted in his seat. Charles shook his head no. "Just the same old Henry."

"Did he tell you about the letter?"

The executives glanced at one another. "What letter?" asked Lyle.

"It warned Henry against taking your company's money, calling it a deal with the devil."

Lyle let out a loud, sharp laugh. "Typical. Here we are, doing the right things, investing in research to save birds, and they still target us."

Arrogant ass. "Do you know a Mr. Lam?" she asked.

Charles had a puzzled look on his face. He didn't seem to recognize the name. Lyle folded his arms across his chest and replied, "Mr. Lam wants to invest in our company, but we're not interested. I don't trust him."

"I'm curious—why did you fund Henry and Michael's research?"

Charles smiled. "As you can tell," he said, pointing to his grey hair, "I'm close to retirement, but that doesn't mean I have antiquated ideas about the oil industry. We need to change to survive, and that means working with people like your husband to improve our industry's environmental record."

Kate thanked the executives for meeting with her. Charles leaned forward and gently patted her hand. "Take care, Kate," he said. Tears filled her eyes, but she quickly blinked them away.

On the drive to the airport, Kate played the recording of her conversation with the Tecktronic executives. "Not much to it," she said. "The president was pleasant, but that CFO, Lyle Sabey, creeped me out."

"Good intuition," said Erik. "Looks like Lyle might be cooking the books."

He filled her in on his phone call with the accountant. "Didn't quite understand it all— something about the same person in charge of accounts payable and receivable. My friend says that makes it easy to steal money from a company, or launder funds through it."

Kate thought through the implications. If Henry had discovered Lyle was defrauding Tecktronic, that could explain why he'd been murdered.

"I know what you're thinking," said Erik, "but proving it is another matter. I did some digging; turns out Lyle was attending an oil industry conference in Texas, along with the company president, the day Henry was killed."

"Lyle could've hired some people to do his dirty work, but you're right, how do we prove it? We'd have to find out who he hired. Damn. We're back to square one."

They returned their rental car and entered the new terminal, funded with oil sands money. Riding the escalator to departures, Kate admired the pine beam ceiling and the glowing northern lights mural. In the departures lounge, Erik resumed their earlier conversation: "There's another possibility. What if Mr. Lam faked the documents to distract us?"

"Why?"

"I'm pretty sure he works for the Chinese government. Maybe he's trying to infiltrate Tecktronic. It'd be a good way to get backdoor access to big oil companies."

"How does that lead to Henry's murder?" asked Kate.

"Maybe Henry found out what Mr. Lam was up to."

Kate didn't know what to think. Would the Chinese government resort to murder on foreign soil? It seemed unlikely. But then again, nothing was simple or straightforward about this case.

37

At the Edmonton terminal, the automatic doors to arrivals slid open and Jeremy greeted them with a wide smile. Kate and Erik wheeled their carry-on suitcases over to him. "I take it you have some news for us?" Kate asked.

Before he could reply, the doors opened again and a group of noisy men with stubbly faces strode out, reeking of beer. They wore work boots and carried duffel bags slung over their shoulders—oil patch workers, buoyed by their leave after gruellingly long work shifts.

"Let's talk at Northern Shipping," said Jeremy. "Brenda's waiting for us there."

They hurried to the parking lot and got in Jeremy's car. At the payment booth, Erik handed over his credit card.

Jeremy shook his head. "My treat. I'm the one with the job."

Kate laughed and Erik rolled his eyes. "Thanks for the reminder."

No one spoke during the short drive to the warehouse, which was only a few minutes from the airport. Brenda stood waiting in front of one of the loading bays. Northern Shipping operated a fleet of courier trucks, along with offices and a dispatch room.

Kate got out of the car and gave her a hug.

"I have a surprise for you," said Brenda.

Kate followed Brenda down a beige hallway toward the offices, noticing how the drab decor had barely changed since Brenda and Conor first opened the business fifteen years ago.

Brenda opened one of the office doors. Inside, Conor leapt to his feet, fists clenched, but relaxed immediately when he saw Kate. "Glad it's you and not the police coming to arrest me," he said.

"What the hell are you doing here?" Checking behind her to make sure Erik wasn't around, she added. "You're going to end up in jail."

"I had to come back after what happened to you and Sam."

"I'm surprised they didn't arrest you coming off the plane," Erik said. Conor spun around to face him.

Erik lifted his hands in surrender. "Don't worry, I'm not going to tell. But I'm not sure how you got out of the airport. Your passport should've been flagged by border security"

"I think it was, but they still let me go."

Jeremy stuck his head in the room. "After he made it through customs, he called me from a payphone. I told him they probably let him pass on purpose—so they could follow him and see who he led them to.

Christina Wong must still consider him the prime suspect, Kate thought. "Do you think they followed you here?"

Conor grinned. "No, I lost the tail."

Brenda gathered a motley selection of chairs in a circle. "You two go first," she said to Kate and Erik. "Update us on Fort Mac."

They took turns recounting the events of the past two days and were met with stunned silence. Brenda took a sip of her takeout coffee and said, "So let me get this straight—eco-activists, a Chinese spy, the CFO of Tecktronic, or an organized crime gang may be responsible for Henry's murder? Oh, and there might be dirty cops involved."

"Yup, that's about it," Kate said, rubbing her temples as a headache throbbed behind her eyes. The situation reminded her of Agatha Christie's novel, *Murder on the Orient Express*, where the passengers conspired together to commit a crime. Maybe that's what's going on here—why it's being so hard to identify the person responsible for Henry's murder.

Jeremy whistled. "Crazy."

Conor shook his head in disbelief. "No way he slept with sex workers."

"I'm not sure about that," said Kate. "The cleaner at the hotel was under the impression he did. And when we showed Crystal his photo, she recognized him."

"Any word from this Janelle?" asked Brenda.

"Not yet."

Jeremy and Brenda exchanged glances.

"What is it?" asked Erik.

"Found out from my security alarm contact that a company called RMS Holdings owns the Gusher," said Brenda.

Kate leapt out of her seat. “RMS was written on the piece of paper we found tucked in the bird.”

“Yes, which makes me think we’re on the right track,” said Brenda. “I couldn’t find any names of people attached to the company, but Jeremy found out some background info on it.”

Jeremy rocked in his chair. “RMS Holdings is linked to an east coast organized crime group that’s involved in street drugs and trafficking of underage girls.”

“How’s Ferenc connected to all of this?” asked Erik.

“Maybe he’s not,” said Kate, “at least directly.”

Erik stood up and started pacing. “Could the Fort Raiders be a puppet club to this east coast group?”

“It’s possible,” said Jeremy.

Erik spun around. “Brenda, when did RMS Holdings purchase the Gusher?”

“Last year,” she said.

“I see what you’re getting at,” Kate said to Erik.

Brenda and Jeremy raised their eyebrows in confusion.

“Turf war,” said Kate.

Brenda slowly nodded. “This new group is moving in on Ferenc’s territory.”

“And he needs to move more product up north to push out the competition,” said Kate. “Which is why they tried to blackmail Conor. They needed Northern Shipping’s airport access.”

And turf wars meant bodies would soon start piling up. Or maybe they already had. Kate turned to Erik. “What if Henry somehow got caught up in this turf war and that’s why he was killed?”

“We need to see if any other recent murders in Fort Mac could be connected,” said Erik. “Jeremy, can you access the police database and pull up Fort Mac murder cases for the past six months?”

“You bet,” he said.

Brenda got up and stretched. “I’ve got a busy delivery schedule tomorrow. Kate, you need a ride to your mom’s place?”

She shook her head. “No, I’m going back to my house. I’ll catch a ride back to the city with Jeremy.

Brenda raised her eyebrows. “Sure you don’t want to see Sam?”

Kate shook her head, “No, I’ll visit her in the morning.” Truth be told, she didn’t want to have to deal with Sam and her anger right now.

"What about you, Conor?" asked Kate, "Where are you going to stay?"

Conor glanced over at Jeremy. "I'm at his place for the time being."

"I've got a tunnel that runs from my basement to the shed," Jeremy said. "If the police come looking for him, he'll be able to escape."

Kate laughed. "Of course you have a tunnel."

She hugged Brenda goodbye and climbed into Jeremy's truck for the ride back to the city. Her place was the first stop, and Erik followed her inside. She didn't have the heart to tell him to go home. Did he think they were a couple again because they'd slept together in Fort Mac? She made up the bed in the spare room and Erik asked if she was going to stay awhile.

"I'm exhausted," she said.

"Sure, no worries. Night."

Kate settled into her bed but couldn't fall asleep. Feelings of guilt bubbled to the surface. For what, she wasn't sure. Sleeping with Erik in Fort McMurray? Or not sleeping with him tonight? Avoiding her daughter? And her job was in jeopardy. She figured it was inevitable she'd be fired. What was she going to do next with her life?

38

When Erik came downstairs the next morning, Kate poured fresh coffee into two stainless steel travel mugs and handed him one. He smiled and reached out to touch her arm, but she pulled away. Not a good sign.

He tried not to think about work. Normally, he'd be sitting at his desk after the morning meeting by this time.

"I'm going to visit the Ranch—alone," Kate said.

He crossed his arms, clearly unhappy with her decision.

"If we're right about a turf war, Ferenc might be willing to share more information," she said. "But he won't if you come with me."

She had a point. "Fine. I'll pay a visit to one of the eco-activists." He checked the list of names Bertrand had given him. "River. What kind of name is that?"

Outside, warmer weather had melted most of the snow, revealing patches of drab brown grass. Along the curb lay clumps of dirt mixed with road salt. Erik leaned in to kiss Kate goodbye before she climbed into her truck. Big mistake. She pulled away and slid behind the wheel. He knew what he wanted, but Kate was obviously conflicted. He realized he had to back off and give her some space.

She rolled down the window and said, "Good luck this morning. I'll call you after I'm done." With that, she pulled away from the curb.

Erik drove towards the Strathcona district. His GPS guided him to a rambling prairie-style house near the university with a large fraternity sign attached to the porch railings. A kid in boxer shorts with bloodshot eyes opened the door.

"Party last night?" asked Erik.

The kid glanced back at the living room littered with beer bottles and pizza boxes. "Minecraft Dungeons tournament. How can I help you?"

"Does River live here?" asked Erik.

"Who wants to know?"

"I'm Erik. I know Bertrand Mickleford and Suzanne Morton.

He jutted out his chin. "I'm River. Come in."

Erik got straight to the point. "I'm investigating Henry Franzen's murder. Your group sent him a threatening letter. Do you remember doing this?"

River's expression shifted. "Hold on here a moment. I thought you were friends with Bertrand and Suzanne."

Erik stepped closer. "Didn't say that. Said I know them. On Saturday, February 28th, your group had a meeting. What did you do afterwards? Kill Henry?"

"This is crazy. I'm calling my dad. He's a lawyer."

"Does he know you're mixed up with this eco-terrorist group?"

River hesitated. "Okay, okay. We met that morning at Aaron's place. Afterwards, some of us came back here. My frat mates can confirm this. We had nothing to do with his murder."

Erik closed the distance between them, thinking, what kind of parents would name their child after a body of water?

The boy's face drained of colour. "I think I'm going to—" He turned and puked all over the carpet.

Erik wrinkled his nose. Did this frat kid really have it in him to kill Henry, plan a home invasion and frame Conor?

"We're trying to reach Suzanne. Where is she?" he asked.

River wiped his mouth with the back of his hand. "Don't know. She emailed the group. Said she was heading out of town for a while."

"Show me."

River pulled up the message and handed over his phone. Erik scanned it, noting the address.

"Thanks." He took out a business card, struck through his office number, and wrote in his personal cell. "Call me if you hear from her."

39

Kate spotted the undercover car parked across the street from the Ranch and felt safer knowing the police were watching. She pressed the buzzer and Tony opened the door. He grinned. "Kate. Long time, no see." He looked her up and down. "Still looking pretty damn hot."

"Hiya Tony. I'm here to see Ferenc."

"He's not here."

"Seriously. It's important we talk."

Tony's phone buzzed. He read the text. "Okay, but we need to pat you down first."

"No way in hell you're touching me."

"You're always such a bitch."

"That's no way to talk to the lady," said Ferenc, appearing behind his nephew. Tony stepped aside so Kate could enter.

She brushed past Tony, wrinkling her nose at his strong body odour. She turned to Ferenc. "I need your help."

"Need to check for listening devices first," he said, waving a frequency detector.

"No problem." She stood with her arms outstretched and legs apart, turning her face away. Ferenc conducted the search with the efficiency of a border security officer, patting her down before sweeping a wand over her.

"Pretty high-tech," she said.

"You're all good. Please leave your purse here while we talk."

Kate turned off her phone so dickwad Tony couldn't snoop.

"You owe Kate an apology," Ferenc said.

Tony's pale, blemished face turned blotchy and he clenched his hands. He looked like he might explode but had to keep his temper in check with the boss watching. "Sorry," he mumbled.

Kate crossed her arms.

"Not good enough." Ferenc's tone was stern, like someone scolding a misbehaving dog.

"I'm sorry for calling you a bitch."

"And the other thing!" Ferenc demanded.

"And I'm sorry about Conor. I didn't know he was your brother. We were just looking to, um, get leverage on someone with security clearance."

"Right, now that we have that straightened out, come with me," said Ferenc.

Tony started to follow, but Ferenc stopped him. "Not you. Go get her surprise." Tony scowled and stomped away. Kate didn't ask what Ferenc meant. She knew she'd find out soon enough.

"Family, what can you do?" asked Ferenc. She understood all too well.

In the years she worked at the Ranch, she'd never been in Ferenc's office. The old-world European décor was a sharp contrast to the rest of the country-and-western club. Persian carpets lined the dark wood floor. A large ornate chandelier with dangly crystals lit up the space. Ferenc led her to an oval table surrounded by upholstered chairs.

"Nice place," she said.

"My refuge from the cowboy culture of the club." He gestured for her to take a seat. "I figured you'd be around to see me after your trip to Fort McMurray."

"How did you know we were in…never mind."

A man set down a wooden tray on the table in front of Kate and Ferenc. It contained a pitcher, two glasses, and a plate of Girl Guide cookies. "Water?" the man asked Ferenc.

"Yes, thank you."

Kate stared at the man as he poured. Why did he look so familiar? She shot a look at Ferenc. "Are you two related?"

He grinned. "No, he's my body double. Acts as a decoy when needed and the rest of the time he works here at the club."

"But…," she shook her head. "Never mind…that doesn't matter right now. What I need is information about the Fort Raiders."

Ferenc rested his elbows on the table and tented his fingers. "I admire your persistence with investigating your husband's murder despite the employment setback."

"All thanks to you. I've probably lost my job and so has Erik."

"A strategic mistake on my part," he said. "It would've been better having you two investigating than Detective Christina Wong. She's not good for business."

Serves him right. "Did you put the bug on my phone?" she asked.

"Wasn't me," he said.

She pressed him. "When you showed up at my place that night, you said you were monitoring us. And you know we went to Fort Mac."

"I'm old school. Over the years, I have cultivated insiders that I pay."

Funnily enough, Kate believed him. "I have a theory I want to run by you." He gave her a nod to continue. "Are the owners of the Gusher Hotel trying to elbow their way into your business?" He shifted in his seat, which Kate took as a yes. "Is that why you needed a new shipment route? To increase supply and take out the competition?"

"And this matters because…?"

"Henry stayed at the Gusher Hotel a week before he was murdered. He questioned some of the sex workers—about what we're not sure. But we think something they told him might've got him killed."

"What are you asking of me?"

"What do you know about the Fort Raiders, and do you think they could've killed Henry?"

He stroked his neatly trimmed moustache. "I'm not going to spill any trade secrets, but I can confirm they are in my territory, and it's not going to last." He reached for his phone. "The surprise I have for you might shed some light on matters."

He sent a text, and a moment later Tony entered, dragging with him a scrawny kid in his early twenties, blood streaming from his nose.

Kate stood up, her hands gripped the edge of the table. "What the hell is this?" she asked.

"Tell her." Tony shoved the kid forward. He went down hard on his knees.

"Don't hurt me!" the kid spluttered.

Kate stared at Ferenc, at a loss for words.

"Tell her what you know," Ferenc said, "and we'll let you scurry back to your cave."

The kid's whole body shook. "I…I…got paid to drive this dude around town. We spent days following the guy that ended up in the news. The professor."

Kate shoved her chair out of the way and strode over to the kid. Blood from his nose dripped onto the wood floor. She looked down at him and said, "His name was Henry." She squeezed her eyes shut, pushing back the grief threatening to engulf her.

The kid whimpered. "Sorry. Henry."

Kate opened her eyes. "This 'dude' that hired you, does he have a name?" she asked, her voice shaky. The kid shook his head.

She clenched her fists. "What did he look like?"

"Older. Wore an expensive jacket and boots."

"What did he tell you?"

The kid wiped his nose with the back of his hand, smearing blood across his cheek. "Hardly talked."

Something snapped. Kate seized him by his shirt and hauled him to his feet. "Did you see him kill Henry?" she demanded, shaking him so hard that his teeth clattered.

The kid's eyes bulged. What on earth was she doing? Kate got her anger under control and let go of his shirt. He slumped to the ground.

Tony kicked him in the side. "Answer her."

The kid curled up into a ball, moaning in pain. "No, I swear—no! I just drove!"

Tony readied another kick, but Kate moved in between them. "That's enough." She looked down at the kid. "Please. Just tell me what you know. Did you follow Henry to the Saxony?"

The kid pulled himself up to sitting, wincing in pain as he leaned against the office wall. "Yeah," he gasped. "We waited in the lot and when the professor—Henry—came out, his arm was around this drunk guy. The drunk guy fell at one point. Went down hard, and I think he cut himself. Henry helped him up and put him in the back of his car. That's when the dude I was driving around got really excited and kept saying, 'This is perfect.'"

Kate struggled to make sense of it. "Did the 'dude' seem to know either of them?"

"Yes. I think he knew them both. That's why I had to do the driving. He kept ducking low in his seat so he wouldn't be seen."

"How did he recruit you?"

"I do stuff for the Raiders. Got a text to meet this dude."

"Is he a Raider?"

"I don't ask questions."

"Then what happened?"

"When the drunk guy fell, he dropped one of his gloves in the parking lot. The dude told me to put on my mitts and pick it up. So I did and brought it back. The dude held open a grocery bag and told me to drop in the glove. That's when he told me he didn't need my help anymore."

"What happened after that?"

The kid shrugged. "The dude got in the driver's seat and followed Henry as he drove out of the Saxony parking lot. Left me there in the cold. I had to pay for a cab home."

Kate's stomach dropped as the pieces of the puzzle locked together with sickening clarity. Somebody had been following Henry, waiting for the right time to kill him, and then intentionally pinned the murder on her brother. And somehow, they were connected to the Fort Raiders.

"You're done here," Ferenc said. "Get out." As Tony dragged the kid from the room, he added, "Sorry you had to see that, but it's more believable coming from him than me, right?"

How had they even found this kid? Better she didn't know.

"Why did they target Henry?"

"No idea. But back to me now. Please convince Detective Wong we're the wrong target."

"Is it all about self-interest?"

"Of course. What else would it be? But I can assure you, you're far better off dealing with me than the Fort Raiders. They're trafficking underage girls as young as my granddaughter. I don't do that kind of thing."

The casual way Ferenc said it made her stomach churn. He knew what the Fort Raiders were up to and did nothing to stop it. Underage girls. As young as his granddaughter. She hadn't even known he had children, let alone a grandchild. Ferenc viewed himself as some sort of gentleman criminal with a moral code. What a load of crap. Children were off-limits but everything else was negotiable to him.

"I'll talk to Detective Wong. Thanks for the information."

"My pleasure."

Outside, the cold afternoon air hit her like a slap. Across the street, a surveillance car idled in the shadows. Kate lifted a hand and waved, deciding that was the fastest way to get Christina Wong's attention.

40

Erik ordered an Americano Misto and a croissant. He nabbed a booth in the far corner of the café next to the window. Perfect vantage point. He could survey the entire room, see outside, and as a bonus, the fire exit was to the left of the table. He took a sip of his coffee and grimaced. It needed more sugar, but he was trying to cut back.

Kate pulled up in her red SUV and fed the meter. When she entered the cafe, a middle-aged woman at the booth across from Erik pointed out Kate to her friend and joked that it must be hard to find a date when you're that tall.

Kate spotted him, waved, and lined up to order her coffee. The woman who had made the comment about Kate's height glanced over at Erik and shifted uncomfortably in her seat. Kate would be terrible at undercover work, he thought. Too memorable.

"You look lovely," said Erik as Kate settled in across from him. She responded by making a funny face. "What's wrong with giving you a compliment?" he asked.

She tossed back her espresso shot and set down the empty cup in the saucer. "Sorry. Thank you. How did your day go?"

Erik glanced around. The woman and her friend at the booth across the way had just left. He lowered his voice anyways, not wanting anyone to overhear him as he updated her about the frat boy encounter and Suzanne's departure from the city.

"How odd," said Kate. "Why would she leave in a hurry? Bertrand must've warned her that we know she's involved in their activities."

"The good news is I have her new email address." He gave it to Kate, and she typed a brief note to Suzanne on her cell, asking her to call.

Erik noticed the dark circles under Kate's eyes had reappeared. This case was clearly taking a toll on her, and he was partly to blame. He regretted getting involved—his motives hadn't been entirely selfless; he'd wanted to spend time with her, maybe even win her back. And it'd worked, briefly. But now there was a distance between them, a new tension he couldn't ignore. But it was too late to walk away now.

"If we don't hear back from Suzanne, would Michael help us find her?" he asked.

"Doubt it. They had a nasty divorce and don't stay in touch, but he might have some insight into why she got involved with the eco-activists."

"How did your meeting go with Ferenc?"

As she filled him in, Erik became increasingly excited. "We're getting close, I can feel it." Henry must've learned something about the Fort Raiders that got him killed.

"How is Bertrand's group connected to all of this?"

"Maybe it's not." Erik glanced out the window and spotted Christina arriving with her new partner, Amrit, in their unmarked police car. He felt a pang of sadness—he missed being on the force.

The cashier was tidying up the counter area when the detectives entered the cafe. "We're closing soon," she said loudly. The place was more of a breakfast spot, opening early and shutting its doors in the late afternoon. Amrit flashed his badge. "Give us half an hour, will you?"

The cashier bit her lip and nodded. The detectives made their way to the booth and Kate shifted over to make room. Christina sat down beside her, but Amrit slid into the seat across the way.

Erik glanced over at the cashier. If they kept their voices low, they should be safe to talk without being overheard.

Christina glared at Erik. "Was it worth it?" she asked.

"What?"

"Destroying your career. The inspector knows you're still working on the case. No way he's going to reinstate you."

"Who told him? Miles?" asked Kate.

Christina shot Kate a furious glance. "Why did you have to drag Erik up to Fort Mac?"

"He has his own mind, you know."

Erik suppressed a smile. "Your investigation is on the wrong track," he said to Christina.

"Where's your brother?" she asked Kate. "There's an arrest warrant out on him."

Kate shrugged. "No idea."

"Why didn't you alert us he was back in town?"

"Thought you knew. I'm surprised you didn't arrest him at the airport."

Christina crossed her arms over her chest. "What were you doing at the Ranch this morning?"

"Trying to get some answers."

"Hear us out," said Erik.

"Go on. Explain yourselves."

Kate and Erik tag-teamed, recounting the leads they'd uncovered. "You believe the Fort Raiders are behind Henry's death?" Christina asked.

"Yes, somehow."

"And Ferenc?" asked Christina.

"He's in a turf war with this group. We don't think he killed Henry," said Kate.

"What about this woman, Crystal? Or Janelle? Any word from them?" asked Christina.

"No."

Christina was silent for a moment. "Look, I can't reveal details, but we've found Henry's car. Burned out just north of Fort McMurray. A wire cable, believed to be the murder weapon, dumped in the back seat."

Erik's jaw tightened. A wire cable. Something deliberate. Surgical. Intimate. He glanced at Kate. Her eyes were closed and her hands clenched so tightly at her sides that her knuckles had turned white. Christina began folding a napkin into neat, accordion pleats, giving them space.

Erik lightly touched Kate's arm. "You okay?"

Her eyes opened. In that moment, he saw it. The terrible image forming in Kate's mind: Henry struggling. Henry afraid.

Kate ignored his question. "What else?" she asked Christina, her voice shaky.

Christina glanced around to ensure the cashier was out of earshot. "We also have bodies piling up in our morgue. A white male with multiple tattoos is a DNA match to the scrapings taken from under your daughter's fingernails."

One of the home invaders. Someone was trying to tie up loose ends. "You said bodies. Who else?" asked Erik.

"An unidentified female in her forties."

"What makes you think they're connected? he asked.

"Both victims had their hands cut off."

"*What?*" Kate's hand shook as she tucked a strand of hair behind her ear.

"Similar MO. No hands. Cut off after death," said Christina.

It seemed clear that someone was making it difficult to identify the victims. Was it possible that the woman was Crystal? Had their awkward line of questioning put her in danger? Erik asked, "Can we see a photo of the female victim?"

Kate got up abruptly "Excuse me," and rushed off towards the washroom.

Erik half-rose, ready to follow her, but thought better of it and slumped back down. His chest tightened. He'd seen her angry, furious, upset—but this was different. She was barely holding herself together and it scared him.

"You think it might be Crystal?" asked Christina.

Erik nodded.

"I don't have a digital copy," she said. "You'll have to come by the station."

That's the last thing he wanted to do. He pushed his plate with the half-eaten croissant towards Christina. She pulled off a piece and popped it in her mouth as he finished his coffee, wishing he could have another cup.

Christina cleared her throat. "Look, I'm sorry the inspector found out. Kate was right, Miles told him. I wouldn't have said anything, even though I don't approve of what you two have done—the affair, the trip to Fort McMurray. What were you thinking?"

Miles. That little shit had had it in for him ever since he'd come down hard on him at the station. Well, he'd certainly got his sweet revenge. And truth be told, he wasn't wrong in reporting them. Twice. Not that Erik regretted his actions. At least Christina hadn't been taken down with him. "Sorry about this mess."

Christina sighed, "So am I."

"How's your new partner?" he asked.

She shrugged her shoulders. "He's fine, but I miss you." Her face brightened. "They're promoting me to sergeant."

"You deserve it. Congrats." And he meant it.

Christina stood up to let Kate slide back into her seat. Erik noticed a faint smudge of mascara beneath Kate's eye. Christina zipped up her jacket. "I don't suppose I could persuade you two to leave the investigating to us?"

"No," they replied in unison.

Christina sighed. "Keep me in the loop, and don't do anything that will force me to intervene."

They watched though the window as the unmarked police vehicle pulled away from the curb.

"Everything okay?" he asked Kate.

"Do you think it's Crystal?"

"Maybe. Why don't we go down to the station first thing in the morning and look at the photos of the victim." He gently put his hand on top of hers, thankful she didn't pull away. "But right now, you need to go home and rest. You look exhausted."

After Kate left the café, Erik ordered another coffee and sat alone, quietly reflecting. The full weight of his situation settled on him—his choices, his future as a former police officer.

41

Kate headed straight to her mother's house in Leduc. The news about Henry's car and the bodies had shaken her. The stark reality of it—Henry strangled from behind with a wire. But why had he been murdered? If only she'd reached the storage locker first. Whatever information he'd stored in that file folder was so explosive it had cost him his life. Kate feared they'd never figure it out. Her mind turned to Crystal. What if their visit to her in Fort Mac had put her in danger, too? What if they'd gotten her killed?

At a stop light, she tapped in Crystal's number, but as she'd feared, it was no longer in service. She thought of the bartender at the Gusher. Maybe he knew Crystal's whereabouts.

Approaching the next red light on the outskirts of Edmonton, Kate called the hotel in Fort McMurray and asked to speak with the bartender. She fumbled with her phone, trying to put it on hands-free. As the light turned green, the car behind her honked. Muttering under her breath, she shifted into gear. "Fucking impatient drivers."

The bartender came on the line. "Who is this?"

"My partner and I spoke to you last week about Crystal. I'm the tall woman."

"I remember. That biker, Jeff, hit on you."

"That's me. I'm just trying to get in touch with Crystal, but her number isn't working. Do you know where she is?"

The line was quiet for a moment. "She's moved on."

"Do you know where she went?"

"You know what these girls are like, always moving around. Sorry, can't help you."

She ended the call. She had a sinking feeling about Crystal.

Kate made the trip down to her mother's place in record time. She rapped on the door, walked in and found Sam and Alma in the kitchen.

"I'll make myself scarce so the two of you can talk," Alma said.

Sam was hunched over her homework at the table, headphones on her ears. Kate placed her hands on Sam's shoulders and looked down at the mathematical equations that filled her notebook.

Sam turned around, her eyes bleary, and pulled off her headphones. "Hi, Mom."

"Hello, sweetheart. I missed you." Kate wrapped her arms around her.

"Sorry about that text." Sam rubbed her eyes.

"It hurt, but you're right. I shouldn't have gone to Fort Mac."

"Auntie Brenda and I had a talk while you were away."

"Oh?" Funny, she hadn't mentioned it.

"She said I had to look at things from your point of view. The police still think Uncle Conor is guilty, so it's up to you to find out the truth. But what if you get hurt?"

I'm an idiot. Sam wasn't angry; she was scared. Kate pulled up a chair and looked into her daughter's eyes. "Don't worry about me, I'm not going anywhere."

Sam's tears streamed down her face as she struggled to get out the words. "I was scared all the time you were away."

Kate pulled her into an embrace. "I'm sorry about all the upheaval. I love you so much."

"I want to go home with you." Sam wiped her runny nose with her sleeve.

Her request broke Kate's heart. What had she done to her child? Abandoned her when she needed her most. "I want you home too but let me first talk it over with Granny."

Sam nodded and returned to her schoolwork. Kate ran her hands through Sam's hair—long and unruly on one side, short and soft on the other—and watched her work on math problems. It hit home that she'd been uninvolved in Sam's day-to-day life for a long time now, ever since she'd moved out of the house. Or maybe even before that. And after Henry's death, Kate became even more withdrawn, consumed by her search for the truth. She vowed to change before it was too late.

Kate found her mother tidying up the spare room. "Thanks for stepping in and caring for Sam over the past few weeks."

Alma fluffed a pillow, dismissing the gratitude with a small shake of the head. "No need to thank me."

"She wants to come home with me." Kate smoothed a crease in the duvet.

Alma settled her hands on her hips. "Is it safe at your place? Why don't you move in here instead?"

"I have a new alarm system. We're perfectly safe." Living at her mom's wasn't an option.

Her mother sighed and adjusted the pillows on the bed. "Whatever you think is best, sweetheart."

They'd only been back home for a few hours when Kate got a text from a number she didn't recognize.

Heard you were looking for me.

Kate's heart raced. Crystal was alive. Or it was someone claiming to be her. She called the number and Crystal answered. "I'm in Edmonton. With Janelle. She's willing to talk, but only to you. Come alone."

Kate felt lightheaded, relieved she'd been wrong about the body in the morgue. "That's fine, text me the address."

After Crystal texted her the hotel address, Kate felt a jolt when she realized they were staying at the Saxony. Of all the hotels in town, why choose that one? Was she walking into a trap? She reminded herself the Saxony was one of the cheapest, most run-down places around—probably just a coincidence.

Before she left, Kate knocked on Sam's bedroom door. "Still working on your math?"

Sam set down her pencil. "Almost done."

"I've got to head out again."

"What for?" Sam asked.

Kate hesitated.

"Please, I want to know what's going on."

"I've got a lead," was all she said, "But it's time sensitive. I have to go now." Sam didn't know about the sex workers in Fort Mac, and Kate planned to keep it that way.

"I don't think you should go on your own," said Sam.

"Not a worry. Erik's coming," she lied and kissed her daughter's cheek. "Might be back late. Don't wait up."

Fifteen minutes later, Kate pulled up in front of the Saxony Hotel and Bar. She scanned the nearly empty lot, remembering that Henry had parked here the night he was killed. After dropping off Conor at their mother's house, he'd been followed. But where had he been strangled? The terror he must've felt. Did they kill him immediately, or did they force him to drive somewhere secluded before using the wire? And why did they use a different vehicle to dump his body in the ditch? What was the reason for driving his car up north and setting it on fire?

Before she stepped out of her truck, she sent a quick text to Erik, letting him know her location. Inside the hotel lobby, she angled her body to avoid any view into the bar as she passed by. She walked past the front desk, climbed the hotel staircase to the second floor, and knocked on the door of room 212.

"Who is it?" asked a muffled voice.

"Kate."

Crystal opened the door a crack and peeked out. "You alone?"

She nodded, relieved to see Crystal instead of a Fort Raiders gang member aiming a gun. She opened the door wider, allowing Kate to slip inside. Kate quickly locked the door behind her.

"It's good to see you. What made you leave Fort Mac?"

Crystal grimaced. "Didn't plan to, but things got real strange. I left in a hurry, without my stash of money. Luckily, for the price of a few blow jobs, a trucker drove me down here."

Their visit had stirred up trouble for her—Kate was sure of it. "Did the bartender tell you I called?" she asked.

"Ya, he's a buddy of mine."

Kate looked around the shabby room. A young woman sat cross-legged on the edge of a double bed. "You must be Janelle."

Janelle glanced at her, then dropped her gaze. The long blond wig overwhelmed her narrow face. She folded her arms tightly across her chest, shoulders hunched, as if she were trying to make herself as small as possible.

God. She looked younger than Sam.

Kate crouched to make herself less intimidating and spoke to her again. "I'm here alone, like you asked." Janelle uncrossed her arms and began biting her nails. A curtain of hair hid her face.

"It's okay, honey," said Crystal.

Kate tasted bile in her throat. What kind of men took advantage of vulnerable girls like Janelle? They deserved to have their balls cut off. "How did you end up in Fort McMurray?" she asked.

Janelle spoke in a soft, hesitant voice, forcing Kate to lean in to catch her words. "Things weren't great at home in Thunder Bay. This guy I'd met at the mall said he was going to take care of me. He bought me things, called me beautiful." She gave a little shrug. "But he lied."

Janelle described how she was forced into a cube van with some other girls and driven out west to work at the Gusher Hotel. "That's where I met Crystal and Tiffany." Janelle briefly smiled, then resumed the nail biting.

"Who's Tiffany?" asked Kate.

Janelle's lips trembled as she struggled to keep her composure. "My best friend."

"Tiffany disappeared last November," said Crystal.

Janelle's face crumpled and Crystal rushed over to comfort her. After some time, Janelle wiped away her tears and resumed her story. "Tiffany was afraid of this one regular and his buddy. They'd only asked for her and were real rough but our boss didn't care."

"Tiffany was only fifteen," Crystal told Kate.

"The last time I saw Tiffany, she was real upset 'cause she had to see this guy and his buddy again." Janelle started softly crying. Crystal placed a reassuring hand on Janelle's back

"I'm so sorry," said Kate. She paused, building up the nerve to ask. "How was my husband involved?"

"He approached me, asked questions about the Gusher," said Crystal, looking at her warily.

Kate let out a breath she hadn't realized she'd been holding. Henry hadn't slept with her. Relief swept through her so fast it made her dizzy.

Crystal picked at a clump of dried mascara on her lashes, one of her blue gel nails was missing. "You thought he was a client."

Kate nodded.

"Wish he had been," said Crystal. "He was sweet."

"What did he want to know?"

"He asked about the cameras in the girls' rooms and whether the Fort Raiders kept the footage."

"And do they?"

"Oh yes, my boss—former boss—had videos of a cop, teachers, even a judge." Crystal fidgeted with the bangles on her wrist. "That's when I told Henry about Tiffany's disappearance and how the boss didn't seem to care."

Janelle spoke so softly Kate couldn't make out what she'd said. "Sorry, sweetheart, can you repeat that?"

"Tiffany nicknamed this guy 'husky-dog-man' because of his creepy grey-blue eyes."

Kate's heart raced. *Could it be?* "Crystal, this is important. Did you mention this guy's nickname to Henry?"

Crystal's brow furrowed. "Yes. That's when Henry got all jumpy. Like you are now. He wanted to know if I could identify husky-dog-man. I'd never met him, but Janelle had. That's when Henry asked to talk to Janelle."

Kate rubbed her forehead. What was it that Bertrand told them? He'd seen Henry meet a young blonde woman, possibly a prostitute, in the Gusher parking lot. Must've been Janelle. It all fit.

Janelle hugged her knees and resumed her story. "I met Henry in his car. He showed me a photo, and I said that was him, the guy Tiffany called 'husky-dog man.'"

Henry had figured out who'd killed Tiffany but why was Henry asking questions in the first place? "What happened next?" asked Kate.

"Henry got real upset and told me my life might be in danger and I had to leave town right away."

"That's when Janelle asked for my help," said Crystal. "The bartender and I arranged things, and she's been staying here in Edmonton ever since."

"I'm sorry, Crystal. Our visit endangered you," said Kate.

Crystal's bracelets jingled as she waved off Kate's apology. "Nah. It was time to move on anyways. Do something else. Thought Janelle and I could set up shop as fortune tellers in Winnipeg."

"We're sorry about Henry," said Janelle.

Kate smiled. "Thanks, sweetheart." She pulled out her phone and searched for the Tecktronic staff listings. She located the photo of the chief financial officer, Lyle Sabey, and handed the phone over to Janelle. "Is this the husky-dog-eyed man?"

Her eyes widened in recognition. "That's him!"

42

Back in the lobby of the Saxony, Kate checked her phone. Erik had sent her a text: Why did you go there without me?

She ignored his question: On my way home. Stop by the house in the morning and I'll update you.

She shut off her phone, climbed back into her truck and gazed out into the darkness. This was just all too much. Gripping the steering wheel, she slammed her fists down in frustration. Fuck, fuck, fuck. Pulling her hands tightly to her chest, she began to cry. Those poor girls. And Henry—how did he get involved in this? She had to talk to someone before she completely lost it. Jeremy and Conor. She decided to go see them. Shivering, she zipped up her coat.

Her brother answered the door at Jeremy's place. "Hey, sis. What're you doing up so late?" That's when she saw how dishevelled he looked. And he was blushing. Bad timing on her part. "Sorry to interrupt. I'll leave."

Jeremy came down the stairs, adjusting his robe. "Kate, come on in. Tell us what's wrong."

Kate took a deep breath and filled them in on her conversation with Janelle and Crystal.

Conor shook his head in disbelief, "So this oil executive could be the killer?"

"Maybe of Tiffany, but Lyle was in Texas at the time of Henry's murder."

"But I don't understand why Henry didn't go to the police," Jeremy said. "Tell them that Lyle might've killed this girl."

Kate rubbed her eyes. She felt bone weary and beyond tears. "Turns out Henry was like the rest of us. Full of secrets."

"But how does it all fit?" Conor counted off all the strange occurrences in the case. "First they tried to frame me, then they bugged your phone, broke into your place, stole the key and raided the storage locker."

And the bodies in the morgue. Still so many unanswered questions.

"All I know is the Fort Raiders are involved somehow," she said. "Maybe Lyle hired them to kill Henry?"

Jeremy suggested they go upstairs to his office so he could show Kate the results from his search for news articles about people who had been murdered or gone missing in Fort McMurray over the past year. He logged in and pulled up a story from last year, dated November 21, 2014. "Janelle and Crystal told you that Tiffany went missing last November. This fits with the timeframe."

The headline read, *Unidentified Teen Found Dead*. They scanned the article. The victim, a female, estimated to be about sixteen, had been raped, beaten to death and left in a ditch.

"Brutal," Jeremy said.

Kate glanced at Conor, trying to gauge his reaction.

A moment later, Jeremy realized what he'd said. "Sorry, Conor. I wasn't thinking about your cousin…"

"It's okay. I'm fine. I'll leave you to it. I'm going to watch TV." He hugged his sister, kissed Jeremy.

"Shit, how insensitive of me," said Jeremy.

"Don't worry. He'll be okay."

As long as there was no alcohol in the house. Still, Kate wondered what would happen between Jeremy and Conor if times got hard again. With Conor's history, a relapse was always a real possibility, and last time, Jeremy had left Conor when he needed support most.

"If you hurt my brother again, I'll kick your ass," she warned.

When she got home, Kate checked in on Sam. Fast asleep. Her side table lamp was still on, a book splayed open beside her. Kate stroked her daughter's cheek. "Love you," she whispered. She closed the book, turned off the lamp and retired to bed.

She woke up to the sound of the doorbell ringing and a murmur of voices.

"Mom! It's Erik!" Sam called.

Kate glanced at the clock on her bedside table—9:00. Shit. She'd forgotten to set the alarm. "Tell him I'll be a few minutes." She scrambled out of bed, grabbed the clothes she'd dumped on the floor the previous evening and pulled them on.

The aroma of freshly brewed coffee in the kitchen greeted her when she came downstairs. Erik and Sam were seated at the island, chatting and sipping their drinks. As soon as Erik saw her, his smile disappeared. She put her finger to her lips, signalling for him to keep quiet about last night's events.

"Bertrand's in town and wants to meet us," Erik said, consulting his watch. "Says it's urgent. And then we should go straight to the station to look at the morgue photos."

Sam glanced at them in alarm. "Morgue photos?"

Kate glared at Erik, who had the decency to look ashamed. "Don't worry, Detective Wong wants us view the body of a gang member to see if we can identify him," she explained.

Sam appeared reassured by Kate's answer and resumed eating her toast. After saying their goodbyes, Kate joined Erik in his car, taking the passenger seat.

As he pulled away from the curb, Erik asked, "Why did you go to the Saxony alone? It could've been dangerous."

"Well …" She was at a loss for words.

"And in a hotel room?" he pressed. "You know that's not safe. All sorts of depraved and deadly things happen in places like the Saxony."

She bristled at the lecture but let it go. "Fine."

"Look, you're a crime analyst, not a police officer."

No kidding.

"And there's a reason we have partners in the field. People to back us up."

"Do you want to know what happened or not?" she said, then told him about her meeting with Crystal and Janelle.

His eyes widened as she told him about the CFO of Tecktronic. "We need to tell Christina."

They drove the rest of the way in silence. Kate studied Erik's profile. The stress of the past few weeks showed: deeper lines at the corners of his eyes, more grey threaded through his hair. She'd been responsible for pulling him into this chaos.

Bertrand was parked in his dented Chevy Malibu at the far end of a Tim Hortons parking lot. Erik pulled up alongside him, rolled down his window and motioned for Bertrand to do the same. As Bertrand complied, a strong smell of smoke wafted out of his car.

"Toke and drive—seriously?" asked Erik.

Bertrand shrugged. “Got a high tolerance. Besides, I need to take the edge off.”

“What’s going on?” asked Kate.

“Suzanne’s missing. Something’s wrong.”

“What do you mean? We know she left town,” said Erik.

“Yes, she did. To her cabin. But when I showed up, she was gone. No car or luggage, but I found this on the floor.” He held out a broken gold chain with a simple amethyst pendant.

“She always wore it.”

Erik told him to head home and said they’d look into it. Bertrand took another drag from his joint, then rolled up the window and drove off.

“What do you think?” Kate asked.

Erik shrugged. “Can’t read too much into a broken necklace.”

43

After their meeting with Bertrand, Erik drove them to the police station. At reception, Paisley handed over visitor badges and escorted them upstairs. Kate had already endured this particular humiliation, but for Erik it was his first time back as a civilian. Colour rose in his face; his hands were clenched at his sides. As they walked by, people glanced up from their workstations. A few murmured greetings, but mostly there were just stares. Kate took mental note of every slight. One day, she told herself, she'd get her revenge.

Christina and her new partner, Amrit, were already set up at the boardroom table.

Erik got straight to the point. "We have some information you might want to hear."

Kate told the detectives about her meeting with Janelle and Crystal. "They're certain their friend Tiffany is dead," she said, handing Christina the newspaper article detailing the discovery of an unidentified woman's body found outside Fort McMurray last November. "I think this could be her."

"How is the Tecktronic CFO connected to Henry's death?" asked Christina.

Kate replied, "I'm not certain. He might not have been directly involved, but it's possible he hired the Fort Raiders."

"Janelle said two men met with Tiffany the night she went missing. Any idea about the identity of the second man?" Christina asked.

"No idea," said Kate.

Christina tightened her ponytail and turned to Amrit. "Contact the Fort Mac police. Ask them to pick up this Tecktronic CFO."

"Will do," he said.

"I'd like to be involved in questioning him," said Erik.

Christina crossed her arms. “Not possible. You’re suspended.” She tapped the folder on her desk. “Now that we know Crystal is alive, we’re back to square one with this unidentified body in the morgue.”

Out of curiosity, Kate asked to see the photo. She must have gasped because when she looked up, everyone was staring at her.

“Who is it?” Erik asked.

She showed him the photo. “Suzanne!”

A moment of stunned silence followed before Christina barked orders to Amrit. “Contact next of kin to get identification. And find out where the hell she has been the past few weeks.”

Kate offered to break the news about Suzanne to Michael. Despite their nasty divorce, she was certain he’d want to know about his ex-wife. At the university, she slowly climbed the three flights to his office. Over a week had passed since she and Sam had packed up Henry’s office—the same day they’d discovered the key. And the burglary happened that night. Kate felt it in her bones that they were close to solving the case. Tecktronic’s chief financial officer had likely murdered a young sex worker, and somehow Henry found out about it. Was that why he was killed? But the bigger picture remained elusive. How were the Fort Raiders involved? Did Lyle hire them to kill Henry? And where did Suzanne and the environmental group fit in? Why was Suzanne killed?

She knocked on Michael’s office door.

He looked up from his desk as she walked in. “Kate. So nice to see you again. Is this business or pleasure?

“Business, I’m afraid.”

“Have a seat.”

She pulled up a chair and pointed to the artwork on the wall behind his desk. “Is that new?”

“No, I brought in the Burtynsky from home. I like to rotate my pictures to keep it interesting.”

“Well, it’s stunning, even though I have no idea what it is.”

“Try to guess.” Michael pushed his chair away from the desk to give her a better view.

She studied the large-scale photograph, a series of concentric circles, grey and brownish with streaks of rusty red, and evenly spaced ridges radiating outwards from the centre. “An extreme close-up of a seashell?”

Michael grinned. “It was taken in a Russian potash mine. The machine harvesting the mineral makes those shapes.”

She tilted her head. “Really?” How disconcerting—though maybe that was the artist’s intention.

Her mouth felt dry. She’d let this chatter about Michael’s artwork go on too long. Time to deliver the bad news. She leaned forward and pressed her palms on his desk. “I have something to tell you.”

Michael reached across the desk and took her hands in his. “What is it?”

“I’m sorry, but Suzanne’s dead.”

Michael yanked his hands away as if she’d burned him. “What? I don’t understand.”

Kate explained what she knew but avoided the grisly details.

“*Murder?* What’s going on, Kate? First Henry and now Suzanne?” He slammed his fist on the desk, causing his pen to fall to the floor. She picked it up, noting the intricate carving along its side—just like the antique silver pen Henry had owned.

“As you know, our divorce was acrimonious. But for this to happen to her…” He lowered his head.

She rose halfway from her chair, then hesitated, unsure whether to offer comfort or give him space.

“Would you mind closing the door behind you when you leave?”

“If you ever need to talk…” Her voice trailed off. Michael had turned to the window. She paused on the threshold. “What can you tell me about Lyle Sabey?” she asked.

Michael spun around. “Why?”

She was taken aback by his sharp tone. “I met him when were up in Fort Mac. Odd guy.”

Michael shrugged. “Don’t know much about him.” He turned back to the window.

Her face flushed. “Sorry.”

She slipped out, shutting the door softly behind her. *I’m an idiot. He just learned his ex-wife was killed and I’m asking him questions about Lyle.*

Instead of returning to her car, Kate walked down the hall towards Jennifer’s office. Just as she reached the door and was about to knock, it swung open. Jennifer, startled at the sight of Kate, threw up her hands, sending papers fluttering to the floor. “Sorry to startle you,” Kate said, bending down to help pick them up.

Jennifer shook her head. "Not your fault. I wasn't paying attention."

That's when Kate noticed how gaunt she looked, her face pale with dark circles under her eyes. "You okay?" she asked.

Jennifer busied herself with straightening out the papers. "You know, good days and bad days. Anyway, I'm leaving town. Got accepted into a post-doctorate program in Montreal." When Kate expressed surprise, Jennifer added, "I thought I could stay, but things aren't the same here without Henry."

Down the hall, a door opened. Michael emerged, phone in hand, absorbed in whatever glowed on the screen as he walked toward them. He glanced up and stopped short.

"Kate, I didn't realize you were still here." He tipped his chin toward Jennifer. "Can you assist me when you're done?"

"Sure, no problem." Jennifer's voice carried a hard edge.

Perhaps, Kate thought, with Henry gone, the department's atmosphere was less convivial.

44

Kate woke up shivering, having kicked her covers off earlier in the night. Her cotton nightgown was soaked with sweat, and her heart raced. She thought back to the day of Henry's funeral. Something niggled at the edge of her mind. *That's it!* She'd been talking to Michael at the gravesite when Suzanne approached. As Michael left, Kate had caught a fleeting expression on Suzanne's face. At the time, she'd assumed it was anger or hatred. But now she realized she'd been mistaken.

It had been fear.

Kate logged onto her computer and typed in information about the Burtynsky she'd seen in Michael's office. An auction house posting came up, announcing the recent sale of the photograph to an anonymous purchaser for $100,000. Michael had lied to her. He'd said he had brought it from home. How could he afford to buy such an expensive artwork on a professor's salary?

Kate ran to Henry's office. Hands shaking, she scoured the desk for his antique pen. Not there. She thought back again to the day of the funeral. Michael had been here in this office with her. He'd picked up the pen, then he'd gotten a phone call from Tecktronic. Could he have taken the pen accidentally? But why not return it? Why keep it on his desk at work?

The hair rose on the nape of her neck. She tried calling Erik. No answer. She left a message for him.

Next, she dialled her brother.

It rang too long. Went to voicemail. She called again. Finally, she heard a click, then a rustle of sheets.

"Kate?" Conor's voice was thick with sleep. "It's one in the morning. What's wrong?"

"Put Jeremy on." Her voice was hoarse. "Now."

There was a pause. "You're scaring me. What's going on?"

"Just get him. Please. It's important."

More rustling, then thumps and muffled voices as Conor passed over the phone.

Then Jeremy, breathless: "Kate?"

"Do you remember Gillian?" she asked.

"Gillian…?" He paused. "You mean the woman who used to work for Victim Services?"

"Yes, that's her. I introduced Gillian to Michael after his divorce. They hooked up but it didn't last long."

"Yeah, I know who you mean." He was awake now. "But why—?"

"I need you to find her. As soon as you can. Wake her up if you have to."

"But—"

"Ask her if Michael was ever rough with her."

The word seemed to hang there in the dark.

"Rough," Jeremy repeated. "Rough how?"

"Just ask her." Her voice cracked. "Please."

"Why?"

She didn't know how to answer.

"Oh," he said. He understood. "You think he's capable of something."

Kate closed her eyes. "I need to know if he has a dark side to him."

"Are you alone right now?" he asked.

"Yes."

"I'll track down Gillian as quickly as I can. And, Kate," he added quietly, "make sure that you keep your doors locked."

After she hung up, she checked the time. Almost one-thirty in the morning. What next? Ferenc. He'd still be working. She pulled on the same outfit she'd worn to his club the day before and left a brief note for Sam on the kitchen island: *Had to see Ferenc. Explain when I get back. Xo Mom.* She made certain to lock the door and turn on the house alarm before she left.

The Ranch parking lot bustled with people. It was two in the morning, and the bar had just closed. A young woman in a tiara was puking against the club's outer wall. One friend held back her long hair, while another rubbed her shoulders—an ignoble end to a bachelorette party. Kate walked around to the main entrance. Inside, Tony and the bouncer were chatting up some scantily clad women sporting cowboy hats. The buttons on Tony's too-tight dress shirt strained across his amped-up torso. "Kate, fancy seeing you again so soon."

"I need to see Ferenc. It's urgent."

He led her to the office. Ferenc was at his desk counting bills. "To what do I owe this pleasure, two times in as many days?"

"Do you recognize either of these men?" She showed him photos of Lyle and Michael.

Ferenc shook his head. "Who are they?"

"I think they're somehow involved in the murder of an underage sex worker, a woman named Suzanne, and maybe Henry as well," said Kate.

"Where do they work?"

"Michael is Henry's co-worker at the university, and this guy works for Tecktronic in Fort McMurray."

Ferenc tapped his pen on his desk. "Both men slept with prostitutes?"

"I wouldn't be surprised."

"And one of them might have killed a girl? Well then, if I were the head of a criminal organization," he grinned at her, "they would be terrific candidates for blackmail."

"Yes, we thought that, but for what? Money?"

"No, for connections. Just like we approached your brother to move product. Finding reliable shipping lines is always a concern for this business."

"Thank you, that helps."

Kate's next stop was Jennifer's loft. She rang the buzzer repeatedly until Jennifer finally answered with a sleepy, "Hello?"

"It's Kate. Can I come up?"

"It's four a.m. Can't it wait?"

"No!"

Jennifer buzzed her in, and Kate rode the elevator to the fifth floor of the converted warehouse.

"You look fancy," said Jennifer when she opened the door.

Kate apologized for waking her up. "I need to know. Did you tell Michael about the home invasion?"

Jennifer crossed her arms. "No. Of course not. After the police questioned me about the key, they told me not to talk about what happened to you and Sam."

Kate poked at the burning spot under her rib cage and thought back to that day she and Erik visited the university. Michael had claimed he heard about the home invasion from Jennifer, but if Jennifer hadn't told him, there was only one other way he could have found out.

"Why are you transferring to a different university?" asked Kate. "Is it about Henry, or is something else going on?"

Jennifer tugged on the cuffs of her housecoat. "Look, I know that Michael is your long-time family friend, but he's been behaving oddly, and it's freaking me out."

Jennifer described a series of troubling incidents in the past few weeks. He'd made some moves on her, and when she gently refused his advances, he began to harass her—constantly criticizing her work, her clothing, and the way she spoke. Last week, he briefly pinned her arm behind her back before letting go and walking away. "He was unhinged."

Kate had pegged Michael as the Casanova type, someone always trying to make a conquest. But the behaviour Jennifer described wasn't a side of Michael she'd seen before. If he could hide his true nature from her—and from his supposedly good friend Henry—what else was he capable of? "I'm sorry," Kate said. "I didn't know."

"Neither did I, until lately. You can tell he's stressed about something. He's constantly on the phone."

"Did you overhear any of his conversations?"

Jennifer shook her head. "He closes his office door."

Kate nodded slowly. "Thanks. This helps." She hesitated, weighing whether to mention anything else. Finally, she said, "Jennifer, please stay away from him. I mean it. Don't be alone with him.

Jennifer frowned. "Why?"

Kate held her gaze. Because I think he might be dangerous."

Jennifer tightened the belt on her housecoat. "One more thing. Michael claims our department van is in the shop, but it's been gone for weeks."

Kate gripped her truck keys. "Does it have one of those tags that gives access to the cargo terminal at the airport?"

"Yes," she said.

Kate thanked Jennifer and left the condo. In the elevator, she leaned back and rested her eyes. If the Fort Raiders had the same motive as Ferenc, to move more product up north, a university van with security clearance was a perfect vehicle for smuggling drugs. What if the Raiders helped Michael kill Henry and in return, Michael assisted the Raiders with their distribution? *Quid pro quo.*

Outside, the sky was still dark. No hint of a sunrise. Kate got into her truck and checked the glove compartment for antacids. No luck. Her phone rang.

"I talked to Gillian," Jeremy said. "Your hunch was right—turns out Michael likes to get rough during sex."

Kate thanked him and ended the call. Hands shaking, she called Erik and told him everything she had just learned about Michael.

Erik swore. "I can't believe it's him. Where are you now?"

"Heading home."

"Right, I'll be at your place within the hour."

When Kate stepped through her front door, she heard voices in the kitchen. Sam stood at the counter in her terry cloth robe, pouring beans into the coffee grinder, chatting with someone out of Kate's sightline.

"Morning, Mom. Guess who's here bright and early?"

Kate felt a cold sweat break across her skin. Erik couldn't possibly have arrived already.

She turned the corner—

—and saw Michael.

He was casually leaning against the counter, cradling a mug, as if he belonged there.

45

Kate forced herself to cross the room, kiss her daughter on the cheek, and pretend nothing was out of the ordinary.

"Michael. What brings you here so early in the day?"

She had to keep calm, give him no hint she suspected him. He was watching her movements carefully.

"I tried to reach you at the station," he said. You didn't tell me you were suspended."

A glimmer of hope. Maybe she could talk her way of this. She shrugged, trying to look sheepish. "Sorry. Didn't think it was the right time."

"What do you mean?"

"After what happened to Suzanne, my news felt insignificant."

He stared at her; she glued a sad expression on her face. *You fucking fucker.* Why was he here? Fishing, maybe—trying to find out how much she knew. Fine. She would treat it like a chess match. Their lives depended on it.

Her eyes flicked around the kitchen. Where was the nearest weapon? The wooden knife block sat on the counter.

Michael leaned in closer to Sam. Her daughter's brows furrowed, as if she sensed the weird undercurrent beneath the conversation. *Got to get her out of the room.* "Honey," she said lightly, "I need to talk to Michael in private. Maybe you can go over to your friend's?"

"Sure?" Sam said, her voice wobbly.

"Stay and visit," Michael said, wrapping his arm around Sam's shoulders. "I haven't seen you in some time."

A wave of nausea hit Kate. She inched a little closer to the counter—closer to the knives.

"Um… I'll just go and change first," said Sam, shrugging off Michael's embrace.

Relief washed over Kate when he let Sam go. She could tell that her daughter had sensed something was wrong. Once she got to her room, she would call for help.

Michael watched Sam climb the stairs. He licked his lips. "She's all grown up. You'd better keep an eye on her."

The comment made Kate's stomach turn.

Then he lifted a phone and waved it in the air. "She left this downstairs. Don't let me forget to give it back."

Kate's heart sank. Sam had no way to call for help. Her only chance was to keep Michael talking until Erik arrived. Lowering her voice, she said, "I'm worried about Sam's mental health. Just trying to keep her insulated. Don't want her hearing too much about the case."

"And what is going on in the case?"

"What do you mean?"

"Henry's dead—and Suzanne—and the police think it's related?"

"It's baffling," Kate replied, trying to sound like she was completely confused by the turn of events. She felt her phone vibrate in her pocket. Good. Someone was trying to reach her. "But I'm on the outside now. They won't tell me anything."

"And what did you find out when you went to Fort McMurray?"

How should she answer? If he's connected to the Fort Raiders, he must know that they'd spoken to Crystal. Maybe mentioning her would calm him—make him think they weren't onto him.

"Well, there was a sex worker at the hotel who'd been seen with Henry. We tried question her, but she wouldn't say anything. Now she's disappeared. We can't find her."

"Yes," Michael said. "Neither can we."

The words hung there. *Shit.* He shouldn't have said that.

Michael slowly set his mug down. Coffee spilled over the rim and seeped across the counter. For a moment, he stared at it, as if deciding something.

Please, Kate thought. *Fix it. Say something that makes sense. Let's keep up this charade. I'll pretend I don't know anything and you need to do the same.*

"Well…" He scratched the back of his neck, studying her. His gaze lingered a little too long. She took a step back, then another. He sighed. The tension seemed to drain out of him. His shoulders loosened, and a strange smile crept across his face.

Kate felt a chill.

Something had shifted. The man she knew as Henry's friend and colleague was gone. In his place was a stranger. Looser, almost exhilarated. As if he'd been holding his breath for days and had finally decided to let it out. The real Michael.

"This is too bloody difficult," he said. "I can't tell if you know or not."

Kate lunged for the knife block and yanked out the largest knife. "Oh, I know," she said.

Michael laughed softly.

"Do you?" He tilted his head, studying her. Not frightened. Curious.

"Go on then," he said, smiling. "Tell me what you think you know."

Kate tightened her grip on the knife. *He wants to see how much I've figured out.*

"You killed Tiffany," she said. "And Henry discovered it."

Michael's smile widened. "Ah," he said. "So you do know."

"Why did you kill them?" Kate asked. Her voice sounded thin to her own ears. "I don't understand." She inched away, putting the island between her and Michael.

Michael rubbed his hands together. His eyes shone with a strange, boyish excitement.

Kate's stomach tightened.

He wants to tell me.

"The prostitute's death was an accident," he said. "Things just got a little too rough." His mouth twitched. "We thought we'd gotten away with it."

As he spoke, he pushed himself off from the counter and took a step towards the centre of the kitchen.

Kate tightened her grip on the knife. Another step and he would be between her and the back door.

"But then Henry had to mess it all up."

"How?" Kate asked.

Michael tilted his head, studying her. "He'd discovered that the CFO of Tecktronic had defrauded the company," he said, "And that the same man had killed a prostitute."

Henry's fatal mistake had been trusting in Michael. "He didn't suspect you were involved?" Kate asked.

Michael snickered, "Of course not. It never even crossed his mind." His eyes glinted with satisfaction. "I was far more cautious than Lyle. Made sure no one saw me with her."

Kate kept the knife steady between them.

"Then why kill Henry if he didn't know about you?"

He shrugged, as if they were discussing a minor inconvenience. "If Lyle was arrested, that weasel would've turned me in within five minutes. Henry had to go."

Michael began to slowly move along the edge of the kitchen island.

Kate shifted with him, keeping the counter between them.

"But planning it was tricky," he went on. "Henry told me he'd hidden some incriminating information about Lyle in a storage locker. Insurance, he called it."

Kate frowned. "I don't understand. Why didn't Henry go to straight to the police?"

Michael smiled. "Because he decided to play detective." His tone dripped with amusement. "He wanted to gather all the evidence first. Put the whole puzzle together before presenting it to the police." He stopped pacing and looked directly at her. "And he trusted me."

The words hung in the air.

Michael's smile widened. "He wanted to explain to me why we couldn't take Tecktronic's money anymore."

Kate felt a chill down her spine. Above them, a floorboard creaked. Kate's heart slammed.

Sam.

She pictured her daughter in her bedroom, maybe digging through her backpack, maybe wondering why the house had gone so quiet. Kate tightened her grip on the knife. *Stay upstairs*, she prayed silently. *Just stay there.*

Michael's eyes flicked towards the staircase for a brief second, then back to Kate. He grinned.

How had they all been so blind about Michael? "You killed your best friend," she said. "But you didn't do it alone. Someone from the Fort Raiders must've helped you."

Michael seemed impressed that she'd guess that much.

"After the prostitute died, Lyle and I told the Fort Raiders about our little predicament. They helped us dispose of her body." He shrugged. "And later, they helped me deal with Henry."

"Murder Henry and frame my brother."

Michael barked out a laugh and Kate shivered at the sound. "Couldn't believe my luck when Henry picked up your drunken brother at the bar," he said. "Perfect opportunity to pin the murder on Conor." He smirked. "And as a bonus, when your brother stumbled in the parking lot, one of his gloves fell off. I slipped it into the crime scene. Sent the police running in completely the wrong direction."

Kate swallowed hard. "What did you do for the Fort Raiders?"

"I loaned them the university van now and then. Helped them move product up to Fort Mac."

"In other words," said Kate, "they had you under their control."

Michael's hands curled into fists. Kate's pulse spiked. Had she pushed him too far? For a moment, the room seemed to shrink. Then his fingers loosened and the tension slipped out of his shoulders.

Kate let out her breath. *He wants to talk more than he wants to hurt me.*

"No," Michael said lightly. "It was a business arrangement." A smile crept across his face. "And I was paid handsomely."

"And added to your art collection."

He brightened. "It's a beauty, isn't it?"

Kate clenched her jaw. *Where the hell was Erik?* Every second stretched thinner. She was running out of questions.

"Who heads the Fort Raiders?"

He smiled and said nothing. His eyes drifted down at the knife in her hand. "That bitch stumbled onto it too," he said mildly, "So I had to strangle her."

Suzanne. Kate forced herself not to react.

"How did she find out?" she asked.

Got to keep him talking.

"Henry's fault." Michael leaned back against the counter again, oddly relaxed. "Turns out he told her about Lyle and the prostitute. After we got rid of Henry, she must've figured out I was involved." His mouth curled. "We used to dabble in S & M, and she left me after I went a bit too far one night."

Kate's stomach twisted. "Did you cut off her hands?"

"Oh no. That was the clean-up crew." He seemed amused. "Gruesome, huh? Too bad it didn't work. She wasn't supposed to be identified for a while."

He watched her carefully. "That's why I was so surprised when you told me she'd been found."

Now his reaction that day made sense. Kate tightened her grip on the knife and shifted sideways again, keeping the island between them.

Michael sucked in his breath. "Oh, how I wished I could give you proper strapping," he said softly. "Henry was completely pussy-whipped."

Her hand trembled. She steadied the knife with both hands and forced her breathing to slow. "Who bugged my cell?"

"The Raiders gave me the virus to load onto your phone. That turned it into a nice little listening device." He grinned. "That's how we learned about the storage locker."

Kate's heart thudded.

Where are you, Erik?

Time was running out.

"When did you even get your hands on my phone?"

"At the funeral reception. I called your phone when I first arrived. You pulled it out of your pocket but didn't answer." His eyes gleamed at the memory. "Then I came over and hugged you."

Kate felt a cold wave wash through her.

"That's when I lifted it," he said. "You were completely clueless." He rocked back on his heels. "When I was alone in Henry's office, I opened an email I'd sent myself, loaded the virus, deleted the message, and slipped the phone back in your pocket."

Kate remembered: Henry's office. Michael's phone call. Her leaving him alone.

And the antique pen. *What a bastard.*

"And the home invasion?" she asked.

Michael rubbed his hands together, his excitement returning.

"When you were packing up Henry's office, I overheard you tell Jennifer about the key under the owl." He chuckled. "And thanks to your bugged phone, we heard you arrange to meet Erik at the locker the next morning."

He spread his arms out wide. "So we had to act right away."

Then he lifted a small scrap of paper and waved it. Kate's stomach dropped. It was the note she'd left for Sam.

"Why were you at the Ranch this morning?"

"Just needed to get out and have some fun."

Michael laughed and lunged at her, punching her in the forearm. She gasped and dropped the knife. It skittered across the porcelain tile. He grabbed at her as she dove for it. Their heads slammed together, a burst of light flashing behind Kate's eyes. She fell hard on her side and heard a dull thud as the back of Michael's head struck the counter on the way down. He collapsed across her leg, out cold. Her whole body shook. *Focus, Kate.* She shoved at his shoulder, trying to roll him off. Too heavy. He groaned.

Shit. He was waking up.

The knife! Where was it? She twisted her torso, searching the floor. There—behind her.

Too far to reach.

"You bitch," he muttered.

Cold fear surged through her veins. Michael shifted, freeing her leg. Kate twisted, grabbed the knife, and drove it into his thigh. He screamed and clamped both hands over the wound as blood spurted between his fingers. Kate scrambled to her feet and ran for the front closet, hoping to reach it before he could recover. She yanked the door open and grabbed the bear spray from the shelf—but fumbled with the safety. Her hands were shaking so badly.

Too late.

She heard him rushing up behind her. Kate spun and swung the heavy canister, smashing it against the top of his head.

Michael crumpled to the floor and lay motionless.

"Mom?"

Kate looked up. Sam stood at the bottom of the stairs, staring at the blood on the floor and the man sprawled beneath her.

Kate dropped to her knees and pinned Michael to the floor. "I need duct tape," she shouted.

Sam didn't move.

Kate spoke again, keeping her voice low and calm. "Sweetheart, please get tape and scissors."

Sam blinked rapidly and dashed to the junk drawer. Together, they bound his wrists behind his back and then his ankles. He groaned and shuddered awake. He swore and struggled to get free. Sam cut another piece of tape to cover his mouth and nostrils. Kate waited a moment, let him flail around in a panic before she rolled the tape away from his nose.

Safe. She stood up and tucked the scissors in her back pocket. Sam collapsed into her arms.

The sudden crash of feet kicking in the front door followed by a jumble of voices sent a jolt through them.

"Hide. Now," Kate hissed.

Sam spun around in panic, searching for a spot.

"Under there." Kate pointed to the large cupboard under the kitchen island. Sam folded her body inside and pulled the door shut just as two men in balaclavas, handguns raised, burst in the house.

Kate turned to face them. *Please, God. Keep my daughter safe.*

A tall, wiry man shouted at her to stay still.

Kate began to shake uncontrollably when she recognized the tattoo on his neck. The man from the bar in Fort Mac who'd put his hand on her thigh. Jeff—that's what the bartender had called him.

Guess he had the last laugh.

The other man, shorter and stockier, walked up to Michael, who was trying to speak through his taped mouth, and shot him in the forehead. Blood and brain matter burst from the exit wound. Kate's heart hammered so hard she thought it might explode.

This was it.

Her end.

"Let's go," Jeff ordered, gesturing with his gun.

Kate slipped on the pooling blood in the front hall. She caught herself against the doorframe, pain shooting up her right arm. "Get a move on." He jabbed her in the back with the tip of the handgun.

The stocky shooter walked past them, his gun now tucked in a back holster, and slid open the side door of a white van parked out front.

They didn't know about Sam.

Kate hurried to the van. The sooner they left, the better.

Jeff shoved her from behind, and she stumbled into the open door, reaching out to steady her fall. Tears clouded her vision.

The men dragged her the rest of the way inside and slammed the door closed.

She lay on the cold metal floor and squeezed her eyes shut as they sped away from her house. What had she done? *Oh Sam. I'm sorry. Please God, keep her safe.*

She'd promised Sam that everything would be okay, and it would've been if she hadn't kept digging. What a complete idiot she'd been.

Kate wondered why they hadn't killed her yet.

It was probably only a matter of time.

46

After ending his call with Kate, Erik grabbed his gun and vest from the safe. On the drive to her house, he tried to call her. No answer. He tried again. And again. Why wasn't she picking up? When his phone finally rang, his hopes lifted, only to be dashed when he saw the number—Jeremy. He put him on his car speakerphone. "I'm on my way to Kate's," he said.

"We're on our way there now, too," Jeremy said. "We're worried that she's not answering her phone. Neither is Sam."

"I'm almost there. Gotta go."

What if Michael was there right now—doing God knows what?

Erik pressed harder on the gas. He clocked a hundred kilometres per hour in a fifty zone, barely slowing for the corner, the back end fishtailing. When Kate's house came into view, he screeched to a halt and saw it immediately—the splintered front door. He leapt out, gun drawn, and ran inside. Michael lay on the floor. A bullet wound marked his forehead; blood and brain matter spattered everywhere. Then footsteps sounded behind. He spun around.

Conor burst in, a canister of bear spray clutched in his hand. Jeremy was close behind, taser raised.

"Easy now," said Erik, lifting his hands.

They stopped short, mouths agape at the carnage. Conor began hyperventilating.

"Breathe," said Jeremy.

"Where are they?" Conor's legs buckled and he dropped to his knees.

Jeremy crouched down to comfort him. A sudden clash of metal pans shattered the silence. Erik aimed his gun at the kitchen island cupboard and barked, "Who's there?"

"It's me," came a muffled voice.

Erik holstered his gun.

The cupboard door creaked open. Sam crawled out, tears streaking her cheeks.

"Did they kill Mom?"

"No, Michael," said Erik.

Conor rushed to Sam and pulled her close, placing himself between her and the front hall to shield her from the gruesome scene.

Sirens wailed outside. A moment later came the pounding of boots and shouted commands as a team of heavily armed officers stormed inside.

"Police! Show me your hands!"

Erik raised his hands. Again.

Sam, Conor, and Jeremy followed suit. Christina pushed past the SWAT team, glanced down at Michael's body, then over at Erik and the rest with their hands in the air. "What the hell is going on?"

"We need to check the rest of the house," Erik said.

Christina shook her head. "Kate isn't here, if that's what you're implying. A neighbour called it in, said she was forced into a cargo van."

Erik closed his eyes for a brief moment. She's alive. For now.

Christina insisted they sit in the living room while the tactical team cleared the rest of the house. Conor held Sam's hand, passing her tissues. He'd calmed enough to comfort his niece.

"Start talking," said Christina.

Erik cleared his throat. "Kate called me early this morning. She'd figured out that it was Michael who'd killed Henry. We'd arranged to meet here before calling the police. When I arrived…" He gestured toward the front hall. "…I found that."

Christina followed the motion of his hand to the bloodstained entryway, then turned to Sam.

"I know this is difficult," she said gently. "But I need you to tell me what happened. It might help us find your mother."

Conor squeezed her hand in encouragement. Sam's voice cracked as she struggled to explain.

"What did you hear when you were hiding in the cupboard?" Christina asked.

"A gun shot." She clapped a hand over her mouth. "I thought they'd killed Mom and I was next." She burst out sobbing and Conor pulled her into his arms.

Christina rubbed her forehead. Erik empathized. This case had just become a lot more complicated.

Jeremy broke the silence. "Then who killed Michael and took Kate?"

Good question. Erik felt his phone vibrate in his pocket. "Am I free to use the bathroom?" he asked.

Christina shrugged.

Erik stepped into the bathroom, locked the door, and checked his messages.

We have Kate. We'll exchange her for Ferenc.

The other text was from Ferenc. Call me. Now.

He called Ferenc. "Do you know where she is?"

"The Fort Raiders took her. They're planning to board a private aircraft bound for Fort McMurray."

"How do you know all this?"

"I have an inside man. I also know they want me in exchange for Kate."

"What do I tell them?"

"Agree to their demands and abduct me from my club. You'll need to bring your gun. Make it look realistic."

That sounded like a dangerous proposition.

"Why are you doing this?" He knew it wasn't out of the goodness of Ferenc's heart. The man wouldn't risk his life to save Kate.

"We're using this opportunity to take them down."

"How?"

"I'll explain later."

The line went dead.

Erik pocketed his phone, splashed water over his face and patted it dry with a hand towel. He stared at his reflection in the mirror. *What the hell was he doing teaming up with a crime boss?*

But he knew the answer: Ferenc had a better chance of getting Kate back safe and sound than the police did. But for this to work, he'd have to lie to his former partner.

He strode back to the living room. "Are we free to go? I need to take Sam to her granny's."

Christina narrowed her eyes, studying him. But they both knew she had no grounds to hold him. "Stay out of this," she said. "Call if you hear from Kate or her abductors."

"No problem."

He led a dazed Sam out of the house. Jeremy and Conor followed behind, both wearing confused expressions. Conor opened his mouth to speak but Erik held up his finger. "Wait."

They helped Sam into the back seat of Jeremy's car. She stared straight ahead, her expression blank. Poor kid. All that she'd been through.

Erik glanced toward the house, then lowered his voice. "Ferenc called me."

Jeremy and Conor exchanged a look.

Erik told them what the crime boss wanted—and what he was asking Erik to do.

"Bring me with you," Conor said. "I can help."

Erik was skeptical. "Sam needs you."

"I can take Sam back to her grandmother's," Jeremy offered.

Erik weighed his options. Kate would never forgive him if something happened to her brother, but he could use someone he trusted to watch his back.

"Fine," he said, crouching to talk to Sam in the back seat of the car. She turned away, refusing to meet his eyes. "Jeremy is going to take you to your granny's," he said. "Your uncle and I are going to get your mother back."

Erik shut the door and Jeremy pulled away from the curb.

"Give me your keys," said Conor, holding out his hand. Erik started to protest, but Conor pointed out that he drove a courier truck for a living. "Besides, you don't want me to navigate," he said.

Erik handed over the keys.

As they pulled into traffic, Erik spotted an undercover police car following them. Christina must've suspected he was planning something and arranged the tail. But Conor proved to be an excellent driver. He pushed through amber lights, executed several U-turns, and took side roads. As soon as they had shaken the tail, Erik called the number from the text.

"How do I know Kate's alive?" Erik asked. Suddenly, he heard a thump followed by a faint cry—Kate's voice. "What did you do?" he demanded, his concern rising.

"Don't worry. I just gave her a little poke," the captor replied.

"How am I supposed to get at Ferenc?" Erik asked.

"You'll figure it out. Call back once you have him."

On the drive to the Ranch, Erik explained the plan to Conor.

"Are you sure this is a good idea?" Conor asked.

"Not really, but I can't think of anything better. Can you?"

Conor shook his head. He pulled up to the back entrance of the Ranch. "Stay here and be ready to leave in a hurry," Erik instructed.

Erik rang the buzzer and as soon as Tony opened it, Erik pulled out his gun. Tony raised his hands and spoke quietly. "There's a Raiders guy across the way in a car. Make sure he sees you're holding a gun."

Erik angled his body so he'd be seen from the street, handcuffed Tony's wrists and pushed him inside, closing the door behind him.

Ferenc was waiting for them in his office. "Safe from prying eyes in here," he said.

Erik removed Tony's handcuffs and they gathered around Ferenc's desk to go over the next part of the plan.

Tony muttered under his breath. His role in the plan was to be tied up and left behind in the office. Ferenc patted his nephew's shoulder. "We both know Erik could never overpower you, but we need the Raiders to believe he did." Tony grunted in response and sat down in a chair. Erik tied up his wrists and ankles, making sure to tug extra hard on the rope.

"Let the games begin," Ferenc said, holding out his hands to be cuffed.

Once they were outside, Ferenc pretended to struggle to get away from Erik. To sell the act, Erik punched Ferenc in the face. Ferenc went slack and fell to the ground. For a moment, Erik worried he had actually knocked him out—until he heard Ferenc whisper, "That fucking hurt."

Erik dragged him over to the car and Conor helped load him into the trunk. By the time they got back inside the car, they were both sweating profusely. Conor sped off, tires squealing.

"Now," Erik said, pointing out the Fort Raider's vehicle, "we've got to lose another tail without making it look like we're trying to lose them."

"Not a problem."

Again, Erik was impressed with Conor's driving skills. Once they'd lost their tail, they drove to the address Ferenc had given them and straight into the attached garage of the house. After the door closed, they let Ferenc out of the trunk. "You didn't have to hit me so hard," he said, rubbing his swollen cheek.

Erik shrugged. "Had to be convincing."

They followed the crime boss inside the house where they were greeted by two men. One small and wiry, the other dark-haired and strangely familiar looking.

"Erik, he looks like you," said Conor, pointing to the dark-haired man.

Now Erik understood Ferenc's plan. "I think that's the point. My lookalike is going to act as a decoy, isn't he?"

Ferenc nodded. "I'll explain in a moment, but first, you've got to call the Fort Raiders and let them know that you have me and that you're at the Esso station, which is only a block away from here, on 109th. If you wait too long, they'll get suspicious."

Erik looked at Conor and put his fingers to his lips, then dialled the number they'd given him. "I've got Ferenc," he said to Kate's captor. "Now what?"

"Where are you?"

Erik gave them the name and location of the nearby gas station.

"Leave your sidekick there. You come alone with Ferenc. Keep him in the trunk."

"Good. I don't want to look at his face anyway," said Erik, "But where am I supposed to bring him?"

"Up to Fort Mac. Call when you arrive, and I'll text you the address where we'll do the exchange."

"But that's a long drive," said Erik. "What—"

The captor cut him off. "Just do it," and hung up.

Ferenc introduced Erik to his double, Sean. "You two need to switch clothes. Be quick about it." They exchanged outfits and Erik grimaced at his new look. Baggy black sweatpants, T-shirt and hoodie.

His double got into the car and backed out of the garage. Erik watched as he drove off, heading towards Fort Mac, drawing the Fort Raiders away while the real operation unfolded elsewhere. "Where did you find Sean?" asked Erik.

"He works as a collector for my nephew," said Ferenc. "His nickname's 'The Cop.'"

Erik shoved his hands in the hoodie pockets. "Why's he called that? Does he impersonate me when he's collecting?"

Ferenc shrugged. "Couldn't tell you." He paused, the hint of smile on his face. "But apparently, people are quick to pay him."

"What's going to happen to Sean when they find out he's a decoy?" Conor asked Ferenc.

"He's a big boy. He can take care of himself," said Ferenc. "We only need them distracted until we get on the ground in Fort Mac. We're heading up there in my plane."

Erik rubbed his face. Not another flight.

"You," said Ferenc, pointing to Conor, "are staying behind."

"No way. They have my sister. I'm coming with you."

Ferenc looked at Erik, who nodded. "Let him."

Ferenc shrugged. "He'd better not become a liability." The warning clear in his voice.

The wiry man drove them to the airport where Ferenc had his private twin-turboprop waiting on the tarmac. Tony was already inside. He rubbed his wrists and scowled at Erik.

"Glad you got rescued," Erik said.

Tony grunted. "Took over an hour before staff arrived."

"Buckle up," said Ferenc. "It's a windy day."

Erik tried to quell the knot of panic in his stomach as the small aircraft roared down the runway and lifted into the air. Once they reached cruising altitude, he loosened his grip on the armrests.

Then the turbulence hit. The plane lurched and shuddered. Erik squeezed his eyes shut as it bobbed and weaved through the gusts.

"You okay?" Ferenc asked.

Erik forced a smile. "Hate planes." He shifted in his seat. "What's your plan when we get to Fort McMurray?"

"We've been planning a showdown with the Fort Raiders for quite some time," Ferenc said. "Kate's kidnapping is… an unexpected complication."

"Why didn't the Fort Raiders just tell me to kill you in exchange for getting Kate back?" asked Erik.

"Let's just say I'm more valuable to them alive than dead," said Ferenc. "That's all you need to know."

"Why do you want them to think I'm driving you up to Fort Mac?"

"It gives us time to readjust our plan. To save Kate, we'll need a diversion."

Ferenc went over the details. When he finished, Erik sat quietly for a moment, thinking it through. “I know who can help with the diversion,” he said.

Ferenc glanced at him. “Who?”

Erik met his eyes. “Someone the Raiders already want dead.”

47

Kate huddled in the back of the windowless van, haunted by the image of Michael lying dead on her floor. She knew that, even if she survived this ordeal, she could never live in that house again. Her emotions swung between hope that Sam was safe and fear for her own fate. If only Sam had stayed at her grandmother's, she wouldn't have had to go through such a terrifying experience. Once again, Kate felt the crushing guilt of having put Sam's life at risk.

Her two captors crouched across from her pulled off their balaclavas. They didn't care if she could identify them.

Not a good sign.

"Where are you taking me?"

No response.

A half hour later, the van stopped, and the side door slid open. Tarmac. The roar of a plane overhead. *They're taking me north.* A knot tightened in her stomach.

"Don't try anything or we'll kill you," Jeff warned.

Her two black-clad captors climbed out and joined three bearded men in biker jackets waiting nearby. Kate was marched across the tarmac and up the steps of a small twin-propeller aircraft with the Tecktronic logo on the side.

Of course. Lyle must be behind this. A chill ran through her. What were they planning to do to her?

Jeff used zap straps to bind her wrists and ankles. "Sit here and don't move," he ordered, pointing to the leather-clad seats. Only then did she feel the scissors in her pocket, the ones she'd used to cut duct tape to wrap around Michael's wrists. She was left alone in the back of the ten-seater aircraft while five bikers sat near the front and played what sounded like Texas hold'em. No point trying to escape now.

An hour later, the plane landed on a single bumpy landing strip. The tall man flipped open a switchblade, making her flinch as he sliced through the zap straps binding her. She was quickly ushered into a waiting truck and driven deep into the woods, arriving at a sprawling warehouse where every sound seemed to bounce around the cavernous space.

They led Kate to the far side of the warehouse and stopped at the top of a stairwell that led underground. A tunnel of some sort, she realized—but leading where?

Jeff checked his phone. "They're on their way," he said to his bearded, black-clad buddies.

A moment later, two figures emerged from the tunnel and climbed the staircase. Kate's breath caught. Shock shot through her like ice water. Lyle she'd expected.

But Charles?

The president of Tecktronic stepped into the light.

Kate had known Lyle was crooked. But the president of the company? She hadn't imagined the rot went that high.

Charles laughed at her expression. "Kate, nice to see you again. Sorry it's not under better circumstances."

She forced her voice to sound steady. "What about the 'Henry was such a wonderful guy' and we need to be 'stewards of the environment' speech?"

Charles laughed again. "We make dirty money respectable. And that requires the occasional lie."

Now Kate understood. They were money launderers. The final piece in the puzzle clicked into place. RMS must be the parent company behind both the Fort Raiders and Tecktronic. "Why bother funding Henry and Michael's research if Tecktronic is just a front?" she asked.

"Good cover for us. And when we learned of Michael's sexual tastes, we thought he might be useful. Until he got too high maintenance."

Kate felt no sympathy. "So why am I here?"

"You're here as bait."

"What does that mean?"

"You'll find out soon enough," Charles replied. He gestured towards a nearby metal pillar. "Tie her up over there." The two executives returned to the tunnel.

Jeff forced Kate sit and zip-strapped her ankles and wrists to the pillar. He then placed a strip of duct tape over her mouth. "That's for being lippy at the bar."

Once Jeff left, Kate waited, straining to hear any voices or footsteps. Silence. Her heart raced. They hadn't checked her pockets—so all was not lost. She twisted and stretched, trying to reach the scissors, but her fingers couldn't quite get to them. Fuck. Now what?

She looked up just as a man in green fatigues sprinted toward her. He crouched beside her, whispered, "I'm with Ferenc," and carefully peeled the tape off her mouth. "Keep your voice down," he warned.

No kidding. "What are you waiting for? Get me out of here—they could come back any minute."

He rubbed the back of his neck. "Can't. Not yet. They've made a deal with your boyfriend."

It took Kate a moment to realize he meant Erik. "What do you mean?"

"He's supposed to capture Ferenc and bring him here for an exchange—trading Ferenc for you. But it's a ruse. We have another plan in motion."

"How the hell is that going to work?"

"Don't worry. But you need to stay put for now." He unwrapped a granola bar and held it up for her. "Eat."

She shook her head. "I'm thirsty."

He unscrewed a water bottle. "I'll hold it while you drink."

"Can't you untie me?"

"No, too risky." He held the bottle to her lips, and she drank. Better. Before she could protest, he pressed the tape back over her mouth. "If anyone comes to talk to you, tell them you want to make a deal with the Tecktronic executives. Got that?"

She nodded, and he gave her a thumbs up before disappearing behind the warehouse shelves. Like hell she was going to stay put. She resumed trying to reach the scissors tucked in her back pocket. It was going to be a long day.

48

Ferenc's private aircraft touched down in Fort McMurray, and the group was whisked away in a cargo van. "Keep your head down," Ferenc instructed. "The Fort Raiders can't know we're here."

As in Edmonton, the van drove into the garage attached to a suburban home. They waited for the garage door to close before getting out. Ferenc led them into the kitchen, where a young man in an apron was pulling lasagne from the oven. "Excellent. Lunch is ready," Ferenc said.

Erik picked at his food, watching as Conor sneaked glances at the well-stocked wine fridge.

Ferenc nodded toward the fridge. "Door's locked."

Conor's cheeks flushed, and he pushed his chair back from the table. He asked the man in the apron, "Where's the washroom?"

Once Conor left the room, Ferenc asked, "Are you sure he's not a liability?"

Erik was wondering the same thing. "He'll do whatever it takes to get his sister back."

Ferenc stroked his chin. "I'll take your word for it."

After their meal, Ferenc reviewed the plan once more. "We'll have the element of surprise on our side," he said. "They don't expect me to arrive until the morning."

"What's going to happen to my decoy?" asked Erik.

"I'll text Sean to lose the men trailing him as soon as we're in the warehouse and our plan is in motion," said Ferenc, "Your double knows what he's doing."

One of Ferenc's men handed Conor the keys to the cargo van and gave Erik a gun. Erik patted his own gun belt. "I already have one," he said.

“I’d advise you to use the untraceable one,” Ferenc said. Erik hadn’t considered that. He accepted the new gun, checked the chamber for bullets, and tucked it into his belt.

Conor drove them north of town, pulling over half a kilometre from the warehouse. “Be careful,” he said.

Erik made his way through the woods to the rear entrance of the warehouse. He tried the door—it was unlocked. Ferenc’s inside man had come through. Erik texted Let's get this started and stepped inside. Shelving units lined the back section of the warehouse. On his right stood a large metal safe with a high-tech electronic lock. To his left, a staircase led down—likely to the tunnel connecting to Tecktronic’s headquarters.

“Behind you,” someone whispered, startling Erik. He turned around, weapon at the ready.

A man in green fatigues approached and said, “I’m with Ferenc.” Erik gave him with a thumbs up. “Follow me,” the man said.

Erik stuck close as they moved quickly along the shelving units. Green Fatigues signalled for Erik to stop and crouch. From their hiding spot, Erik could see Kate tied to a pillar. He had to fight the urge to rush over and free her.

They didn’t have to wait long before they heard voices. Good, it was all going to plan. The inside man, on security detail, had managed to lure the executives to the warehouse by telling them Kate wanted to negotiate. But when Charles and Lyle emerged from the staircase, flanked by five Fort Raiders on security detail with weapons ready, Erik’s heart pounded. How could he rescue Kate safely now?

“The one wearing the bandana is with us,” said Green Fatigues. Bandana coughed. For a split second, nothing happened. Then Green Fatigues stepped out from behind the shelves and fired. The Tecktronic president’s head snapped back. He collapsed where he stood.

Bandana pivoted and opened fire. One security guard dropped. The second went down a heartbeat later, his gun still holstered.

Erik ran over to Kate and flipped open his pocketknife, sawing through the bindings at her wrists. One of Tecktronic’s men swung his weapon toward them. Erik fired first. The bullet slammed into the man’s shoulder.

The man in green fatigues finished him with a shot to the head.

"We've got to get down those stairs," Erik said, pointing to the tunnel entrance. "Cover!"

He grabbed Kate's hand and they ran.

Behind them, Green Fatigues and Bandana poured gunfire into the room, forcing the remaining guards back as Kate and Erik thundered down the staircase and into the dark tunnel.

The sounds of the gunfight faded behind them.

Their footsteps echoed in the narrow passage. Erik slowed and moved ahead of Kate, gun raised, sweeping the darkness.

Kate screamed.

Erik spun around.

Lyle stood there, one arm locked around Kate, a gun pressed to her temple.

"Looks like I get the last laugh," said the CFO.

Kate dropped her weight and twisted. The judo moves broke Lyle's balance for a split second. Long enough.

She drove the scissors into his neck.

The blades punched into his jugular. Blood burst between her fingers.

Lyle's cold blue eyes widened. A wet choking sound escaped him. His grip loosened.

He crumpled to the tunnel floor.

Kate stood there, breathing hard, the scissors still clutched in her hand. Blood ran down the blades and over her fingers.

"Where did you—" Erik began.

More gunfire echoed down the tunnel behind them.

He gently pried the bloody scissors from Kate's hand and tucked them into her pocket. Her fingerprints and DNA were all over them. They couldn't leave them behind.

"Keep moving," he said.

They sprinted down the tunnel. As they neared the far end, Erik heard voices above them, chanting. "Hey ho! Hey ho! The polluters have to go!"

Their diversion plan was working.

They climbed a narrow wooden staircase that led into an empty room.

Kate stopped. Her breathing went ragged. She stared down at her blood-stained hands. "I killed someone."

He clasped her shoulders and looked her in the eyes. "You saved us. It was self-defence."

She bit her lip and nodded. Erik took off his hoodie and handed it to Kate to cover her blood-stained top. "Keep your hands in the hoodie pockets. We're almost out," he reassured her. "Bertrand's creating a diversion. Follow me."

Erik took a deep breath and pushed opened the door into Tecktronic's front lobby.

Bertrand broke into a grin when he saw them. They slowly manoeuvred through the crush of protesters towards the glass entrance doors. Outside, the local TV news van was pulling in behind several police cruisers.

As planned, across the compound, beyond the security gates, Conor waited in the cargo van. The police now blocked the main entrance.

Erik nodded toward it. "Your brother. Walk straight to him. I'll be right behind you." He kept his eye on the guard at the security gate as they passed. For a moment, Erik feared the man might be one of the Fort Raiders. But the guard barely looked at them. He seemed rattled—probably concerned he was going to be fired for letting a swarm of environmental protesters overrun the compound and wreak havoc.

Kate climbed into the passenger seat of the van. Erik slid open the side door.

"Where do you think you're going?"

He froze.

A police officer stood just inside of the chain link fence, gun raised.

Erik tossed both guns into the van and shouted, "Go! Now!"

Kate grabbed the handle, trying to climb back out, but Erik slammed the side door shut and Conor hit the gas.

The van surged forward, tires spinning in the slush. It shot past Erik, through the open security gate, and onto the access road beyond the compound.

Kate was gone. Safe.

Erik turned.

The police officer stood ten yards away; the gun aimed straight at him.

Erik recognized him immediately—the officer who had questioned them the last time they'd been in Fort McMurray.

A cold weight settled in his stomach. One of the blackmailed cops.

"Put down your weapon or I'll shoot!" the officer shouted.

Erik slowly raised his hands. Empty.

For a moment, the officer hesitated. Their eyes met. Then the officer's finger tightened on the trigger. The gun cracked.

White-hot pain exploded through Erik. His knees buckled. Then the world went black.

49

N*o, this can't be happening.* Kate twisted around in her seat, desperately trying to see out the back window as the van sped away. "Stop! He's been shot!"

Conor ignored her, gripping the wheel tightly and pushing down hard on the accelerator. Sirens blared all around them as an ambulance and several police cars raced past. Kate rolled down her window and craned her neck to see where they were headed. The ambulance turned left into the oil company's headquarters, while the police cruisers continued straight, likely towards the warehouse.

Conor drove them through downtown Fort McMurray, passing the Gusher Hotel where smoke poured from broken windows and the roof. Staff and guests huddled outside on the sidewalk, looking shaken. Firefighters rushed to connect hoses to hydrants and climbed ladders into the smoky building. Kate stared in disbelief at the chaos surrounding them, her entire body trembling.

Conor glanced at Kate repeatedly as he drove. "He'll be okay, sis. Erik arranged for us to go to Mr. Lam's house. He's expecting us." When they reached a gated estate, he stopped the car and pressed the buzzer. The gates opened, and Mr. Lam was already waiting for them on the front porch.

Conor stepped out and supported Kate as she got out of the car. She struggled to steady herself, barely managing to put one foot in front of the other.

Mr. Lam took her other arm, helping her up the stairs.

"Thanks for sheltering us," Conor said.

Inside, Mr. Lam handed Kate a silk robe. "You can wash and change in the powder room. Leave your clothes on the floor. My trusted maid will clean them for you."

Kate slid closed the pocket door and tore off her bloody clothes, her breathing jagged. The scissors fell from her pocket and clattered onto the white tiled floor. She avoided looking at them as she scrubbed her hands raw in the bathroom sink. *I killed someone.*

A soft knock. "Kate, you okay?" whispered Conor.

Far from it.

She tied on her robe and opened the door. When she spoke, her voice was hoarse. "Did Erik survive?"

"Yes, don't worry," said Conor. "Mr. Lam spoke to a contact at the hospital. Erik's vest took most of the impact. He'll recover."

Kate's knees buckled. Conor wrapped an arm around her waist and guided her into a nearby room where Mr. Lam sat on a curved modular sofa facing a television set. The screen was paused on an image of Erik.

Kate stared at the TV. "Is that..."

"The shooting was caught on camera," said Mr. Lam. "I recorded the news story. Would you like to watch it?"

"Sis, maybe you shouldn't..."

"Yes," she said, ignoring her brother's warning. She joined Mr. Lam on the sofa and he pressed play.

The footage was shaky, the camera jostling as protesters shouted offscreen. For a moment it was hard to tell what was happening.

Then Kate saw him.

Erik stood beside the chain-link fence, his hands raised.

She knew what was coming.

The officer lifted his gun.

The screen jerked. A flash. Erik's body folded out of the frame.

Kate sucked in a breath. Erik wasn't holding a weapon when he was shot. Then she remembered her daughter. She pressed a hand to her mouth. "Oh my god—Sam!"

"And Jeremy!" Conor added.

She had to call her daughter, let her know that they were okay. She looked down at her silk robe. Panic set in. *Where was her phone?* Then the memory of the kidnapping came rushing back. Her phone was still on the kitchen counter, right beside where Michael had been shot.

"I'm on it," said Conor.

Kate eased back into the sofa. Conor called their mother first, reassuring her—and Sam—that they were safe. Then he called Jeremy.

"She's there with you?" Conor asked.

He listened for a moment, then straightened. "Oh—hello, Detective Wong. Yes, Kate's here."

He held out the phone to his sister.

"How are you?" asked Christina.

"Exhausted. Worried about Erik."

"We have a team on our way up. We'll be there soon."

Mr. Lam set down a food tray on the coffee table as Kate ended the call. Kate's mouth watered. She hadn't eaten anything since early that morning. She eyed the contents: a large glass of water, a red ceramic teapot with cups and a plate filled with red bean buns.

"Thank you for all your help," said Kate.

Mr. Lam slowly poured the tea. When he finished, he kept his hand resting on the lid of teapot for a moment and lowered his head. "Henry's death is my fault," he said softly.

Kate looked up sharply. "What do you mean?"

He handed her a cup. She finished it in two gulps. He offered her the plate of red bean buns. She took two.

"I gave him Tecktronic's financial documents," said Mr. Lam. "I thought he'd take them to the police right away."

He poured more tea. This time, she sipped. Henry must have reached the same conclusion they had: Lyle had been cooking the books. But instead of going to the police, Henry had kept digging. That must have been when he discovered Lyle's visits to the prostitutes at the Gusher.

If only Henry had confided in her instead of Michael.

Kate's stomach tightened.

That was what had gotten him killed.

"Why did you show Henry the financial documents in the first place?" Kate asked.

"I could see he was a decent man," Mr. Lam said quietly. "I meant to warn him away from Tecktronic."

"You were only trying to help."

Mr. Lam gave a slight nod. "I'll leave you to rest."

Kate drained the glass of water and devoured the sweet buns. Then she sank back into the sofa, curling her long legs beneath her.

Her eyelids grew heavy. She struggled to keep them open.

But soon gave up the fight.

50

Erik woke up in a hospital bed with Christina sitting on the edge, holding his hand.

"Welcome back. How do you feel?" she asked.

"Shitty."

"You're lucky to be alive. Good thing you turned at the last minute, or the bullet would have missed your Kevlar vest."

The events at Tecktronic came flooding back. "A police officer shot me."

Christina scowled. "Just wait until you see the news coverage."

"So he's—"

"Under arrest for attempted murder."

Shocking. How could one of his own, a member of the police, ever cross the line like that? He must've been blackmailed. But then, who was he to judge? He'd slept with a subordinate, lied to his partner, and worst of all, teamed up with the head of an organized crime group to rescue Kate from the kidnappers. "How's Kate?"

"She's fine. Resting up at the private home of a Mr. Lam. How do you know him, by the way?"

"Long story."

"I have time. You need to start talking. Tell me what the hell went on here in Fort McMurray."

51

Conor drove Kate to visit Erik in the hospital. In his room, the nurse was changing the bandage on his shoulder. Kate's cheeks flushed at the sight of his bare torso.

"You're a fine mess," she teased.

"Glad to see you."

She kissed him on the cheek. "Thanks for saving my life."

He grinned. "My pleasure."

They sat in silence while the nurse finished taping the fresh bandage and helped him back into his hospital gown. Once the nurse left, Kate leaned in. "Have you heard from Ferenc?"

Erik shook his head.

"A fire burned down the Gusher. Think he's behind it?" Kate asked

"Probably. By the way, Christina paid me a visit."

Kate glanced over her shoulder to make sure no one was listening. "What did you tell her?"

"Don't worry, I didn't say much. Told her I was too groggy from the meds to talk. We're supposed to see her in the morning. We need to get our stories straight before we talk to her."

She bowed her head. "We have to deny any knowledge about what happened at the warehouse. It's not to protect Ferenc—although he did save my life—but to protect us."

"You don't have to explain. I get it. But we can never work with the likes of him again."

"Agreed."

While they discussed what to say, Kate struggled to keep her eyes open. Erik looked just as tired. "I need to get some more rest," she said.

Erik shifted over in his bed and patted the empty spot beside him. "Snuggle in. I promise I won't try anything."

At some point, they'd have to talk about the future of their relationship, but she wasn't going to refuse the offer of a comfy spot to catch some sleep. She kicked off her boots and nestled in next to him.

EPILOGUE

One last glance around her empty house. So many memories. Kate locked the door and handed the key to the real estate agent waiting on the front lawn. A cab pulled up to the curb, followed by a Mercedes with tinted windows. Kate thanked the real estate agent and made her way to the Mercedes. The back window slid open, and she peered into the dark interior.

"Hello, Ferenc. Welcome back. You must've been somewhere sunny."

He gave a hearty chuckle. His normally ruddy skin was tanned and his face looked thinner, with fewer lines. Less stress now that he'd eliminated the competition in Fort Mac.

"Why don't you tell the cab to leave?" he asked. "I'll give you a ride to the airport. That way we can talk."

She regarded him for a moment, uncertain, then shrugged. "Sure. Why not?" She handed the cab driver a twenty and climbed in the back seat of Ferenc's Mercedes. "Hey Tony," she said to the driver. He grunted a reply.

"You're travelling light," said Ferenc.

"The family went on ahead with the luggage. I'm to meet up with them just before noon." She checked her watch. Running a little behind.

"We will get you there in time."

Tony pulled out onto the roadway. She looked out the side window and watched her home disappear as they rounded the corner. She turned to Ferenc. "So where did you go after Fort McMurray?"

"I had some business to attend to abroad and wanted to see how matters played out here before I came home. Thanks for keeping my name out of it."

Kate shifted in her seat. She had to tread carefully—be as diplomatic as possible.

"I owe you that for saving my life," she said. "But seven people were slaughtered that day, and all those hotel employees lost their jobs when the Gusher burned to the ground. My kidnapping turned out to be a convenient excuse to go in and wipe out your competition."

"Trust me, you wouldn't have wanted them around. The eastern group running the Fort Raiders was vicious."

Kate almost pointed out that he was vicious too. But she held her tongue. Funny what people tried to justify—like the things she and Erik had done to solve Henry's murder.

Part of her still believed that, in their situation, the end had justified the means.

But where did you draw the line?

"Now we're even, but I can't condone what you do, Ferenc. Please don't ever use any of my family or friends again."

Ferenc stroked his moustache. Tony glared at her through the rear-view mirror. How she hated that man.

"Rumour has it you and Erik are starting a private investigation firm," Ferenc said.

Kate clenched her purse handles. "How did you find out about that? Never mind. I don't want to know."

He still seemed to have tentacles everywhere.

He smiled. "I guess we won't be outsourcing any of our work to your company?"

"I think you know the answer to that."

He fidgeted with his blue-and-pink-striped tie. "I do now, but I thought you might consider it. I hope we can stay out of each other's business."

"You know I can't promise that."

Tony pulled the car up to the international departure terminal doors. Ferenc leaned over and patted her hand. Kate flinched at his touch.

"Take care of yourself, my Amazonian," he said with a faint smile. "I suspect this isn't goodbye."

She stepped out of the car and didn't look back.

ACKNOWLEDGEMENTS

Thank you to retired Edmonton Police Service Deputy Chief Mike Bradshaw for reviewing an early draft of my manuscript and to Jared Brentnell for answering my questions about crime scene forensics. To Tim Gunning, my Northern Ireland expert, your feedback was immensely helpful in shaping the story and characters. Thanks to my friend and first editor, Kiki Yee, who patiently read and edited several drafts. Kiki, along with Kathryn Sutherland and Sophie Yendole, are part of the Friday Warren. Your support and encouragement at our weekly gatherings gave me the confidence to keep going. Thanks to the Alexandra Writers' Centre, where I learned how to write a novel. A special shout-out to Lori Hahnel's critique class. Thanks to commissioning editor Doug Whiteway who listened to my pitch and took a chance on me. To my dear friend Rhonda who urged me to follow my dream. I miss you. And last but not least, to my husband, a.k.a. my continuity man, and my daughter, who reminded me that she came up with the title to the book.

ABOUT THE AUTHOR

Off the Mark is Linda Sanche's debut novel. Her mystery short stories have been published in several anthologies, and "The Electrician" was a finalist in the 2025 Crime Writers of Canada Awards of Excellence. For over seventeen years, she worked as a producer, writer, and director of factual series television, including three seasons as senior story producer on the true crime series *Murder She Solved*. Working on the series inspired Linda to retrain as a crime analyst, but she discovered that she is better suited to writing about crime than investigating it. After living in Vancouver for many years, Linda now calls Calgary home.

Eco-Audit
Printing this book using Sustana Enviro100 Book
instead of virgin fibres paper saved the following resources:

Trees	Water	Air Emissions
3	563 kg	74 kg